DESERTER

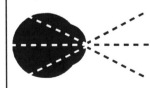 This Large Print Book carries the
Seal of Approval of N.A.V.H.

DESERTER

PAUL BAGDON

THORNDIKE PRESS

An imprint of Thomson Gale, a part of The Thomson Corporation

THOMSON

GALE

Detroit • New York • San Francisco • New Haven, Conn. • Waterville, Maine • London

LIBRARY OF CONGRESS CATALOGING-IN-PUBLICATION DATA

Bagdon, Paul.
   Deserter / by Paul Bagdon.
     p. cm. — (Thorndike Press large print western)
   ISBN-13: 978-0-7862-9599-9 (alk. paper)
   ISBN-10: 0-7862-9599-6 (alk. paper)
   1. Soldiers — Confederate States of America — Fiction. 2. Sheriffs — Fiction. 3. Large type books. I. Title.
PS3602.A39D47 2007
813'.54—dc22   2007008281

Published in 2007 by arrangement with Leisure Books, a division of Dorchester Publishing Co., Inc.

Printed in the United States of America on permanent paper
10 9 8 7 6 5 4 3 2 1

To Jaye Chambery,
who would never desert me.
She's my inspiration,
and a whole lot more.

CHAPTER ONE

July 2, 1863
Gettysburg, Pennsylvania
Evening

The screams and moans of pain and the cries for water from the boys still sprawled on the battlefield no longer seemed to be locked in combat with the cacophony that poured forth from the rapidly erected and acutely undersupplied hospital tents. The soldiers bleeding into the rich, fertile soil approaching the jagged stone outcropping known as the Devil's Den were dying where they lay; those who'd been carried to hospitals or surgeons would live perhaps a bit longer.

"Jake, over there," Uriah said, voice controlled, "right near where they're draggin' the artillery piece — at maybe two o'clock. A blue belly on an awful fine horse — too damned fine for a cavalry hound."

Jake Sinclair shifted slightly on the thick

branch upon which he sat, a leg on either side of it, his back against the massive trunk. The tunnel he'd created through the leaves and branches didn't give him a great deal of peripheral vision, but he scanned the two o'clock area with his spyglass until the burnished-brass coat of the leggy, proud-looking horse came into view. The man astride the animal wore no insignia on his navy blue uniform, but the coat and trousers appeared clean and well maintained. There was no saber at his left side — that would have been as much a giveaway to Reb snipers as would symbols of rank on his shoulders and chest. "Yeah," Jake grunted. "I see him. Good eyeballin', Uriah."

Sinclair plucked a small leaf from the branch above him, held it out to his side, and released it. It was a matter of form, actually — a matter of double-checking for any vagrant breeze that may have developed. The leaf fluttered downward quickly, parting the moist, sluggish air as it sought the ground. The day had been mercilessly hot since sunup, and now, well into the evening, the heat remained stultifying and unremitting. Jake and Uriah Toole, his spotter, had, since early morning, observed men slowly drop to the ground in the loose, floppy manner that signaled heat prostration, so different from the quick, jerky, crazed puppetlike reaction of a body struck by minnie ball or canister shot or fragment of artillery shell.

The 1862 Sharps rifle rested securely across Jake's upper thighs, wrapped in a section of tanned and oiled deer hide. The rifle, equipped with the set of triggers prized by buffalo hunters and sharpshooters, fired a .54-caliber slug that was larger than a man's thumb with unerring accuracy to effective ranges of almost three-quarters of a mile. The triggers, side by side in the trigger guard, served a pair of functions: The one on the left readied the rifle to fire, and the one on the right actually discharged the bullet. Jake was fond of saying that the finger pressure required to operate the right trigger was equal to that of a weak butterfly's heartbeat.

Jake eased the Sharps from its wrap and raised it to firing position. The weight of the rifle, slightly over eight pounds, and the precisely cut butt that tucked tightly to Jake's shoulder provided a stability, a sense of unity, of oneness, between man and weapon that Sinclair had experienced with no other rifle — not the Spencer, not the Henry, not the Winchester.

The rich scent of the polished cherry

wood stock and the tang of gun oil brought an unconscious half smile to Jake's face. He reached forward and flicked up the ladder sight mounted at the end of the octagonal barrel, the barely audible *click* the sound of quality craftsmanship. He estimated the shot at two thousand feet. He'd make no allowance for wind; there wasn't any. It was a middling-long shot from the tree to where the target sat atop his horse. The humidity could have an effect on the slug, dropping the trajectory a tad more rapidly than normal. Jake made the slightest adjustment to the height of the barrel.

It was impossible for Sinclair's naked eye to make out any actual features of the target other than the blue of his uniform. A head shot would be difficult, but the officer's chest and body were essentially a sure thing. Jake wet his lips with his tongue and drew in a long breath. His right index finger tugged the left trigger home and moved to rest ever so gently against the curve of the right. He released the breath, drew another not quite as deep, and fired.

The Union officer was plucked from the back of his horse as neatly and as cleanly as he would have been had an invisible giant's hand snatched him. A barely discernible reddish mist floated momentarily in the air where the man had been, and then it, too, was gone. The briefest bit of a second later, the horse, riderless now, reared. Vague blue forms disappeared behind the cannon as soldiers scrambled for cover.

The report was thunderous but familiar, as was the stinging blowback from the breech that tickled Sinclair's face like a swarm of insects. The thick smoke of the discharge rose slowly, lazily, toward the top of the tree, its pungency sharp in Jake's nose, leaving a metallic taste — like that of blood — on his tongue and in his mouth.

"Good," Uriah said. "Right nice shooting, Jake."

"That's why President Davis pays me all that money." Jake grinned. He glanced upward and his smile disappeared. "Get down," he snapped, rewrapping the Sharps and tying a horsehair cord around it, sling-fashion. "That smoke is gonna hang there like a finger pointing at us. Come on — move!"

Uriah hustled down the tree, using the trunk and branches as hand-and footholds to keep himself from falling through the foliage to the stony ground below. He dropped the last six or so feet, landing lightly, immediately stretching his arms upward to receive the rifle Sinclair was lowering. When the Sharps was secure in Toole's arms, Jake scrambled downward, less gracefully but more rapidly than his partner had — almost in a free fall, clutching branches to slow his descent rather than using them to lower himself. His boots had barely touched soil when the tree began to disintegrate. Leaves, twigs, and chunks of bark exploded from branches that seemed to be in the grip of hurricane winds, shaking, swinging wildly, some fracturing under the onslaught and tumbling to the ground. A large-caliber slug slammed into the upper trunk, gouging away a slab of wood the size of a dinner plate. Another burst of canister — tiny steel balls fulminated outward from exploding shells — shook the tree, tearing more pieces from it.

Both men huddled behind a boulder on the side opposite the onslaught. "That Yankee sharpshooter isn't bad," Jake commented. "His round would have taken me down as sure as you're born." After a moment, he added admiringly, "Good eye."

"Light artilleryman ain't so bad either," Uriah said. "He's purely tearin' the piss outta that ol' tree."

"Makes me a little nervous," Jake admitted. "Let's put that rise between us and the Yanks. Seems like those boys must be awful mad if they put that much firepower on a single sniper. Let's make sure they don't get lucky."

"We're the lucky ones, Jake. We hit them good an' hard all day."

"We did. We surely did," Sinclair agreed. "Some Southern boys who maybe wouldn't have are going home after we win this war."

"Damn right. An' some Yankees — they ain't going home."

Jake nodded but didn't respond.

The Confederate encampment was an erratic, broken line of tents and wagons arrayed beyond the profusion of trees that fronted the ridge called Seminary because of the stately and hastily abandoned Lutheran theological school located a thousand yards from the crest. Lee's Army of North Virginia had been sweeping across Pennsylvania, intent on taking the capital at Harrisburg, pillaging their way through the countryside. The men hadn't eaten so well in months and many wore boots or shoes for the first time that summer. The miniscule Yankee towns and villages fell before the Confederate army without resistance, and the Rebs took what they wanted, carrying off livestock, casks of whiskey and wine, bundles of clothing, and anything else that struck their fancy on wagons taken from farmers — and drawn by horses or mules also stolen from farmers. The routing of the Union forces the day before in spontaneous, impromptu battles had driven the spirits of the Confederates yet higher; talk of abandoning the Harrisburg campaign and swinging about to take Washington and crush the Union there rattled through the ranks like gossip over backyard fences.

Skirmishes crackled behind Jake and Uriah as they strode together through the fading light in the woods to where their commanding officer — General George E. Pickett — had established bivouac for almost fifteen thousand men. Smoke from cook fires rose rifle-barrel straight in the cloudless sky in front of them; behind them the gray pall of battle still hovered over the fields, softening the hues of the sunset.

Guards nodded or waved to the two men. The Sharps over Sinclair's shoulder and the brass telescope on a lanyard around Toole's neck gave them recognition as sharpshooter and spotter and guaranteed easy passage to the camp. Fear of infiltration by enemy spies was close to nonexistent. The Union knew where the Confederate troops were just as the Rebels knew that the Feds were spread along the rise called Cemetery Ridge, a long pair of miles away.

They walked well together, rifleman and spotter, with the easy, matched strides of a pair of men who'd gone many miles together on foot. Jake Sinclair, twenty-six, a few months older than Uriah, at an even six feet, three inches taller than Toole, was a hard-muscled Georgian dressed in a buckskin shirt, soiled and torn tan trousers, and boots. Toole wore a shirt of Confederate gray, but his pants and boots had been scavenged over the last year and a half. At this point in the war uniforms were rare and hard for anyone but ranking officers to come by. One item was abundantly available for some reason, however: leather belts with brass CSA buckles attached. Both Sinclair and Toole wore the belt and so did a high percentage of Pickett's troops. A sheath carrying a bowie-type knife with a foot-long blade hung at Jake's right side. At Uriah's, a converted Army Colt picked up from a dead Yankee at Antietam was holstered. Jake's hair, nut brown and shaggily shoulder length, flowed like a mane behind him as he walked, while Uriah's hair was cut raggedly — with Jake's knife — quite close to his head. Both men shaved — again using Jake's knife — when it was possible. Today both their faces were dark with the growth of four or five days.

The men had been partners for almost two years. They'd gotten drunk together, they'd killed together, and they'd watched friends die together. Their bond was strong, although unspoken. The only real dispute they'd ever had between them was over General Robert E. Lee.

"He spills Southern blood like it was no more important than well water, Uriah — you know that. You've seen it at Manassas, at —"

"A general has got to send men into battle. That's his damn job. There ain't no war goin' to be won without some blood is shed. That's too bad an' all, but that's the way it is. Nobody loves the South or the Confederacy more than Bobby Lee."

"President Davis does," Sinclair argued. "And it won't be long before he comes to his senses and pulls Lee out of command. I just hope he does it while there's still some men left to fight the Yankees."

Toole's words came faster, hotter, and his usually benign blue eyes had flames of anger behind them. "That's horseshit. Bobby —"

"Bobby, my ass," Jake snapped. "It's because boys like you hero-worship that old fool that so many of you get killed. Maybe it's his fancy West Point education that taught him men's lives can be tossed away to gain some lousy piece of ground that doesn't mean a thing in the long run of the war. That's what I'm saying, Uriah — and you're too thickheaded to listen to reason."

"General Lee's got better'n seventy-five thousand men standin' right behind him ready to —"

"Behind him? Lee hasn't even been close to a single battle! He *watches* the damned war, Uriah, he doesn't fight in it. He sits his ass down on that fancy horse and watches boys die through his binoculars, is what your General Robert E. Lee does."

Neither one of them was quite sure how it happened, but suddenly they were standing, face-to-face, fists clenched, ready to swing, ready to end a military partnership and, more importantly, a burgeoning friendship. Their breaths rasped in their throats and their eyes were locked together, fused by passion, livid with righteousness. The stand-off lasted for a pair of minutes — perhaps the longest minutes Toole or Sinclair had ever passed.

As if the move were choreographed, each man took a step back, but their gazes held. Another eternity passed and then they both began to speak at once. The jumble of words brought quick smiles and the moment, the intensity, was gone.

"We can't talk about General Lee, I guess," Uriah said quietly.

"I guess not."

"Good thing we wasn't drinkin' when that started," Uriah said, shaking his head as if in wonder. "Could have been a big mess."

Jake extended his right hand. "Yeah. It could have," he said. Uriah took his hand and they shook almost formally, as if they were sealing a business deal.

"You ain't heard a word of what I've been sayin', right?"

Jake pulled back to the present, realizing Uriah was correct. "Sure I have. I was just thinking a bit."

" 'Bout what?"

"Nothing real important, partner. Just kind of drifting. Sorry."

Uriah sniffed the air and smiled. "Smell that? Somebody's cookin' up chicken. Reminds me I'm damn near starved." He was silent for a few strides. "What I was sayin' was that it seems like the war is drawin' down to the end, 'specially if this Pennsylvania campaign keeps on goin' the way it has. Hell, we're knockin' on Lincoln's front door, Jake." He paused again. "What're you gonna do when it's all done?"

"I'll go back home for a bit," Jake said.

"Sit around with my feet up and watch that cotton grow and go out target shooting and hunting with my pa. I'll eat good and sleep in a real bed and forget all about the goddamn War of Northern Aggression."

"Ain't none of us goin' to ever forget this war, Jake," Uriah said very seriously. "Thing is, I'm still thinkin' of us partnerin' up after all this. Maybe going into a business or taking some land out West and runnin' some beef an' maybe some horses for sale. There's always a call for good stock horses out there."

A wave of pure emotion washed over Jake Sinclair. The differences between himself and Uriah Toole were profound, but in the final analysis, meaningless. Jake's two years at college and the multi-thousand-acre plantation he'd been raised on seemed far more grand than Uriah's family's hardscrabble West Texas and their local whiskey business. But those were economic differences and nothing more — the result of birth, not accomplishment. Could they partner after the war? Jake thought they could — and he realized that after twenty months with Uriah Toole, he'd learned more about life than he had in his previous twenty-six years. Uriah found pleasure — even joy — in a cup of good coffee or the smooth power of a fine horse at speed, while Jake worried about patching a hole in the sole of his boot or the outcome of a dicey campaign. Jake's fancy words and book learning served little purpose beyond impressing ladies at cotillions, while Uriah's sense of fairness and his homespun intelligence gave him a certain stature that wealth or birthright couldn't instill in a man.

"I can't see the pair of us in a mercantile selling ribbons to women and cut plug to cowhands," Jake said. "I like your idea about a ranch, though. I like it a lot. Flat racing is big in the West. I know some about breeding and we might could raise some good horses, make a nice living with them."

"Maybe so." Uriah nodded. "Maybe we could just do that. Be a good life."

"That's assuming we both make it out of —" Jake began.

"Whoa, now!" Uriah interrupted. "They ain't made the Yankee bullet that'll end either one of us, Jake. I know this for sure. Some things a man just knows — and that's one of them."

Sinclair had no response to that, and Uriah knew that he wouldn't. The two men continued on to the encampment.

Rumors — Lincoln is dead, Lee is dead, a wagonful of whores is on its way, the war is over — ran about in army camps like a plague, leaving no man untouched, whether he believed what he heard or not. The predominant topic — the one that caused battle-jaded eyes to widen and hands reaching for pieces of fried chicken to tremble — was the story of General Lee's plan for the next day.

"We'll soften them up with artillery till they're staggering, an' then we'll go right on up the chute — it ain't but a mile, give or take — an' we'll shoot their asses off when we're over that Cemetery Ridge," a new sergeant told his men, pacing back and forth in front of where they sat and sprawled on the ground.

"Ain't but a mile, give or take," a grizzled and bearded soldier with a soiled, bloody bandage wrapped around his right wrist mocked. "Shit! Might as well be a hundred miles! There won't be a man left standing to engage the Yanks on the ridge."

"But the artillery — there'll be a barrage like no other before that'll —"

"It's gonna be a damn slaughterhouse, nothin' less an' nothin' more," the private argued. "I won't believe none of this till I hear it right from Bobby Lee's own mouth — an' even then I'd tell him he's pure crazy."

"Lookit here," the sergeant said. "Lemme say something. Tell me if it's not true that General Lee always done right by us, by the Confederacy. We're goin' through the Yankees like shit through a Christmas goose this campaign, ain't we? Answer me that. Go ahead an' tell me we ain't — if you can say it without God striking you dead for lyin'." He glared into the group, knowing there could be no valid response that proved other than what he'd just stated. The grumbles, low, quick, anonymous, ". . . stupidest plan I ever heard," ". . . impossible," ". . . pure craziness," died out.

"It ain't our place to question orders," the sergeant said, pacing again. "General Lee tells us to march on an' take Cemetery Ridge, and that's what we'll do."

"Or get our heads blowed off," someone mumbled, "followin' a damn fool half-crazy order."

Jake Sinclair ran a cleaning rod with an oiled cotton patch at its end through the barrel of his Sharps, inspecting the residue it removed in the flickering light of the cook fire. "It's another rumor." He grinned. "I'd as soon believe Abe Lincoln's going to join up with us tomorrow."

"Jake's right," Uriah agreed. "All you boys seen that field, that slope up to the ridge."

The dozen or so men around the fire, some still eating, some smoking pipes or building cigarettes, a few sucking at a canteen of whiskey that was being passed around surreptitiously, watched as Jake set his rifle aside and smoothed a square of dirt in front of the fire. Using a pebble he scribed a shaky line at the top of the area and another at the bottom. "Here's Seminary Ridge," he said, pointing at the lower line. "Right behind it is where we are right now." He pointed to the top line. "Here's Cemetery Ridge." He swept his hand across the space between the two lines. "This is about a mile. It's wide open — no cover of any kind once Seminary Ridge is left behind. The Yanks" — he pointed again to the top line — "have perfect cover — the ridge itself — and their artillery has a clear and open field of fire. If we got into musket or rifle range, the Yanks would make mincemeat out of us. And look: Even if our artillery is placed here" — he punched a couple dozen holes at the sides of the cleared area and several more in front of the bottom line — "dropping canisters or balls over the ridge and onto the troops would be a problem. Plus, it's an uphill run all the way from where we are, which would slow us down, make us easier, better targets, tire us out quicker." He looked around. "Anybody here fancy joggin' a mile uphill in the kind of heat we've had, through cannon and rifle fire, to a perfectly protected ridge with maybe twenty thousand Yankees behind it?" He sat back. "I sure as hell don't. And neither does General Pickett. He's not crazy. He wouldn't do something like that — wouldn't even think about it. He's too good of a soldier. Like I said, the whole silly thing's only another rumor."

"Damn it, Jake, it isn't either!" One of the men stood and faced Jake. "My cousin Horace, he was right there when Longstreet was tryin' to talk General Lee out of his plan. Horace even wrote down what Longstreet said." He crouched close to the fire, its light illuminating the half page of paper he held. "Here's what Longstreet told General Lee — listen up, now: 'It is my opinion that no fifteen thousand men ever arrayed for battle can take that position.' " He carefully folded the paper and put it back into his shirt pocket. "Horace," he added, "is a church-goin' man. He wouldn't lie. He said Longstreet had tears runnin' down his face when he rode away from General Lee."

Jake looked down at his diagram in the dirt. "I'm not calling your cousin a liar," he said. "But I'd be willing to bet that he misunderstood what it was he heard. A man would have to have no more sense than a chicken to go into a battle like that."

"You talkin' desertion, Jake? Disobeyin' a direct order?" a voice asked.

"No. I'm not. What I'm saying is that I don't believe Lee would concoct such a shit-for-brains battle plan, and I'm no big supporter of Lee. You boys know that."

"It's true, men," Lieutenant Xavier Lewis said, stepping from the darkness up close to the fire. "General Pickett will lead a major attack on the Union troops at Cemetery Ridge tomorrow afternoon. It's a well thought out plan that has the backing of General Lee and all of his officers. Our artillery will pound the Yankees as long as it takes to weaken them, and then our ground forces will sweep over them like a new broom. We will be successful. We will devastate the Army of the Potomac in their own backyard." He emphasized the word "will" in both sentences.

Much the same words, delivered in much the same fashion, were being spoken by officers to men throughout the encampment. Here and there a ragged cheer erupted, but for the most part, the news was greeted with silence. Many Catholic soldiers made the sign of the cross; those of other denominations bowed their heads. Some men sat as if dazed, staring at nothing, picturing the impossibly long grassy slope that ran uphill to the crest of Cemetery Ridge.

Jake and Uriah stopped to allow a wagon loaded with cases of ammunition and kegs of gunpowder to pass in front of them. Sitting at the fire had become like being caged. Even aimless walking seemed better, if for no other reason than to escape the comments and projections of their fellow troops. The arguments were hot and strident and more than a few ended in fistfights. Those who were convinced that the charge would crush the Yankees punched, bit, and kicked those who were certain that they'd be dead within twenty-four hours — and were in turn battered and beaten by soldiers who saw the operation as a hideous and bloody mistake. The fights were short-lived. The men, ultimately, seemed to realize that they were comrades — and that they'd need one another the next day.

Men drifted away from groups and huddled near campfires or lanterns, scratching out letters to mothers, fathers, and sweethearts. Some knelt, unashamed, heads bowed, lips moving silently in prayer. Others sought the casks of whiskey they'd hidden in the woods, filling their canteens with

Pennsylvania's finest, swilling it until they vomited or, preferably, passed out to a dreamless sleep that carried them at least until morning, far from Cemetery Ridge.

"Damn. Lookit that," Uriah said, nodding toward a wagon creaking by, heading toward the rear lines of the camp. It was pulled by two stout horses, the coats of which gleamed with frothy sweat. The gaits of both animals were unsure, toes of their steel shoes dragging the ground from exhaustion. The driver, in a business suit and wearing leather gloves to handle the reins, looked straight ahead, ignoring the ripple of disgust — of fear — he and his wagon raised in the troops he passed. The wooden sign affixed to the sides of the wagon read:

EMBALMING & SHIPPING
FAST — ECONOMICAL — SANITARY —
ODORLESS
MENDON H. DURFEE, MD
FAIR RATES

"Sons-a-bitches are like flies buzzin' around a dead dog," Toole said. "You'd think the army would chase them the hell away."

"Might be they do some good," Sinclair said. "I talked to one once, early on after I joined up. What they do is have a big stock of cheap coffins at the nearest railroad depot and haul the corpses they embalm to the coffins and send the dead away to their homes so their families have something to bury."

"Makes me queasy an' scared, Jake. Like I seen a ghost or somethin'."

They walked on, watching the back of the embalmer's wagon until it turned off into the deeper woods, the yellowish light from the two lanterns mounted above the driver barely piercing the darkness. "I s'pose he'll do some business tomorrow," Uriah said.

"I suppose he will."

"Gonna be bad, ain't it, Jake?"

"Yeah. It's gonna be bad."

It was as if Toole had to force out his next words. "You ever think of skeedaddlin', Jake? Sayin' the hell with it an' grabbin a horse an' lightin' out? Goin' home or wherever?"

"Think about it? Sure," Jake answered. "Just like you have, partner, and like all the men in the whole damned army, and in the whole Union army, too. Some — maybe many — have done it. Hell, after a big battle so many men are killed and ripped up that it's impossible to tell who is who. All a man has to do is leave something with his name on it on a body that can't be identified and he's all set. He just chooses a new name and goes off to wherever he decides to go."

"Well. But he can't go home an' he can't claim what was his before the war. When folks see a deserter comin' back they know he's yellow and that he run off. It's like slappin' President Davis's face. Folks liable to lynch him."

"There are lots of places to go, a whole lot of land out there. I've heard a man out West doesn't need a last name and doesn't need a history." Sinclair hesitated. "Thing is, I — we — signed on to defend a way of life we believe in. Neither one of us can walk away from that." He shook his head slightly, negatively. "Nobody said anything about following orders that're so stupid that a man's pretty much guaranteed not to walk away from a battle, though."

"Seems like you're saying two things at once, Jake."

Sinclair sighed. "Maybe I am."

The night of July 2 and into July 3 passed slowly for the Confederates who sat awake and too quickly for those who slept. A selfish breeze that began an hour before dawn and lasted barely an hour did little beyond disturbing the white ash of dead cook fires, not cooling the men or horses in the least. The heat, even in predawn, was a malignant force, a weighty blanket of stifling, humid air that turned breathing into labor and drew sweat from every pore. Flies plagued the horses and descended in clouds on the latrine ditches. Cooks, dizzy from the combined heat of their fires and the ambient temperature, drew from their rapidly diminishing supplies of biscuits, hardtack, and coffee, cursing at their slow-moving helpers.

Men and horses, drenched with sweat, had been dragging artillery and ammunition into place since the first vestiges of light. The cannons of all the Rebel divisions — every piece that could be moved and that could be coaxed to fire — were needed for the initial barrage. Mounds of canister and ball rounds as tall as a man were fronted by wooden kegs of black gunpowder, tops already wrenched off, awaiting the siege. Movement along the entire length of the Confederate encampment at Seminary Ridge seemed chaotic, frenzied, as if the army was in a race with time. Officers rode in and out of battalions and companies of soldiers; General Pickett and several of his aides rode the length of the camp, waving as cheers and Rebel yells rose at the sight of him. General Lee, seated on his magnificent horse Traveler, observed the preparations, acknowledging the thunderous hurrahs he generated with nods of his head and sweeping waves of his arm.

Pickett's officers, on foot and on horseback, weaved through the masses gathered to the rear of the forest that fronted Seminary Ridge. Orders were given, repeated, modified, and contradicted. That made little difference: The plan was one of the most basic simplicity. Well over eleven thousand Confederate soldiers would march at double time in ranks as orderly as practicable across a mile of uphill terrain that even this early baked and shimmered under the burgeoning strength of the morning sun.

Uriah Toole worked gun oil into the action of his Henry rifle, a weapon he'd brought to war from his home in Texas but hadn't carried since he began as a sniper's spotter for Sinclair. Now cloth sacks of ammunition sagged from his belt on either side of his body, the left with rifle rounds, the right with .44-caliber cartridges for his Colt revolver. Sinclair, a similar sack bulging with the big .54-caliber cartridges that would feed his Sharps slung across his chest bandolier-style, sipped at acidic, overboiled coffee in a tin cup. There would be no

Confederate sniper deployment today; all men able to walk and shoot other than the artillery units would march in the assault on Cemetery Ridge. A buzz of activity and a low hum of conversation was pervasive, but the huge gathering was strangely quiet.

Toole peered around from where they sat in the skimpy shade offered by a young oak. "Damn," he said almost reverently, "I've never seen so many men in one place in all my life." Without pausing, he swung to a totally different topic. "Funny how you an' me ended up in Pickett's division, ain't it? With all these Virginia boys, I mean — you bein' from Georgia and me from Texas, an' all." To someone who didn't know him well, Toole's voice would probably have sounded normal. To Sinclair, the minute quiver of nervousness and the speed of the flow of words stated that his friend — the man who trusted Robert E. Lee implicitly — was plain scared.

"I guess that's the army for you," Jake said. "It worked out, though. I never met a man with eyes like yours, Uriah. I swear you could count the hairs on a gnat's balls at a hundred yards — at dusk."

Toole's smile was both quick and very obviously forced.

"Look, Uriah," Jake said quietly. "We're

both going to walk away from this battle. It'll be a pisser, there's no doubt about that. But like you said, the Yankee round that'll take either of us down hasn't been made yet." To Sinclair's own ears, his words sounded artificial, spoken for impact rather than credibility. Nevertheless, they seemed to cheer Toole slightly.

Jake fervently wished he believed what he'd just said.

Some of the light came back to Toole's eyes. "Be good to run some cattle 'long with raisin' horses," he said. "After the war, I mean — after we see our folks an' then meet up again. A man can always turn a dollar if he's got a few head of beef to sell."

Jake had to force the words at first, but as he spoke — rambled, in a sense — the pretense of normalcy, that this was merely another casual conversation with his best friend — paid the dividend of eliminating the image of the mile of open field leading to Cemetery Ridge. "That's true," he said. "It takes some time to raise up a horse, break him to saddle, and train him to race. That's better than a two-year process. Even a small herd of hardy stock — longhorns, maybe — would pay the bills while we . . ."

The hours passed as molasses flows in the dead of winter, slowly, thickly, barely moving. The position of the sun changed as slowly as the minutes and hours passed. The temperature continued its way upward, leaving the nineties of the previous day behind, reaching for the hundred-degree mark. About noon, officers began moving men into the woods, ready to form quickly and efficiently into lines when the order was given. The rare report of a Yankee sniper's rifle was the only sound louder than the shuffling of feet and the quiet conversation of Pickett's troops.

At one o'clock the Confederate artillery fusillade began. It was more than an ungodly racket, more than a wild cacophony of sound. It was a physical force that made the very earth tremble before it, shook the trees, shattered the air, tore the color from the sky, and turned it from deep blue to the hazy darkness of thunderclouds. That such a furor could continue for more than a few moments was impossible. Yet the clamor continued. Blood seeped through the balls of raw cotton stuffed in the artillerymen's ears from ruptured eardrums. Most were deaf within the first minute of the opening volley. But they needed no sense of hearing to obey their order: Fire! Buckets of water were dashed against barrels of cannons and directly down their maws — followed by the next canister and the powder and the torch. Beards, hair, eyebrows smoldered in the heat from the cannons and skin blistered when it inadvertently touched the guns. The thin glass of windows shattered in the Seminary building, not from being struck but from the sheer force of the waves of sound. The Union response to the Rebel enfilade, rolling thunder in itself, was feeble by comparison to the Confederate onslaught.

Two full hours later the cannonade was over. Longstreet, atop a knoll adjacent to the rear cannons, waved an arm to Pickett and then formally saluted him. Pickett returned the salute, spun his horse, and issued the order that started the troops from the woods and onto the grassy, uneven field leading to Cemetery Ridge.

Jake and Uriah stood side by side, watching the soldiers ahead of them move out from the cover of trees into the sunshine. It was an eerily quiet spectacle. There was no Rebel yell, no hollering back and forth between the men. Instead, the steady tramp of boots on soil and grass was the only sound — a steady, rhythmic beat that grew neither louder nor quieter as men poured out and extended the lines.

It took Jake a moment to assimilate what

was happening in front of him. He'd never seen his army march like this, with such discipline, in such order. Confederate marching — after more than two years of war — had degenerated to a shuffling walk covering the miles between battlefields, a shambling parody of a military movement of troops. Yet here, the march seemed to be precisely synchronized. A scattered volley of rifle fire from overly enthusiastic Yankees greeted the first Rebel lines out into the field, but the range was such that the Rebs didn't flinch, knowing that the minnie balls and slugs couldn't reach them. Jake tapped his left trigger as his line began forward, keeping his finger outside the guard and away from the second trigger. He glanced for a quick moment to his right. Uriah matched strides with him, the Winchester clutched across his chest, his face a pasty white, in spite of his heavy tan. There were perhaps twenty lines of men ahead of Sinclair and Toole, spaced twenty-five feet apart. Jake looked to his left and then to his right. The lines appeared to be a good half-mile long.

It seemed like the damage began all at once, like a quick rain shower from a cloudless sky. The man to Jake's left went down making a gurgling sound, blood bubbling from a rend in his throat. The deadly hail of Yankee canisters swept through the advancing army, tearing holes in the lines. Soldiers sidestepped to fill the gaps and kept marching. Yankee riflemen, placed on both flanks of the marching horde, picked off Confederates almost as quickly as they could — fire and duck behind the cover of gullies or slight knolls. Jake stopped, raising his rifle to his shoulder. He fired at a Yankee uphill from him at 150 yards and hurried to catch up with his line as his target was hurled backward by the impact of the slug. Around Jake men were returning fire now, mostly to the flanks, snapping shots, doing little more than keeping some of the Yankee's heads down.

The Union cannonade became constant, shells whistling past, canisters exploding with flashes of white light seemingly everywhere in the sky. A half dozen men a few yards ahead and to Sinclair's right went down together, blown to bloody bits of flesh and bone by an exploding round that struck the ground a few feet in front of them. Their screams were swallowed by the blast and by the ongoing roar of the cannons on the far side of Cemetery Ridge.

The weather, too, was a formidable enemy. Men gasped and wheezed as they struggled to maintain the rapid advance, but the uphill angle and the 101-degree temperature sapped their strength and blurred their vision.

Uriah fired steadily at Jake's right, aiming carefully, making his rounds count. His face was no longer pale, Sinclair noticed, and his lips, tense, tight lines, were slightly parted, looking as if he was about to smile.

The front line of the Confederate troops reached the halfway point before the very worst of the slaughter got under way. Jake, aiming, stumbled over a ragged severed leg and fell clumsily onto a pair of downed men who were barely distinguishable as human — who resembled the carcasses of sloppily butchered animals. Sinclair scrambled to his feet, his arms and chest painted with blood, a loop of glistening viscera from one of the fallen soldiers grotesquely hooked around the grip of his bowie knife. Instinctively he swept the length of gut away and as his fingers touched it, the warmly wet and slippery surface filled his mouth with bile and vomit and he staggered, releasing a keening, panicked wail he couldn't hear over the furor of the battle.

Like mindless machines they hustled onward up the grade, Yankee cannon and rifle fire sweeping through the lines like terrible, death-dealing winds, soaking the ground with blood, littering it with limbs and bodies. Cemetery Ridge, still far ahead, was no longer a distinct geographical feature: Gunsmoke shrouded it so completely that only muzzle flashes were visible through the gray, roiling fog.

Uriah shoved roughly at Jake's shoulder, bringing him out of where he'd been for a brief moment, urging him onward. He sleeved the blood from his face, clearing his eyes, and raised his rifle, aiming at a white flash on the ridge. It wasn't the lack of sound — he hadn't been able to hear the throaty roar of his Sharps for several minutes over the clamor of the fight — but the absence of recoil against his shoulder that told him he'd squeezed off a nonexistent round. He loaded with spastic fingers as he lumbered forward.

Hundreds — perhaps thousands — of dead and dying men were strewn about the killing field. There were no more Rebel lines — instead the troops were a seething mass stepping on, over, and around their fallen comrades. Even above the acrid stink of gunpowder and sweat and fear, the heavy, metallic odor of fresh blood hung damply, pervasively, enveloping the now formless assault.

Rifle fire was a devastating, incessant storm from the ridge. The shuffling, hollow-eyed Rebs were no more difficult targets than dairy cows standing stupidly in an enclosed lot, awaiting their personal bullet or minnie ball.

Jake shouldered his rifle and pointed it at a cluster of flashes within the wall of smoke ahead of him, ignoring the sight at the end of his barrel, and jerked the pair of triggers back together. He was no longer a marksman, a sharpshooter. He was a poorly tuned mechanical device that sent .54-caliber slugs toward no particular target, with absolutely no noticeable effect.

A wash of warm liquid slapped Jake's face on the right, stinging him with its force. His eyes flicked in that direction, to his partner's position. Uriah stood, swaying, rifle dropping to the ground in front of him. Jake screamed.

Uriah Toole had no head. It was simply gone. His neck, a ragged stump of flesh with tiny tendrils of smoke rising from it, erupted gushets of blood. After an eternity the body fell forward, coming to rest on the twisted remains of another soldier.

Jake Sinclair's mind — all his senses — shut down. He raised his rifle to his shoulder perfunctorily, unthinkingly, not because he needed to fire it but because that's what he'd been doing for what seemed like all his life, and because that's what he was supposed to do now.

A slug slashed a groove along the left side of his head. Another slammed into the breech of his Sharps, shattering the metal and grinding into the polished wood of the stock, splintering it. A round from his flank gouged a channel along his right cheekbone. Something — maybe a fragment of an exploding cannonball — struck the barrel of his rifle, tearing it from his hands, sending it spinning away into the smoke.

Sinclair went down, face and head bleeding into the dry dirt. In a moment a one-legged corpse with a gaping hole in its chest fell on top of him, and a moment later, another corpse followed, this one amazingly intact.

CHAPTER TWO

Sinclair drifted in and out of the battle that surged around him. He wasn't at all sure where he was — the crashing, incessant furor of the weapons, the screams and curses, the quick movements of the corpse that covered him when it was struck by rounds or steel fragments — twisted him back and forth between the edges of awareness and darkness. The pain in his head was something that had always been there, torturing him, and would always be there. Beyond that, his senses had deserted him. There was no passage of time, no end to the battle. Images of Uriah Toole, alive, drinking coffee, arguing, laughing, flickered occasionally in his mind, along with vestiges of scenes from his own home, his youth. His dog, a noble old collie long since dead and buried in the family cemetery, fetched a chewed knot of rawhide to him, dropping it at his feet, liquid, intelligent eyes asking that it be thrown again. Jake scurried from the kitchen to the front veranda with the cut-glass tumbler of bourbon and branch water his pa took at the end of each day, the cook cautioning him to be careful not to spill a drop, her voice rich and warm. The lawn in front of his pillared home stretched, green and lush, to the quiet little hook the river made, the place where Jake fished with his father, hauling catfish the size of small dogs to the shore. The scenario of leaving the relative safety of the trees forward of Seminary Ridge and jogging into the march, his Sharps at port arms, stepped on the panorama of his home, recurring, becoming more vivid and real each time it appeared.

It was a battlefield scavenger that brought Sinclair to full consciousness. The deadweight of the soldier on top of him was dragged away and rude hands slapped at Jake's pockets. He felt a tug at his waist at the haft of his bowie knife, strong enough to send lightning bolts of pain to his head. Jake's right hand closed on the offender with all the strength he could muster, and even through the pain the feeble size of the wrist registered. *A woman?* The flesh was smooth and the bones small and slender.

The boy yelped and fell back from his crouch next to Jake, his voice high and frightened. "I didn't know! I didn't know you was alive!" Jake's eyes, crusted with dried blood, opened, fixed on the boy's face. He was perhaps ten or eleven, his flesh pale, his eyes as wide as those of a panicked horse. Jake released his grip and the boy was gone.

The sounds of the battle were gone, as well, and the texture of the light told Sinclair that dusk had fallen. He turned over from his face-to-the-earth sprawl very slowly, head screaming in pain, and struggled to a half-sitting position.

The broad field was strewn — littered — with dead men lying together, in small masses and individually. Arms, legs, heads dotted the landscape like afterthoughts. The reek of gunpowder was all but overpowered by that of blood and viscera, a queasily metallic stench that hovered like a malignant fog. Sinclair, upper body balanced by his hand on the ground, palm pressing against still blood-damp soil, watched without passion — without much interest — as a soldier aimed, fired, and picked off a scavenger, the shooter's hoarse cursing louder than the report of his rifle.

Jake Sinclair made his decision at that moment, with little thought or consideration. *No more. No goddamn more. I'm done. Fin-*

ished. The voice within him was quiet and strong and, he fully realized, irrevocable. His father's face flashed before him, the old man's mouth set in rebuke, his eyes showing his shame at his deserter son. *No more,* Jake told him. *A man can only see and smell and feel just so much and no more. Then something shuts down, turns off like a blown-out lantern, and everything about him changes and he's a different man. I won't bring my cowardice home to you. You'll think I got torn apart on this field like all these other men, that I died for President Davis and the Confederate States of America, and you'll be proud of me for the rest of your life. After the war is won and the South prevails you'll believe that I gave my life for a just and noble cause. But, Pa, I can't do any more than I've done or give any more than I've given. I have nothing left to give. I'm finished.*

Even the slightest bodily movement sent stunning blasts of pain to Jake's head. He raised his left hand — still supporting himself in a sitting position against his right — and touched first the slash across his cheekbone. The flesh above and below the cut seemed numb, but the open line that followed the bone seemed a yard wide, raw and crusted and slightly damp in places along its four-inch length. He probed very gently at the left side of his head, above his ear. The furrow there continued to bleed along its length, but slowly, the blood seeping rather than flowing. He knew he had to do something about both wounds; infection killed almost as many men as did canister shot and rifle rounds.

There was a fuzziness, a lack of definition, to the sounds around him. The moans of the wounded boys were soft, without the stridency of the pain that forced them from the soldiers' mouths. Surgeons in their once gray and now bloodied dusters moved through the battlefield. One, not twenty feet from him, Jake noticed, wore a Union uniform and a sagging apron, dripping blood. Litter bearers followed the surgeons, grim-faced, walking away from dying men in order to carry those who could possibly survive, to the hospital tents. The surgeons, working mechanically, crouched next to men, inspected their wounds, checked pulse or heartbeat, and either shook their heads or nodded before moving on to the next mangled soldier.

Jake struggled to his feet and stood swaying dizzily, feeling his yelp of pain in his throat but unable to actually hear it himself. The Yankee surgeon lowered the corpse he'd been examining and weaved his way over and around bodies to where Sinclair stood. The doctor's mouth moved but Jake heard no words. The doctor's eyes were red and his face an expressionless mask as he leaned close to Jake, inspecting his wounds. Again, Jake saw the man's mouth move but heard nothing.

"I can't hear," Jake said.

The surgeon moved directly in front of him, close enough to him so that Jake could smell whiskey on his breath. He formed the words carefully: "Clean your wounds." When Jake nodded slightly, indicating he understood, the doctor and his litter bearers moved on.

Darkness was rapidly encroaching on what little light of the evening remained. The heat seemed as intense as it had at noon, and no breeze stirred. The line of trees that had been the Confederate starting point of the charge was impossibly far away. A cavalry horse, its chest white with frothy sweat, a single rein dragging, the other torn off at the bit, danced across Jake's line of vision. Jake began to raise an arm and the animal caught the motion and bolted uphill, toward Cemetery Ridge, hooves missing some fallen men and stepping on others.

Step by staggering step, Sinclair moved toward the woods, the slight downhill grade offering some degree of assistance as he shambled around corpses. Once a hand reached up to him. Jake stopped, saw the hand was at the end of a severed arm lodged against a dead soldier's side, and stumbled on.

There was no longer an encampment. Here and there a cook fire burned beyond the trees, but even the rough order of the pre-attack Pickett's Division was absent. Men, many — perhaps most — of them bandaged, wandered about, dazed, mumbling, making no attempt to gather together with what was left of their units. Some carried weapons. Strangely, most did not. Bits of Jake's hearing were coming back. A shouted phrase pierced the buzz in his head, then a few spoken words.

Lanterns hung from the front of a hospital tent drew Sinclair. A large cluster of men awaited treatment, many carried or at least supported by friends, all with cloths wrapped around their heads or arms or legs. The screams from within the tent were loud enough for Jake to hear. Amputation was the treatment for severe wounds to limbs; to the rear of the tent a growing pile of battered legs and arms sawn off with no anesthetic beyond a few desperate gulps of whiskey grew like a mass of discarded scrap lumber. Jake walked away from the tent and the lanterns and the screams, moving aimlessly, as if in a dream. At a fire several men had torn the top from a small keg of Pennsylvania whiskey and were scooping it out with tin cups. Jake found the bandana he'd stuffed in his pocket, pulled it out, and reached inside the keg with it. He brought it out dripping with whiskey and used it to rasp across his cheek and head, the alcohol burning like a touch from a white-hot branding iron. When he moved back toward the keg with the cloth one of the soldiers shoved him — hard — away. The man's mouth moved and Jake heard angry sounds, but the words didn't yet register. Handkerchief hanging from his hand, he lumbered off toward the woods.

He may have seen Pickett, hollow-eyed, broken, cavalry hat gone, face bloodied, riding among the men. He may have seen General Lee, too, weeping, apologizing to the troops. Or he may have seen neither. Perhaps both were only feverish apparitions, parts of a surreal dream. It didn't matter one way or the other. It didn't matter at all.

He found his way to the woods, stumbled in as far as he could, tripped over a rock, and was knocked unconscious by the pain that screamed through his head as he hit the ground. He slept there for several hours.

The first thing Jake was aware of as he awakened was a low-hanging cloud of dew that hovered a few feet from the ground. It was deliciously cool under the protection of the floating mist. The sharp snap of a twig as it broke assured Jake that his hearing had returned. He looked toward the sound and saw a tall bay horse, saddled and bridled, the reins draped over the crest of the animal's neck. The horse pulled at a clump of grass next to a tree.

Jake took a slow inventory of his body. He'd apparently hit the ground with a good deal of force last night: His right shoulder radiated pain down his arm and his hip was sore, throbbing slightly. He touched his head wounds with tentative fingers. Both were crusted with dried blood, the one on the side of his head weeping blood slightly. All his limbs moved as he tested them. Other than the pounding in his head and the suddenly intense thirst that had come upon him, he'd survived Pickett's Charge and the three-day Battle of Gettysburg.

Survived as what? he wondered.

Jake had no intention of rejoining the ranks, of returning to the fight for the Confederacy. He realized that he no longer much gave a damn which side won the war.

Uriah wouldn't be less dead if the South prevailed, nor would the multitude of others who had died here. Sinclair felt oddly disoriented, as if he'd stumbled into a situation that was far beyond his ability to understand. But his decision to run, to desert, to leave the fighting to those who could still do it, didn't waver. The logistics were ridiculously simple, Jake knew that. Desertion was as easy as walking away from a job on a ranch or in a store in a town: A man simply moved on without giving notice. The army wouldn't miss him. So many men were killed and so many shredded by canister shot and explosions that a high number of bodies and parts of bodies would never be properly identified. Many of the Rebs carried no identification papers or personal effects, or lost those to scavengers after the battle. *One body isn't much different from another, especially one of those with a face that took a direct hit.* The hideous picture of Uriah Toole standing, swaying before he collapsed, headless, flashed in Jake's mind. He pushed the thought away as best he could.

The horse's movements helped Sinclair refocus. He inspected the animal with the unconscious scrutiny of a horseman, taking in the smooth lines of its body, the broadness of its chest, the lithe musculature of its legs. *Not a bad mount,* he thought. *I need a horse real bad and it's a sure bet the owner of this one won't come after me for horse theft.*

A mare, he noticed, when the horse swung her rear end toward him and her tail swept a fly away, revealing her gender. *A gelding might be better — but a beggar can't be a chooser.*

There was a furrow of raw flesh across the mare's hip, and flies plagued it, keeping her full tail in almost constant motion, flicking the insects away.

Jake pushed himself to a sitting position, ignoring the jolt of pain to his head the move precipitated. The horse turned toward him, inspected him for a long moment, and then lowered her head to continue grazing.

Good. Not too spooky.

The mare tore up a mouthful of grass, snorted, and focused her eyes on Sinclair, as if asking him where her morning ration of grain was — why it was so late today.

Jake struggled to his feet and stood with his boots well spread, balancing himself. Red spots danced in front of his eyes for a moment and then were gone. The mist was rapidly dissipating and he immediately noticed the difference in temperature between the ground and where his head was now. The July sun was beginning its onslaught for the day. It was already heavy, stifling.

Jake stood motionless, watching the horse, wondering if one of his clumsy steps would send her skittering away from him. He wet his lips and whistled a quiet note. The mare's eyes pinned him for a pair of seconds before looking away. He whistled again and took a half step toward the mare, placing his boots carefully, moving slowly. She continued calmly cropping grass, although the pointing of her ears at him clearly indicated that she was aware of every move he made.

Jake took another step — a full one this time. He paused and when the horse did nothing, took another step, and then another. When he was close enough to smell the dried sweat on her coat and the fresh scent of the grass she was crushing with her teeth, he stopped.

"Hey, mare," he said, his voice barely above a whisper. "I'm glad you got through the shit storm yesterday."

He reached out his right hand and grasped the one-piece rein that was tangled into the mare's mane. He tugged her head gently upward and moved in front of her, rein secure in his hand. Her eyes, the deep, shiny brown of a fresh autumn chestnut, met

Jake's, assessing him, taking his measure. He leaned forward and exhaled gently into her nostrils. The horse lowered her head to his chest level and snorted but didn't back away, apparently satisfied with Jake's introduction.

Sinclair stepped to the mare's left side. The stirrups were about right: The horse's rider had been about Jake's height. The military saddle was deeply stained across the seat and down onto the fender facing Jake, the blood partially dried but still sticky, its metallic scent mixing with that of the polished leather. He raised his left boot and eased it into the stirrup, his left hand gripping rein and mane, and swung onto the horse's back. He was dizzy for a moment, and the thirst returned as he settled into the saddle. It felt good to be mounted again. At home, horses had been a part of his life, not only for transportation but for the glory of the animals, their terrific speed and strength and the sensation of invincibility they gave him as he raced them against those of his friends, and as he bred and raised them, improving his stable with each pairing of stallion and mare and each birth. A sharpshooter in the Army of Northern Virginia didn't rate a horse — and actually didn't require one for what he did. He and

Uriah had slogged along with the foot soldiers, accepted by them but always viewed a bit askance, in the same way men perceived undertakers. It was a necessary job, the soldiers admitted, but still . . .

Jake nudged the mare lightly with his heels and moved out, checking the sun for directions. It was then — at that very moment — that he decided to take the news of Uriah's death to his family in Drumlin, Texas. It was, of course, a long, long haul to West Texas from Pennsylvania. *Going to take some time,* he thought. *That makes it all the better. The truth is, I have nowhere to go, nowhere I want to be. Drumlin's as good as anywhere else, and Uriah's people deserve to know what happened to him. I'll tell them . . . hell, I don't know what I'll tell them. But when I leave them, they'll believe that Uriah died a full man, with all his parts still attached. No family should have to know their boy died like Uriah did.*

From behind him, back toward the encampment, military-type sounds reached Jake: the whinnying of horses, the creak of dry axles as wagons and carts were moved, shouted orders softened by the distance. Lee and his army had nowhere else to go but back South now. That's where the remnants of the army would head.

Jake figured due west as well as he was able from the sun and began his journey, the mare moving smoothly under him, picking her way through the trees and brush, her hooves quiet on the ancient blanket of leaves and pine needles.

Much of the day passed with Jake half aware of his surroundings. Other than checking the mare occasionally when she wandered off course, he slumped in the saddle like a sack of grain, only his years of riding experience and his innate horseman's sense keeping him aboard. When a pheasant flushed directly in their path, exploding from a hackberry bush, wings thundering, the startled horse skittered to one side and attempted to spin away from the threat. Jake's body moved with his mount and his legs and hands brought her back into control easily, without actual awareness of doing so on his part.

It was the scent of water that made Sinclair acutely aware of his parched throat and the thick, arid, dryness of his mouth. The mare, too, smelled water and she was as parched as her rider. Jake straightened in the saddle, reined in, and looked around. He'd been following a deer trail simply to avoid plowing through heavier brush. It wasn't as much an actual decision as it was selecting the way of least resistance.

He tried to generate saliva as he sniffed the air. The cool perfume of water seemed to be all around him, coming from no particular direction. The mare snorted and scraped impatiently at the dirt of the game trail with a front hoof. Jake gave her all of the rein and for a moment she stood stock-still, realizing she was no longer controlled — restrained — by her rider. Then she snorted loudly and cut off the trail, her gait cautious yet hurried as she jogged through brambles and scrub growth, small saplings, and stepped over or jumped fallen trees. Branches slapped meanly at Jake's body and head as the mare plunged onward, head held high, drawing in the scent she followed. A bough swept the length of the left side of Sinclair's head and he cringed, cursing, but didn't slow his mount.

Before long he could hear it — the tinkling, mellifluous sweetness of water moving over rocks and sand, splashing lightly, causing his throat to constrict painfully, as if he were struggling to swallow a mouthful of dry gravel. The mare, too, heard the water. She increased her gait, ignoring the thorns and branches that drew blood from her chest and front legs and lashed at her sides, clumsy now, her breath punching from her dilated nostrils in sharp snorting exhalations.

There was no transition. One moment they were bushwhacking through dense, clinging growth and the next they stood on a sort of sandy apron a couple of yards from a quick-moving stream. The mare lurched forward, rushed into the stream until the water reached her belly, and then droped her head, sucking noisily. Jake slid down the horse's side, even in his thirst clutching the rein, crouched, and pushed his face under the sun-sparkling surface. The water was the most wonderful thing Jake Sinclair had ever tasted — would ever taste. There was the muskiness of minerals and moss to it, and it was arctically cold. He swallowed huge mouthfuls, barely stopping to breathe, until the keenest edge of his thirst was dulled. Then he stood and muscled and hauled the reluctant horse out of the stream and onto the shore. Allowing her too much cold water too fast could lead to founder, he knew, and founder caused the inner structures of the hooves to swell, rendering the horse lame, unable to carry weight — and useless. He was able to interest the mare in the tall, lush grass that grew at the periphery of the sandy apron. As she grazed he released the cinch buckle and the horse took a grateful breath, shook her body, and resumed tugging grass. Fifteen or so minutes later Jake led the mare back into the stream. She drank again, but less hungrily, far less frantically. When he pulled her back to the grass she followed him without an argument. After another ten minutes and another trip to the water, she was sated and content to graze. Jake fashioned rough hobbles from his belt and slipped them around her front legs. Obviously used to hobbles, the mare made no protest.

Jake sat on the sand in the shade of an oak branch above him. Now that his thirst was satisfied he realized that he hadn't eaten in more than twenty-four hours. His stomach grumbled loudly, reminding him of that fact. And, he realized, he stank. The heavy reek of fear-sweat and dried blood permeated his clothing. The armpits of his shirt were wet and foul and his pants were still damp with piss released either during the battle or afterward, when he fell. He touched the palm of his hand to his head wounds and then sniffed carefully at his hand. There was none of the sickly odor of infection. *Good ol' Pennsylvania whiskey.*

Jake stood and moved in a slow circle, peering into the forest around him. There wasn't a sound beyond birds and the quiet ruffling of leaves when a breath of air touched them — no military sounds, no human sounds at all. He sat back down and wrestled his boots off, setting them aside, leaving the gold eagle he'd placed in each of them the day he left home to sign on with General Lee. He put his knife and sheath in a boot, then stood again, shucked off his shirt and pants, bundled them up, and walked into the stream. In the center the water was about a yard deep — perfect for bathing and clothes washing. He scoured his body with handfuls of sand and, avoiding his wounds, squeezed water and sand through his hair and let the impatient flow of the current rinse his body and head.

Back onshore, clothes a dripping mess in his hands, Sinclair checked the sky. He had maybe three hours of sun left for the day — more than enough to dry his pants and shirt. He draped them over a bush, sleeves of the shirt extended to the sides, the legs of the pants as far apart as he could spread them. The mare, sloppy hobbles properly in place, had moved a few feet to another patch of grass and was grazing happily. Jake returned to the spot under the branch of the oak and sat on the sand. His hunger prodded at him, but he did his best to dismiss it, at least for now. If he had his rifle, or even a pistol, he could take a rabbit or a pheasant . . .

And if I were a cow I'd have tits and then I could draw a glass of milk. Or if I could find someone to butcher me, I could have a nice beefsteak.

He looked more closely at the shore where it met the edge of the stream. His own boot tracks and those of the mare's hooves were the most prominent, but there was a map of others: the marks of small claws, the skittery trails of birds, some pug-marks of a bobcat, and the distinctive footprint of a bear — a small one, from the size of the tracks. Jake got up, fetched his boots, and brought them into the shade with him. He took his knife from inside one and removed it from its sheath. He tested the edge with his thumb from habit: He knew full well the bowie was sharp enough to shave with. He sat back down to wait. It'd been a while since he'd last thrown at a target, but he recalled winning a few dollars — prewar Yankee currency — in a contest with a young fellow back home who'd gotten handy with a nicely made Mexican blade. Jake hefted his knife, flipped it in a half circle, and grabbed it just behind the point between the thumb and forefinger of his right hand. He let the length and weight of the knife rest along the line of the side of his hand and wrist, the haft well up his forearm. Then he waited.

For what seemed like a long time, the only sound Sinclair heard was the movement of the water over and past the rocks that poked up here and there in the current like the heads of watching sentinels. Then the sounds of the forest returned, the calls and songs of birds, the chittering arguments of chipmunks, the breathy swaying of branches as squirrels leaped to them and launched from them. The shifting movements and the occasional quiet snort of the mare melded with the natural order of the woods — she offered no threat to any of its creatures. A hognose snake — a big one, perhaps a five-footer, slid past Jake's feet, inches away, unafraid, its bright red tongue testing the air as it moved. Only Jake's eyes moved, following the reptile. The rest of his body was as still as a gravestone.

I hope I don't regret letting that boy go by. He'd have been an easy throw and snake isn't half bad when it's cooked right. Thing is, making a fire'd take forever and I'm hungry right now. Still, empty as my gut is, the idea of raw hognose snake makes me want to upchuck. What I need is a nice fat rabbit to stop by for a drink. And that'll happen — that's what those tracks tell me.

After an interminable hour and a half of waiting, Jake's eyelids grew impossibly heavy. Twice he snapped them open, fetching himself back from sleep. The third time he drifted into a doze, still sitting statue-still, right forearm and hand resting in his lap, knife in place and ready, chin on his chest, shoulders slumped forward.

"The toughest part of hunting — especially for a young boy —" his father told him, smiling, "is to remain motionless. That's damn near impossible for a kid with ants in his drawers." They were in a tree stand, high above a deer trail, on an autumn morning. The early, tentative sunlight was diffused into speckles of gold as it peeked through the branches, the air sweet and cool. Jake's first rifle was across his lap, muzzle pointing safely away from his father and himself. He felt grown, if not in manhood quite yet, then certainly coming close to it, and the fact that it was the first time his father had taken him out for deer added to the glory of the day. "Let's start practicing that right now, Jake. It's coming full light — the deer'll be moving. Don't you shift an inch until you raise that new rifle of yours to your shoulder, hear, son?" The buck that stepped into view was a ten-pointer and every detail of his body, of his majestic rack of

antlers, seemed to sparkle with a radiance, a diamond brilliance, in Jake's mind. His hands, suddenly wet with sweat, eased his 44.40 into position, butt snug to his shoulder. The buck's natural instinct told him that something was amiss. He stopped, and the does behind him stopped too, watching him for the cue to go on or to bolt back into the thick woods. Jake swallowed and eased his finger around the trigger, placing the front sight on the chest of the buck, beginning to squeeze — not jerk — the trigger . . .

It was no longer a deer in Jake's sights. It was now a man in a blue uniform, a saber at his side, a dull black telescope raised to his eye. Jake's sights were on his head, nose high. Jake heard the oiled click as his trigger touched home and the hammer of his rifle snapped forward — and he saw that the man in the uniform was Uriah Toole and it was too late to stop the bullet he'd fired —

"Looks like I got me a nekkid run-off here," a voice that was neither Jake's father's nor Uriah's rasped. Jake's eyes opened. A massive figure stood in front of Sinclair with his back to the stream. Even in the murky, cloud-obscured light of night it was easy enough to see that he held a rifle in his hands, pointed at Jake's chest. "Don't think about movin'," the voice said. "You do an' you're dead."

Jake straightened his back but otherwise remained motionless. The big man spat to the side, and the earthy smell of cut plug tobacco reached Jake, mixed with the after-scent of whiskey.

"No reason to hold that rifle on me," Jake said. The man took a step closer as a string of clouds moved away from the full moon's face. A thin shaft of light that penetrated the leaves of the oak showed Jake the size of the man, his full, unkempt beard that reached halfway down his abdomen, the profusion of dark hair on his bare chest and arms, and the bush of greasy hair that surrounded his head. He looked like a bear and stood like a grizzly, feet apart, body leaning slightly forward, head upright.

"Like I said," Jake repeated, "you have no reason to hold that rifle on me. I don't have anything worth taking."

"That horse back there is worth taking — a hell of a lot better than the crow bait I been ridin'." After a moment he added, "You ain't gonna be needin' no horse."

Jake squinted, making sure of the distance between them. His right arm had tensed. He forced it to relax until the muscle of his forearm was no longer tight, until it would move smoothly when he needed it to.

The bear spit again, this time directing the stream of saliva and bits of tobacco next to Jake. "You Reb or Union?"

Jake didn't answer. He took in a breath and held it.

"Don't much matter to me," the bear said. "Either one, you're dead. I never had no use for a soljer — wearin' blue or gray. An' a coward what would run off ain't hardly worth the bullet it takes to kill him."

The click as the bear drew back the hammer of his rifle was as loud as a thunderclap. Jake made his move. His arm flashed out as if he were pitching a ball, and at the same time he threw his body to his left. The jagged white flame that erupted from the barrel of the rifle lit the scene for half of a heartbeat, the bullet slamming into the ground behind Jake. The bear gurgled wetly, dropped his rifle, and clutched at his neck with both hands. Blood that appeared as black and glistening as oil pumped from around the six inches of blade that pierced his throat. He gurgled again, fell to his knees, and dragged the knife free. He may have cost himself a few seconds of life; the flow of blood increased until it gushed several inches in front of him, spattering to the ground. His eyes, Jake saw, glowed hotly for a part of a second and then that light was gone and the bear fell forward, the top of his shaggy head inches from Jake's feet, a river of blood flowing toward him over the sand. Jake shoved himself back and got to his feet.

Behind him and off to the side the mare reared, startled by the gunshot and now the scent of spilled blood. The belt-hobbles held and she stood breathing fast and hard, the whites of her eyes exposed in the moonlight. Jake walked to her, hand extended.

"Hey, mare," he coaxed the horse, "no reason to get all fired up. You settle down now, mare. You're OK — no more surprises. You're fine, mare — nothing to worry about." He continued the quiet, assuring babble, moving until he stood in front of the horse. He stroked her neck until he felt the muscles relax and the quivering slow and then stop. Jake continued to stroke her until she dropped her head to graze, fear forgotten. He was pleased with how quickly she'd calmed, but not surprised. *Cavalry horses are trained to keep their heads under gunfire — but not at midnight with no fight going on, no other sounds of battle. And yesterday this mare had her owner shot off her back in the most horrendous engagement she'd ever see. She's a good horse, OK. A fine horse.*

The sound of bushes moving and a soft snort told Sinclair that the man he'd just killed had left his horse a distance back in the scrub and had come upon Jake on foot. *He must have been following me — waiting until I went to sleep to get a drop on me.* He returned to the facedown body and stood looking at it. The bear had been tall — approaching six and a half feet, it looked like — and broad, heavy, with wide shoulders. A bandolier was draped over the man's shoulder and must have crossed his naked chest. Moonlight glinted softly on the brass of the cartridges. A military holster held a sidearm at his hip. Jake could use the gun, and the rifle, too. But he didn't take them now. The morning would be plenty of time. Just now, the fetid odor of death and warm blood permeated the air around the corpse and Jake felt his gorge rising in his throat. He moved away, finding the bush upon which he'd left his clothes, and pulled on his pants and shirt. The fabric was dry and slightly stiff and felt good next to his skin. His boots weren't far from the dead man. They'd be there in the morning.

Lots of these crazies around, Jake thought as he walked down the stream. *They follow the campaigns, watch the battles, strip what they can from the dead of either side, killing* and robbing soldiers who wander off — or desert — from camps. They were like vultures, carrion eaters, defilers of the dead, the dying. Men on both sides of the conflict shot them down with impunity, just as they'd kill rattlesnakes or rabid dogs.

Sinclair sat with his back against the cool surface of a boulder, waiting for his heartbeat to return to normal, hunger again gnawing at him. The man whose life he'd just ended was his first close kill — the term soldiers gave to the killing of an enemy close enough so that his eyes could be seen. *Sharpshooting's a different proposition — not real far from target shooting. So is firing into a bunch of Yanks, knowing the slug would take down at least one of them. There was none of the smell of blood or the dying sounds or the extinguishing of the light of life in the man's eyes.* He sighed. *A rifle's cleaner and a long shot cleaner yet. That damned knife . . .* He sighed again. *Him or me,* he thought. *It was him or me.*

The flow of the water and the gentle night sounds had a calming effect on Jake Sinclair. He stretched his bare feet out in front of him and his fingers found the wound on his face and then that on the side of his head. Both were dry, the flesh coming together well. There was no heat, no indication of infection. Thoughts and images flickered and flashed in Jake's mind as his body relaxed. Already he'd begun building a wall around the Battle of Gettysburg and the death of Uriah — a self-protective device that he believed — hoped — would allow him to retain the vestiges of sanity he still possessed. He found it remarkable, quite strange, that his desertion had so little real impact on his feelings. His simple *I've had enough* seemed to cover it, both emotionally and intellectually. The Confederacy, the Union, the war itself, had become abstractions, like thoughts not fully shaped, concepts without definitions. He wondered, for a very brief moment, how far back south the Army of Northern Virginia had gotten in the past day. Then he slept.

Jake hauled his boots onto his sockless feet, tugging and cursing. The morning sun sparkled in the stream and the forest seemed to be a place of calm and peace. The only discordant note was the sprawled corpse of the man Jake had killed the night before. Flies had already gathered in the stream of blood and on and around the body's face and the rend in its throat. The dead man smelled, not yet of death and decomposition, but of moldy pants, sweat, stale whiskey, and tobacco juice. Jake crouched, grabbed at a shoulder, and turned the corpse over, faceup. Jake's bowie knife, sticky with blood, had spent the night under the body. Jake picked it up carefully, making as little contact with the drying blood as he could, took it to the stream, and rinsed it, scrubbed it with sand, wiped the blade on his pants, and slid it back into the sheath. He put the sheath in his side pocket; his belt was serving temporary duty as a set of hobbles.

Sinclair returned to the body and stripped off the holster and belt. The pistol, mismatched to the army holster with the Union symbol of the eagle embossed on its black leather flap, was a converted Colt .44 revolver with bone grips. The weapon appeared to be in very good shape. It was clean and gave off a faint aroma of gun oil. When Jake spun the cylinder it revolved smoothly with a quiet whirring sound. He noticed that the cartridges in the loops of the gun belt were Colt issue, not army-contracted ammunition. He strapped the belt around his waist and buckled it so that the pistol hung comfortably at his side. He tapped at the dead man's packets, which held nothing.

Jake's gaze stopped at a strange-looking

necklace the bearlike corpse wore. A dozen or more clumps of flesh of various sizes and in varying degrees of desiccation hung from a rawhide cord around the man's chest and now rested on the blood-soaked and matted hair of his chest. Jake leaned forward for a closer look, and then recoiled as if struck by an unanticipated, invisible punch to the face. Two of the lumps of flesh were fresh. They were human tongues. Hot bile rose in Jake's throat as he backed away, scrambling, almost losing his balance. He turned his back on the body and took a series of deep breaths to attempt to quell his revulsion. It didn't work.

Afterward he walked past the corpse, eyes averted, to where the rifle lay in the scrub, an inch or so of its stock protruding onto the sand. It was a Henry repeating 44.40, in decent condition. Jake held the butt to his shoulder and the sun-warmed weapon felt good and natural as he peered down the sights.

Removing the bandolier of ammunition from the corpse left Jake with the sour taste of vomit in his mouth and a sheen of sweat on his face. He had no more thought of burying the body than he would have had the corpse been that of a cottonmouth.

As he rinsed blood from the bandolier and

the cartridges it held, a skinny roan horse clambered out of the brush and into the stream and began to suck water. One of the animal's reins dragged a thin, wrenched-away branch. Even from ten feet away, Jake could see the gauntness of the animal and the raw spur marks on its flanks. The horse carried a highly polished, full double-rigged Western stock saddle that looked as out of place as a diamond tiara would on a gin-mill whore. Jake waded out into the stream and grabbed a rein before the horse noticed him, and even then, didn't look up or slow its drinking. Jake give the animal another minute and then led him back to shore and onto the sand. The obviously fatigued gelding followed docilely. When Jake stopped and raised a hand to stroke the emaciated neck, the horse flinched and attempted, weakly, to rear. The roan's flanks trembled in fear as Jake approached from the side. He quickly released the two cinches and tugged the saddle and blanket from the horse's back, revealing several festering saddle sores.

Jake dumped the saddle to the side and examined the sores more closely. They were fresh and wet, but now that they were exposed to the air and given that they wouldn't be abraded further by a blanket and saddle, they'd heal. Jake led the roan into the stream again to drink, and again, after a few minutes led him out. After one more such repetition, Jake worked the buckle on the bridle and removed the bit and headset from the roan. When Jake slapped him on the rump, the horse skittered into the stream, crossed it to the far bank, and disappeared into the woods. Jake smiled and set out to fetch his mare.

While she drank, Jake released the cinch on the army pancake saddle and eased it and the blanket off the mare's back. There were no saddle sores. He tossed the saddle aside. As the bay grazed, hobbled once again with Jake's belt, he went through the saddle-bags attached to either side of the Western saddle with lengths of latigo. They were survival treasure chests, bringing a broad smile to Jake's face. One was half filled with strips and thick knots of jerky. When he tasted it he grinned again: It was beef jerky, not venison, and it was no more difficult to chew than a tough steak. Under the dried meat was an unlabeled quart bottle of amber-colored whiskey. Jake pulled the cork and filled his mouth with the warm liquid. When he swallowed, the heat traveled down his gullet and into his gut as smoothly as silk over a fine lady's shoulder, washing away the bitterness of the bile that had arisen earlier. A cloth sack of rifle ammunition had rested against the bottle. A pocketknife — a Barlow with a well-sharpened blade — went directly into Sinclair's pocket.

The second saddlebag held a ten-foot loop of horsehair rope, more jerky, a sack of tobacco and papers, and a real find — a cylindrical tin container of lucifers with a tight cap that would keep them dry in any weather. A few .44 cartridges, a bandana that stank of sweat, and a single lady's leather glove comprised the final yield.

Jake carried the bottle, a handful of jerky, and the horsehair rope to a shady spot and went to work fashioning a pair of hobbles for his mare. He left the saddle in the direct sun, at least for a while — he swore he could still smell the stink of the dead man on it. He hated to cut the rope. It was a fine piece of work and it'd taken someone a good long time to put it together. As he worked with his knife and the rope, he lowered the level in the bottle a good three inches and finished and replenished his handful of the jerked beef. After an hour or so he walked, not too steadily, to the saddle, hefted it, and brought it into the shade. If there had been vestiges of the odor of the bearlike killer, there no longer were. The saddle smelled of itself — of perfectly tanned, blemish-free leather cut and assembled by a true craftsman. He ran a finger over the ornately rendered initials cut into the inside of the left fender of the saddle: JTW. *A man who knows quality,* he mused.

Jake realized that everything he'd gained from killing the insane scavenger was the result of someone else's loss. The saddle and jerky had no doubt been the property of a Pennsylvania family whose farm the Confederate army had swept past — with the scavenger following it. The rifle may have belonged to a soldier. The pistol wasn't military issue, but that meant little. Men on both sides carried weapons they owned into battle. Even the horse Jake rode wasn't his. Beyond the occasional ripe melon from a neighboring plantation's patch, Jake had never stolen anything. Now things were different — totally different.

Sinclair switched hobbles on the mare, the new set giving her a few more inches between the restraints, making walking easier, but still precluding any gait beyond a walk. He threaded his belt though the loops of his pants and the cut in the sheath of his bowie knife. The blade had been at his side so constantly that he felt less than dressed without it.

The saddle fit the mare well. Her withers were wide and accepted the saddle well. She flinched as Jake drew the unfamiliar back cinch, swung her head back to see what the strange-feeling thing was, and then, satisfied, forgot about it. The blanket that had been under the military saddle on the mare's back, Jake realized, was a bit small. It'd do for now, but he'd replace it as soon as he could.

The release the whiskey provided was welcome. Jake tipped the bottle again and again, but was quite surprised when he noticed that it was empty. He hurled it across the stream onto the far shore, where it struck sand, rolled a few feet, and came to rest, reflecting the bright sun in spikes of light that hurt Sinclair's eyes. He drew the .44, considered blasting away at the bottle with it, and decided against doing so. He'd already attracted one crazy — why draw another with gunfire? He aimed down the barrel of the pistol, enjoying the weight of it in his hand, acutely aware of the potential power it possessed. He spun the cylinder to hear the oiled whir, which reminded him for some reason of the workings of the silver-cased watch his father had carried in his vest pocket.

He eased down onto his back, put his right

hand, still holding the pistol, on his chest, and slept soundly, dreamlessly.

CHAPTER THREE

It seemed to Sinclair that the damned heat would never break. The sun had a good start on the day when he awakened from his drunken sleep, the pistol still resting on his chest. A shaft of white-hot light through the canopy of leaves and foliage above him pinpointed his left eye as soon as he opened it, skewering his brain, setting off spasms of headache pain he suspected would be with him for several hours, if not for most of the day. He shifted his head to avoid the spear of sunlight but couldn't avoid the heat. A greasy sweat had already broken on his face and neck, and his body felt like it was wrapped in a thick, damp blanket.

His mind took him back to when he'd first experienced the effects of sapping, unremitting heat. Jake and his pal Todd St. David had, for a couple of nights, snuck out of their beds well after midnight, met halfway between their respective plantations, and visited the slave quarters beyond the main barn at Todd's place first, and then the quarters on Jake's father's land. They'd rained handfuls of pebbles on the shanty roofs and raced between the shacks, moaning eerily. The highly superstitious field hands and their families had been paralyzed with fear. After the second night of haunting, many of the slaves had nailed dead chickens to their doors to scare off the evil spirits. After huddling in corners shivering with fear all night, the field workers were lethargic in the hundreds of acres of cotton the next day. Overseers reported the problem to the fathers of the boys, and night guards were posted at both plantations. Jake and Todd were identified as the spooks. Their punishment: two full days each picking cotton with the field laborers. No special treatment of any kind was to be given to them — they'd work sunup to sundown with the slaves they'd frightened. Both boys discovered what the field hands already knew: Hell existed on earth. It was August in the endless expanse of cotton in Georgia.

Jake had dropped before noon the first day. A white overseer — under strict orders from Jake's father — had doused him awake with a splash of tepid water and put him back to work. A hand working alongside the boy offered him a misshapen, falling-apart woven straw hat that was already sopping wet with sweat — Negro sweat. Jake had thanked the laborer but turned the offer down. After passing out a second time, Jake wore the hat, Negro sweat and all. It kept him on his feet the next day and a half.

He remembered the heat as an evil force — more evil than the stingy cotton bolls that tore his fingertips and left them raw and bleeding. More evil than the powdery dust and grit that fouled his eyes, his throat, his nose, his ears, that made a deep breath impossible and generated an unquenchable thirst that refused to yield to the scoops of water a boy brought around every couple of hours. The sun had pounded at him — at all of those in the fields — relentlessly, without mercy. Jake staggered, sweated, puked, and picked — for two eternal days he dragged his sack up and down the symmetrical rows of cotton plants, hating each one a bit more than he hated the plant before it.

Todd St. David was carried back to his mansion bedroom the morning of the second day, his skin sallow, dry, all its moisture gone, where he stayed in his bed for almost a week. Jake finished his two days.

He remembered his conversation with his

father the evening of the second day.

"Long days, Son?"

"Yessir. Real long. One of the hands gave me a hat. At first I didn't want to wear it. Then I did."

"So I heard. That boy went without a hat for the rest of the day, you know."

"Yessir."

Jake's father sipped at his bourbon and branch water. "What do you think of that, Son?"

"It was nice of him, Pa. Thing is, they're used to it, used to picking all day, the heat, the dust, all that. Still, it was awful nice of him."

"Used to it, Jake?"

"Sure. Todd's pa said slaves have thicker skulls and smaller brains and the heat can't penetrate as much as it does on white people. And their skin — it doesn't get as hot as ours does. He said they like it out there, singing and carrying on."

Mr. Sinclair considered for a moment. "You ever listen to the words of those songs the hands sing, Jake?"

"Well . . . some, I guess. They're sure not happy songs. A couple are about dying and being carried away to heaven. There's one about a river that's cool and sweet, too."

His father leaned forward in his chair,

closer to his son. "It's my belief that those Negroes suffer from the heat and dust as much as a white person, Jake. That they experience the same pain you did, the same muscle ache, the same thirst — everything."

"Then why do we put them out there, Pa?"

"Because the cotton must be picked, Jake. Because someone has to pick it. And because they're slaves. Slaves are supposed to sweat for their masters. The Bible tells us that. The South didn't invent slavery — it's been around for thousands of years, and it'll be around for thousands more. And — our way of life has its roots in slavery, Son. The South as we know it was at least partially built by slaves. We need them, just as they need us to look after them, feed them, keep them safe."

"Kind of tough on the slaves, though," Jake observed.

"Maybe," Jake's father said. "But it's not your place nor mine to question the Bible, Son. What is, is." He looked into his empty cut-glass tumbler. "I believe I'll have another toddy this evening," he said, holding the glass out to his son.

When Jake returned with the drink he handed it to his father and took his seat. "Todd's pa says slaves are animals — maybe a step up from a horse or a dog, but not people like we are. Is that true, Pa?"

Mr. Sinclair took a long drink. When he looked back at his son his eyes were strangely sad, as if he'd just heard some very bad news. "You go on out and look in on the horses, Jake — make sure the hands gave each of them fresh water. We'll talk again about this."

Jake swallowed the questions he had. On the way to the barn the scent of roasting pork reached him from the mansion's kitchen, and two of the cook's young children chased one another about, naked, laughing, as carefree as a pair of puppies. *The Bible and the way of the South are good enough for me,* Jake thought. *Good enough for all of us. Maybe some things a fellow just doesn't question.*

Jake moved sluggishly, carefully, keeping his throbbing head as still as possible. He stripped at the shore of the creek, waded out to the center, and sat down, his body and head completely submerged; the sudden, sharp chill and the pressure of the current were almost orgasmic in their intensity. The rushing water not only washed away the sweat and dirt; it lessened the pain in his head to a barely noticeable dull throb. He spent a half hour in the stream, alternating between sitting on the bottom and whooshing into the sun to gulp air. When he left the creek and stood on the sand, dripping, squeezing the water from his hair, the residue of the whiskey in his system had been scrubbed away. As he dressed he noticed that some meat-eater had gotten to the corpse of the scavenger. Jake turned away quickly and didn't look back.

He led the mare from where she'd been foraging to the stream and let her drink before he saddled her. His hunger didn't amount to much and the sight of the partially ravaged dead body hadn't helped. Jake ate a handful of beef jerky, washed it down with stream water, and mounted up. Picking a true course through a dense forest was impossible, but he rode generally west, becoming acclimated to the saddle, marveling at the quality of it: There was no squeaking of leather that there would be in a lesser piece of gear, and the cut of the seat and placement of the stirrups felt as if the saddle had been crafted specifically for him.

Mare — he'd begun calling her by that unimaginative name — proved to be a superior trail horse. Agile and smooth-gaited, she moved through the patches of thick brush and trees surefootedly, head up, alert, ears in almost constant motion. Jake gave her all the rein she needed to wend her way, checking her rarely to keep her pointed west. About midday they crossed another stream, this one smaller and narrower than the other, and not flowing as rapidly. Nevertheless, the water was clear and cold, and man and horse drank thirstily. It was about then that Jake's hunger began to nag at him. *A rabbit would be good — or a pheasant, or even a damned old woodchuck. I have matches. I'd chance a fire without worrying about smoke. I haven't heard nor seen a sign of civilization in two days.* Another thought struck him. *And so what if someone does see smoke and show up at my camp? I'm just a drifter passing through — no more and no less.*

Jake lifted the flap on the holster and drew the pistol. Again the weight of the weapon felt good in his hand, the bone grips warm. He reholstered the .44 and urged Mare ahead, following the shore of the creek, noticing the tracks of small animals etched in the sand. When he came to a wider spot, about the size of a good, big dinner table, he urged his mount fifty yards into the trees, struck a small clearing, and hobbled her there, leaving her free to graze. He loosened the front cinch before walking back toward the stream. He left the rifle he'd taken from the scavenger in the saddle scabbard. It wasn't a Sharps, and it — and any rifle other than a Sharps — would never feel right, never perform right. He decided that he needed to learn to use the pistol, at least well enough to pot supper with. *How difficult could it be? Aim and squeeze the trigger — that's all there is to it. Hell, I'm a sharpshooter.*

Jake found a good spot behind a scramble of blackberry bushes and scrub growth, twenty-five feet or so from the sandy spot. The tangles were too thick to shoot through: They'd easily deflect a well-aimed bullet. He shifted himself along in the dirt to where the bushes and weeds diminished to a height of a yard or so and settled in, pistol in his right hand, resting in his lap, legs extended in front of him. It wasn't long before forest sounds resumed.

The first creatures that approached the water were a mule deer doe with a stick-legged fawn at her side. The mother stopped before entering the clearing, one front hoof raised a couple of inches above the ground, as she surveyed the area around her. There was no breeze; Sinclair's scent didn't reach her. Satisfied she was safe, the doe left the cover of the trees, crossed the clearing, looked around again, and then lowered her head to drink. The fawn watched her for a moment and then mimicked her stance, face plunging a bit too deeply into the water. A smile tickled at the edges of Jake's mouth. The fawn shook its head and tried again, this time finding drinking depth.

An image of a haunch of venison dripping fat into a roaring fire flashed in Jake's mind, but there was no real temptation to take the doe. For one thing, the meat would rot before he could use even a quarter of it, and secondly, the fawn would starve to death without its mother's milk. He watched as the two deer finished drinking and crossed to the far side of the stream, the mother gracefully, the baby clumsily, tripping over submerged and slippery rocks. They entered the woods and were gone.

The rabbit was summer-fat and edged into the clearing without a whole lot of regard for predators. Most animals that would take him for a meal were nocturnal, and the sun was barely past its peak for the day. Jake raised the pistol slowly and sighted on the round, paunchy abdomen of the rabbit. He knew that the tiny *click* as he eased back the hammer would grab the animal's attention, and it did. The apple-sized head with the inquisitive ears turned to him and Jake fired. A spout of sand erupted a foot to the rabbit's left and more than a foot short of where the animal stood. The white tail flashed and Sinclair's meal was gone.

"Shit," he said aloud, getting to his feet, the pistol hanging uselessly at his side. He raised the gun and inspected the front sight. It was straight and true and showed no sign of being damaged or bent. The rear sight was equally intact. Jake shook his head. "Shit," he said again.

Walking back to Mare he recalled a conversation he'd had with Uriah a year or longer ago about revolvers. "Best gun hand I ever saw," Toole said, "told me you don't aim a handgun — you point the sumbitch. The fella told me that any range beyond fifty feet made a pistol 'bout as handy as tits on a boar hog, and that the only way to become any good with a handgun is to forget all about aiming and to let your hand and arm do everything the way it wants."

"Where's this fellow now?" Jake had asked.

"I heard he got shot in the back — killed, he was — by a storekeep he was robbin' in Yuma. Still, what he said about pointing a pistol makes good sense. . . ."

Jake holstered the Smith & Wesson and continued walking to where he'd left Mare. He filled his pockets with .22 rounds from the saddlebags, ate a few pieces of jerky, and made his way back to the stream.

At first the whole process was unnatural, awkward — and without the desired effect. He sprayed lead all around the rock he was firing at twenty feet away, on the opposite shore. The pistol felt like an anchor in his hand, a foreign weight that could never become an extension of his body, as his Sharps had been. Jake stood in the sun, firing, reloading, sweating, firing again, ears ringing so that he barely heard the reports. He went back to replenish his pockets with cartridges, mumbling curses to himself that he couldn't hear.

An hour and a half later — and after two more disgusted walks for bullets — something changed. Jake wasn't completely sure what it was, but something definitely was different. It began when he lowered his extended arm from midchest level and began shooting from slightly above his waist, seeing the smoking barrel in his mind, looking at the target rather than at the weapon. The major transformation was that his shots were coming closer to and even chipping pieces from the rock. And the pistol no longer seemed like a deadweight in his hand. Some of the time the .22 seemed to act on its own, seeking the target — and finding it.

The less he thought about what he was doing, Jake realized, the better his shooting was. He'd always had a feel for firearms, an intrinsic and unstudied ability to make them perform as he needed them to. He'd been raised with long guns; his father never quite trusted handguns. "Clumsy damned things," he'd said. "Prone to misfire or not fire at all, and when they do work they have no more accuracy than a woman throwing a stick at a crow."

Maybe so. But this Smith & Wesson .22 is growing on me, Pa.

When the rock was scattered shards and smoking pieces, Jake ejected the final six empty cartridges, reloaded, and holstered the pistol. As he tucked the flap over the weapon, he saw that getting the .22 free from the holster and ready to fire was an overly long process — one that could cost a man his life in a tight situation. Most of the Texans who carried sidearms, he recalled, favored open holsters, deep enough to keep the pistol securely in place, but that made the grips easy to grab and the weapon easy to pull free. *First chance I get I'll replace the military issue, pick up one of those open holsters. If I'm going to carry a pistol I want to get at it when I need it.*

He tightened Mare's cinch and swung into

the saddle. There was lots of daylight left and no reason not to cover ground while he could. Within a couple of hours the ringing in his ears was gone. Mare picked her way west with little direction from her rider, leaving Sinclair with nothing but memories to occupy his mind.

Uriah Toole's strange sense of humor, his way of bizarre exaggeration, brought a grin to Jake's face. *We was so poor that my ma fed us on a stew she made up from rocks, dirt, an' horseshit. Wasn't half bad — needed salt, is all.* Jake remembered how his partner described Texas. *Bigger than heaven, hotter than hell. Jackrabbits taller at the shoulder than a stout head of beef, pigs a man could toss a saddle on an' ride fifty miles in a day. And Texas women — they'd purely wear a man out — screw his ears off till he cain't hardly move, then get him all randy and ready again in half a minute. . . .*

Sinclair's smile disappeared as the Gettysburg images pushed the joking and laughter from his mind. It was like suddenly falling into the brackish, slimy water of a swamp: the bodies scattered over the slaughter lane of Pickett's Charge, the evil air alive with steel and lead and blood and clumps and pieces of men. The all-encompassing fear swallowed Jake and closed over him.

He fought his way back to the sun-speckled forest somewhere in Pennsylvania, felt his good horse under him, smelled leather and pine and hot dirt, and wiped the sweat from his face with a sleeve.

A leafy branch high in a tall oak a hundred feet ahead sagged with the weight of the gray squirrel that had landed on it. Jake stopped Mare with a light drag at the reins and shaded his eyes from the glare of the sun with his hand. Squirrel was a treat to the folks in the quarters back home. Since they weren't allowed to own firearms, it was up to the whites to drop off the results of a day's hunting in the woods, and Jake and his father had done just that many, many times. Jake recalled the sweet-tangy taste of squirrel stew and the slightly gamy but not at all unpleasant taste of a piece of squirrel broiled on a stick over flames fed by dripping fat. His right hand fell to the flap of his holster, paused, and then reached to the stock of the rifle in the scabbard at his knee. *Pistol's fine — but I'm hungry and that squirrel's a small target.*

He fit the butt to his shoulder, levered a round into the chamber, and placed the front sight on the squirrel's chest. He felt Mare tense under him as she heard the lever of the rifle work. Jake squeezed the trigger.

The squirrel swung backward, the instant-of-death convulsion locking its claws to the branch for a moment, and then it dropped through the limbs and leaves to the ground. Mare stood stolidly, without flinching at the report, showing her cavalry training. Jake patted her neck, slid the Winchester back into the scabbard, and sent his horse forward to where the squirrel had fallen.

Jake skinned the squirrel right where it'd hit the ground. It was early to end the day, to make camp, but his hunger was gnawing at him, and there was adequate grass for Mare in patches under the trees. *Plus, I'm not on a schedule — I'm not a soldier anymore. It doesn't matter when I stop for the day or when I start in the morning. As a matter of fact, not much of anything that mattered before Gettysburg means a damn thing to me now. I always kind of looked down on the drifters and saddle bums — saw them as aimless and pointless men who couldn't make a life for themselves. Now — maybe keeping moving isn't such a bad thing. Maybe drifting makes good sense. I guess,* he told himself, *I'll find out about that.* He unsaddled and hobbled Mare.

Gathering dry branches and a handful of kindling took only a few minutes, and digging a small pit with his bowie knife a few minutes more. He structured a campfire in the hole and dropped extra wood next to it. The soil below the surface was dark and rich and moist. Jake figured that if the land could somehow be cleared, cotton would just about leap out of the ground after a good spring planting.

He used one of his matches to start the fire and sat back to watch it catch and grow. While it burned down to white embers, Jake skewered pieces of the squirrel meat on a green stick cut from a young tree. There was a good bit of meat, but he figured he'd finish every last morsel; a constant diet of jerky left a man with a strong yearning for hot, greasy, flavorful, red meat. The fat squirrel didn't disappoint him. The flesh was tender and marbled nicely and the flavor took him back to his boyhood. He ate the entire carcass, wasting nothing. Sated, Jake leaned back against a tree and watched the shadows lengthen and the light diminish. Just before dark, he picked up on the slight difference in the rhythm of the forest, the hushing of some of the birds, the cessation of the movement of the small creatures in the brush. If he hadn't noticed, Mare's questioning snort would have warned him. His eyes swung in the direction the horse was looking — and in which her ears were pointing — but could make out nothing but shadows and murky shapes. He unholstered his pistol, clicked back the hammer, and waited. Mare huffed again, but this time she was staring in a different direction. *Two men coming in from different angles? More than two?* He watched as her muzzle rose and she drew air and the scent of whoever was approaching. *One man shifting around, maybe, trying to make me think there's more than one out there?*

Jake got his feet under himself, keeping his back against the tree. He reached out to the saddle, eased the rifle from its scabbard, and placed it on the ground in front of him. His right palm began to sweat against the bone grips of the .44. He relaxed his grip a bit, loosened the tension in his wrist. When he heard a twig snap in the direction Mare was peering, the sound was sharp and loud and he swung the barrel of his pistol toward it. Another twig broke under weight and a muffled curse followed.

"I've got you covered," Jake called out. "You might just as well walk on in. I'll want to see your hands raised up when you do."

The voice that answered was deep, almost hoarse, but calm. "No need to be so twitchy, friend. I ain't armed and even if I was, I don't mean you no harm. I smelled that squirrel of yours cookin', is all. Hope I'm in time for maybe a bite or two. Maybe we can barter. I got me some coffee. It ain't army, neither — it's right out of an Arbuckle's sack."

"Come on in, then. And like I said, keep your hands where I can see them. Hear?" Jake kept the pistol trained on the voice and pushed wood onto the dying embers of his fire with his other hand. The dry fuel caught and flared almost immediately, giving Sinclair a good look at his visitor. He was about five feet eight, neither skinny nor fat. He wore a shirt that had once been a different color — perhaps white — that was deeply stained under the arms and across the chest. His denim pants were tucked into the tops of boots that were scuffed and worn. He was about Jake's age — maybe a couple of years older. His face showed hard planes, prominent cheekbones, and a strong, protruding jaw. His skin had a light copper cast to it, and Jake could see that his eyes, even at a distance of ten feet, were obsidian, like nuggets of polished coal. His hair hadn't been cut in a long time. There was what looked like a messenger's satchel hanging at his side, suspended from a leather cord that crossed his chest. A canteen hung from his belt on the side opposite the satchel. He held his hands at shoulder height, palms out. His teeth showed white in the firelight as he spoke.

"Mind if I set down?"

"I'd be a lot happier if you'd empty that sack here by the fire," Jake said.

The man took some steps closer, crouched, moved the cord holding the sack over his head, and emptied the satchel onto the dirt near the fire. The contents consisted of a sheathed knife, a spare shirt, an empty and unlabeled tin can, a paper bag with its top rolled tightly closed, an empty canteen with its cork in place, a pocket Bible, and a block of lucifers with their heads encased in paraffin, making them waterproof. "Like I said, I ain't armed," he said. "Now can I set?"

Jake nodded. He still held the .44 but the barrel no longer pointed to the stranger's chest.

The fellow settled onto the ground, his legs crossed Indian-style. "About that cookin' meat I smelled . . ."

"Nothing left but a good taste in my mouth, I'm afraid. I've got jerky I'll trade for some coffee, though."

The fellow grinned, again showing his teeth. "Hell, I can't afford to be choosy. Jerky's better than nothin'." He picked the tin can from his pile of belongings, dumped ground coffee into it from the paper bag, and filled it with water from his canteen. He set the can on the edge of the fire, on embers. "My name's Ferris," he said.

"Mine's Jake," Sinclair said. Neither man offered nor expected a surname. Sinclair eased the hammer of the .44 back into place but didn't holster the pistol. Instead, he rested it in his lap. If Ferris noticed, he didn't comment.

Jake pointed to his saddle. "The jerky's in the saddlebag closest to you. I figure one good handful ought to pay for the coffee. Fair enough?"

"Fair enough," Ferris repeated, working the buckle on the saddlebag and digging his right hand into it. He pulled out as much jerky as his hand could hold and set it in front of him. He closed and buckled the saddlebag before he began to eat. His jaw worked up and down rapidly as he fed sticks of dried meat into his mouth. "This ain't that deer shit," he said around a cud of beef. "This come from a cow." By the time he'd finished his meal the coffee was boiling and bubbling in the can and its aroma made Jake's throat move as if he were already swallowing a mouthful. Ferris took a pair of sticks from Jake's extra wood, maneuvered the can from the embers to the dirt, and grinned. "We'll just let it set till we can hold the can without raisin' blisters."

The tin can was on the very cusp of being too hot to hold, but Jake hadn't tasted coffee in three days. He scorched the inside of his mouth with his first gulp and paid no attention to the pain. He set the can down and wiped his mouth. "Damn, but that's good. No chicory cut — just good coffee."

"I told you it didn't come from no army," Ferris said. "I'd almost rather do without than drink that slop they call coffee. Them cooks . . ." He let the sentence die.

"Cooks for what side, Ferris?"

A long moment passed before he answered. "Doesn't really make no difference, does it?"

Jake didn't answer. The two men sat in silence, taking turns with the can, until the coffee was gone. "Maybe we could make a deal, Ferris," Jake offered. "How about another couple handfuls of jerky for about half of that coffee?"

"Cain't do it, Jake. I'd sooner trade away my grandma's ass than what little coffee I have left. Sorry."

Jake nodded.

"Thing is, I could make up another canful in the morning, though. If you don't have no problem with me sleepin' close to your fire, course."

Sinclair thought about the proposal. *Better having him here where I can keep an eye on him than out there wandering around in the woods, maybe drawing a bead on me with a gun he hid out there before coming in.* "I don't have a problem with that, Ferris. Long as you stay on your side of the fire and I stay on mine, we'll be just fine."

Conversation dwindled along with the embers of the campfire. Jake stood, replenished the fire with most of the last of the wood he'd gathered, and walked into the darkness to relieve himself. His toe struck an embedded rock and he almost went down. He cursed, took another couple of steps, and stopped. He turned back, found the rock with the help of moonlight, and pulled it free of the grass and soil. It was about the size of a large man's fist, cool to the touch, with no sharp edges. He pushed it into a side pocket before going deeper into the woods. When he returned to the fire and sat down, Ferris spoke.

"You wouldn't have any liquor, would you? Now, there's something I'd trade some coffee for — a few snorts of good whiskey."

"Can't help you there. I'm not carrying a drop."

"I was in a little town a couple days back," Ferris said. "I woulda bought me a bottle then, but it turns out I didn't have no money. Sons-a-bitches wouldn't extend me no credit, either."

"What town was that?" Jake asked. "Where is it?"

"Kinda west and east, I guess. Name of Penderson or somethin' like that. Ain't much more than a spot of fly shit on a map. Lots of them little farm burgs around. Most of them ain't real hospitable to a travelin' man."

"Oh?"

"Or any stranger, for that matter — travelin' man or not. Hell, if you ain't married to their sister they don't want nothin' to do with you."

"You've been moving around for a while, then?"

"Some, I guess." The tone of Ferris's voice indicated he had nothing further to say on the subject. Some moments passed.

Ferris poked at the fire with a stick. "I been tryin' to figure somethin' out, Jake," he said. "I kinda hear a touch of South in your words, but not too much of it. You a Southern boy?"

"Two years of college in the East washed my accent away. The professors called

Southern talk 'mush-mouthed babble' and wouldn't allow it. I guess what they taught me stuck."

"See? I knew it! You from way deep? Maybe Mississip or Georgia or such?"

Jake looked away from the fire and into the man's eyes. "Let's let it go."

"Sure, sure," Ferris said hastily. "I didn't mean to pry none." He waited a couple of minutes. "I'm gonna have me a piss an' then stetch out here and get some shut-eye, Jake. Be the first good night's sleep I've gotten in a bit. Saw a good big black bear a few days ago and I've been leery ever since. Your horse will set up a racket if one of them comes close, though, and the fire'll help, too." He stood and strode off into the darkness.

Jake'd had enough conversation. He pulled his saddle closer to the fire and stretched out in front of it, head resting against the side of the seat. He placed his pistol on the grass next to him, within easy reach of his right hand. He sighed. He didn't expect to get much sound sleep that night. The man named Ferris had seemed a little too set on sleeping near Jake's fire. *Could be he's just a harmless drifter looking for somebody to talk to for a bit.* Another thought struck him: *Maybe not, too. Seems like the war and the time that led up to it put a herd of crazies on the roads — gunfighters and wanderers and preachers and abolitionists and men with flat, dull eyes — or strange, too-bright eyes.* He shifted his shoulders against the warm earth under him, relieving a burgeoning cramp in the back of his neck. The air had cooled somewhat with darkness. The temperature remained high and the humidity cloying, but after the heat of the day, the night felt good. Ferris's breathing from the other side of the fire, sibilant, not quite a snore, was as regular as the working of a good clock, as much a part of the forest sounds as the minute shuffling of the higher leaves touched by wisps of breeze.

I wonder how my eyes will look to the people I meet.

It was probably the change in the tempo of Ferris's breathing that nudged Jake back to full consciousness. Through barely opened eyes he saw that the embers of the fire no longer cast much light — a soft-white glow that didn't quite penetrate the darkness. Ferris was next to the fire now, a shadow, poised, moving so slowly and carefully that he seemed still. Jake kept his breathing regular, waiting. His right hand moved as imperceptibly as the man sneaking toward him. The sting of anger tightened

Jake's muscles. *I knew* this, he chided himself. *I even prepared for it, got ready for it, but I let it happen. It'd be easy enough to pull a trigger, but maybe I've seen enough killing for a while.*

The slits Jake watched through made the moonlight on the silver shape appear brighter than it actually was. The shadow-form was closer to him now, although Jake hadn't actually detected motion. He focused on the silver form, keyed his body to it.

For a long few seconds he could smell Ferris's foul breath, feel the heat of it on his face. Then, as the silver glint moved upward and then began to arc down, Jake put every iota of strength he had into his right arm, swinging it upward, his fingers locked over the rock. It seemed, to Jake, like a long time before he felt the impact, but it was actually the quickest part of a second. He'd expected a sharp sensation, a jolt the length of his wrist and into his arm — but instead the blow was softer, concurrent with the sound of stone grating against stone — a quick crackling. He drew back the rock and slammed it at its target again, and this time the shock he'd anticipated tingled down his arm. The screech was high, piercing, feline. The silver shape — the knife in Ferris's hand — dropped to the earth and the man fell back, clutching at his face, even as bits of enamel, blood, and saliva sprinkled Jake's face. Sinclair threw the rock at the writhing, keening mass and was rewarded with a satisfying thunk.

Sinclair picked up his pistol from the grass, stood, and walked around Ferris to the man's satchel, which he dragged close to the bed of embers. He emptied the bag and picked out the coffee and the tin can. Filling the can took the rest of the water in Ferris's canteen. Jake added coffee and set the can in the middle of the embers, where the almost moribund fire looked the hottest. His glance fell back to Ferris's possessions scattered on the dirt. He picked up the empty canteen and tossed it over toward his saddle. Then he hunkered down and waited for the coffee to brew.

Ferris sat where he'd fallen, hands to his face, rocking back and forth from his waist, his initial yowling now a sporadic moan. Blood gushed from an open cut at his hairline and from his mouth through his fingers. "Almost killed me," he said. His words were wet and slurred and his voice was that of a whining child.

The coffee began to boil. Jake smiled as the aroma reached him. "You're lucky I didn't kill you, you son of a bitch. There's nothing lower than a backstabber."

Ferris's rocking picked up speed. "No," he slurred. "Seems to me a yella belly who runs off from a battle leavin' his friends to die is 'bout as low as a man can get."

Jake wrapped Ferris's spare shirt around his hand to pick the tin can out of the bed of coals. Ferris caught the motion and flinched backward, as if avoiding a blow.

"What makes you think I'm on the run?"

"Think? Think, my ass. I ain't blind. That bridle on your horse is Confederate issue, and the holster you wear is army, too. Plus, what's a Southern boy doin' in the deep woods a couple of days after Lee got his ass shot off at Gettysburg? Maybe attendin' a goddamn church picnic? Huntin' wildflowers?"

Jake drank some coffee, breathed a long *ahhhhh,* and set the can down. "What're you doing out here?" he asked.

Ferris lowered his hands and glared at Sinclair, the anger in his eyes momentarily pushing aside the pain. "I ain't no deserter, I'll tell you that. I joined up with Mr. Lincoln's army in '61, but they kicked me out 'cause I wasn't real good at rules an' all."

Jake peered at the man's face in the light of dawn that was beginning to suffuse through the trees. The forehead wound was still leaking blood. Ferris's lips were like a pair of shredded, swollen sausages. Jagged chunks of his front teeth were still seated in his gums, looking like a crumbling picket fence. Jake noticed that the man winced as he drew air to speak.

" 'Least I ain't no yella belly runnin' off from my sweared duty."

Sinclair chuckled. "You figure it's more honorable to kill a fellow with a knife who shared his fire with you for a night?"

"Could be I do." The voice was petulant now, even more childlike than it'd been earlier.

Jake sighed and stood up. He drank the rest of the coffee and tossed the empty can to where his saddle and the canteen rested. He picked up the paper bag of coffee with his left hand. With his right he drew his pistol and stepped to Ferris. He placed the muzzle against the man's temple and thumbed back the hammer. "Smartest thing I could do right now would be to put a bullet in your brain. You tried to kill me. I got the right. The thing is, I don't see that you're worth killing. I'm going to saddle up and go on my way and leave you sitting here like the lump of shit you are. But hear this: If I see you again, if for some insane reason

108

you try to follow me, sneak in on me, I'll gut-shoot you and leave you to die." He eased the hammer down and started around the injured man.

"Goddamn deserter," Ferris mumbled.

The punch was short and not particularly powerful. Jake was in a clumsy position and he had to lean down to deliver the blow. Even so, Ferris's upper lip split like a balloon full of blood, and Jake's knuckles removed a couple of already fractured teeth. There was no scream this time. Unconsciousness came mercifully quickly. Jake gathered up the canteen and the bag of coffee, hefted his saddle, and shoved through the brush to where Mare waited for him.

It felt good to be in the saddle. Mare was perky and fresh and had grazed well. Jake wanted to get some grain into her, and he'd do that as soon as possible, but right now her energy hadn't flagged and she moved easily, responding immediately to any cue Sinclair gave her. They came across water early — a small pond in a clearing that encroached on the water, with oak branches overhanging it. Horse and man drank; Jake filled the canteen and slung it by its cord around his saddle horn.

Jake's thoughts strayed to Ferris and the

night and early morning just past. He shook his right hand as if the memory caused the little cuts from the jagged stubs of Ferris's teeth to heat up. He rubbed his knuckles lightly against his shirt, ending the itching. *Maybe I'm supposed to feel some guilt about what I did to that fellow. I don't — he would have cut my throat and taken everything I have just as happily as he'd drink a shot of whiskey. He deserved what I gave him, and more. Guilt? Hell. I don't feel any guilt about the crazy I killed with my knife, and I have none about Ferris. Come to think of it, I don't feel anything about being a deserter. I sure didn't like hearing the words from that turd, though.*

Something was different, Jake realized, but he couldn't bring whatever it was to mind. The sun cast its hazy light through the canopy of trees over him, and the forest air was still but fresh and sweet. He began to feel some hunger. *Rabbit will do fine — or maybe a pheasant, if I can get a shot at one. Maybe I'll stop later in the day and see if I can wait out a bird. It'd take some sitting still and baking in the sun, but a pheasant makes awful good . . .* It came to him: The difference was the heat, or the lack of it. Mare's neck was dry as he patted it, and his own shirt didn't stick to his skin when it touched his back or chest. His forehead was dry under his fingertips. He grinned and took a long, deep breath. *About damned time the weather broke. It's been an oven since the end of June, right through the three days of the battle, and the days since.*

Leaves began to move behind a new breeze. The temperature dropped another few degrees and Jake sniffed the air, standing in the stirrups: rain. How far away it was, or if it'd come his way, he didn't know. Nevertheless, it smelled good. It seemed like a long time since he'd last seen rainfall.

Mare began getting a little nervous about the time the first deep, resonant rolls of thunder reached Jake's ears. He couldn't see much sky through the tops of the trees, but what he could see had turned from blue to a washed-out gray, tinged with black. The quality of the light changed from its cheerful morning presentation to a murky, dusk-like texture. Lightning flickered; the air became heavy with the smell that followed the flashes. The lightning became more frequent and more intense, washing the woods with pure white light, scaring the hell out of Mare, seething and hissing what seemed like a few feet above their heads. A tree twenty yards away was struck with a tremendous tearing sound, and chips and pieces of wood and leaves and small branches sprayed outward from the trunk. The image of the tree the Yankee artillery had ripped up after he'd dropped the officer Uriah had spotted darted into his mind. He shook it off, using the reins to keep Mare from bolting, attempting to talk her down from her near panic.

Hail the size of minnie balls pelted down, barely slowed by the trees above. The cold, driven ice stung Mare like a cut from a quirt, increasing her fear, raising the voice of her instinct that told her to flee the storm. Jake muscled her head to her left side, not at all sure that he could hold her against her fear. His voice was useless in the crashing of thunder and the seething of lightning and the pounding clatter of the hail against leaves and trees.

Mare did her best to run, but Sinclair was able to hold her head close to her body and she lumbered in a clumsy circle, hooves flinging mud in all directions. Panic touched the rider as well as the horse. Jake's arms and shoulders were about to give out — he was no match for the strength of the healthy young horse. Her frantic, scrambling attempt to run escalated among the treacherous lengths of root and half-buried rocks that could snap a pastern like a dry stick.

The hail gave way to rain — sweeping, howling sheets of rain that were whirlwinds of driven water, blocking out the forest, the lightning, everything but the constant bombardment of the thunder.

Jake's arms and shoulders were on fire, trembling now, approaching the end of their ability to endure. The mud had become oily soup; Jake felt hooves slip as his horse spun crazily. He didn't like what he was going to do, but he knew he had to do it. He knew he wasn't going to win a battle of strength against this animal — to save her, he had to use her instinct against herself.

Jake leaned his weight into his left stirrup, twisting his body awkwardly, maintaining his trembling death-grip on the reins. The force of the spin brought his upper body close to Mare's neck and to her head, so close he could hear the raspy whistle of her breath through her widely dilated nostrils. He leaned the slightest bit more, fighting for balance, struggling to maintain his seat, and closed his mouth over the velvet of an ear. Then he bit down — hard — hard enough so that he felt hot liquid in his mouth and tasted the salt and metal mixture of the flavor of blood.

Mare straightened her front legs, skidded in the mud, slipped sideways, fought for balance, and recovered — and stood stock-still, her flesh steaming as the rain sluiced over it, her eyes open impossibly wide.

Trickles of blood dripped from between Jake's lips to the back of the mare's head. He felt her shiver under him with both panic and fatigue, but he kept his teeth in the tender flesh and cartilage of the ear. His father had taught him well. He could hear the man's voice: *A horse has a small brain, Son. He can't concentrate on more than one thing at a time — and if that one thing is hard pain, it'll take precedence over fear, over panic. That's why a runaway horse can be brought to a halt by twisting hell out of his ear, twisting it hard enough so that it feels to him like it's going to be torn clean off. . . .*

The cruelest part of the storm had moved away before Jake released his aching jaws and stepped clumsily down from the saddle. Mare, splay-legged and shaking, looked dumbly at him, her respiration still much too rapid, but slowing now. Jake's legs gave out and he fell to his knees, still clutching the reins. He shook his head to clear it and looked up at Mare.

"Damn," he said. "That was somethin', wasn't it?"

Chapter Four

The storm had chased away the days of stultifying heat. The air in the woods was cool and damp and the dripping of water seemed to replace all the natural sounds of the forest. Footing was dangerously slippery and Jake was weary from his wrestling match with his horse, and from the after-effects of the adrenaline surge.

Jake stroked his horse's neck, marveling at the resilience — or perhaps the innate stupidity — of the equine species. A very few hours before, the mare was doing her best to run herself to an almost guaranteed broken bone or perhaps worse, in a state of abject terror. Now Mare was none the worse for the experience. Beyond shaking her head a bit more than usual because of flies pestering her tender left ear, she had apparently forgotten the entire episode, with no repercussions.

Jake wasn't quite as fortunate. He stopped

early to make camp, scrounged about for an hour seeking dry wood for a fire, and found none. It was as if the entire planet had been submerged in a vast ocean and nothing remained dry. After unsaddling and hobbling Mare, he ate a few pieces of jerky from his diminishing supply, drank a few swallows of water from his canteen, and leaned back against a tree, resting, his thoughts as bleak and lifeless as the soaked and saturated world around him. He dozed on and off through the late afternoon and into the night, but never entered into a deep sleep. A sensation in his right hand — not pain, actually, more of an itchy tightness, a sense of heat — nagged at him like a hangover headache. The passing of time seemed sluggish, but in the many times Jake jerked awake from a doze, he noticed that the length of the shadows generated by the moonlight had changed, as had the position of the moon itself.

Near dawn he found himself shivering as if he were sitting naked on a block of ice. His teeth clattered together with such force that jolts of pain ran through his jaw, and his entire body shook in a frigid palsy. Bizarre snippets of dreams and images flickered in his mind: the rainstorm, Ferris grinning at him, saying something Jake couldn't quite understand, a Union officer standing for a moment before he toppled, his chest gushing blood, a wrathful President Davis, his eyes a fiery red, cursing Jake, Uriah's bodiless head resting among a pile of severed arms and legs.

When Jake awakened the next time, he was drenched in sweat, disoriented, not able to separate what was real and present from the panorama his mind had unfolded. Dawn was hours past and the sun high when he struggled to his feet and fought off the dizziness that threatened to drop him. He shook his head to clear the floating red shards that blocked his vision. His hand throbbed in unison with the pulse he heard in both his ears. He raised his hand to his face and inspected it. It was swollen, but not hugely so, and without much difficulty, he flexed his fingers and formed a loose fist. He held his knuckles under his nose and sniffed: There was none of the sickly sweet stench of infection. Still, the dull red trailers from the tiny lacerations bothered him.

"It wasn't a cottonmouth, Pa. I'm sure of that. It wasn't anything more than a big old grass snake. I stepped on him and he bit at the back of my leg. I grabbed him and looked at his mouth — he had those little snake teeth but no fangs at all. Just a grass snake. It was

my own fault for stepping on him. I let him go on his way." He grinned at his father. "If somebody tromped on me, I guess I'd bite him, too."

Pa didn't smile. "When was this, Jake?"

"Day before yesterday, early morning, I was going to the barn for my chores."

"And you noticed the redness — those red lines — just today?"

"Yessir. Doesn't hurt so much as it itches. It itches like crazy, Pa."

"It's infected, son. I'm going to send a rider for Doc Turner. I want you in your bed and staying still until he gets here."

"Pa —"

"Do as I say."

Jake's father wasn't a man to hurry. He took everything in stride, made decisions calmly, acted decisively after sufficient thought. But he all but ran from the great room where they'd been talking, calling to a servant to fetch a rider. Jake had never heard a tremor in his father's voice before.

A day later Jake was in his bed, his nightgown and sheets soaked in sweat. The stink of the infection, even through the thick poultice that wrapped his lower leg, made the servants who looked after him gag. "Same damn thing up an' killed my ma," Cicero, an elderly houseman, told the boy. "Wasn't no Doctor Turner *for slaves, Massa Jake. You's lucky."*

Jake swam back from his memories. It suddenly seemed very important to him that he get moving, although he wasn't sure he was strong enough to saddle Mare — and even if he did, to keep her headed in the right direction. Still, the almost frantic urgency was there. His clothing, still soggy from rain, dew, and fever-sweat, stuck to his body like a loose, diseased second skin.

He muscled his saddle to his shoulder, stood weaving for long moments, and then lumbered through the brush to where Mare was cropping grass. He tripped once and went to his knees. When he looked back he saw that nothing beyond low weeds had been in his path. *I fell like a goddamn rummy in a saloon. I can't ride today,* he thought. *I'll topple off Mare, knock myself silly, and lose my horse and saddle. Goddamn that Ferris's mouth — it must have been as foul as shit house runoff. I should have gunned him instead of punching him.*

Mare watched without much interest as Jake stood precariously, tottering in the sun, and stripped off his shirt. When he sat to take off his boots and pants, she went back to grazing. Jake spread his shirt and pants over a bush where the sun would hit them and found a piece of shade to rest in, gun belt buckled and draped over his shoulder.

The shivers started again the moment he sat down. He considered moving out into the direct sun, but before he could act on the thought, his face was running with sweat and jagged black spots were floating in front of his eyes. He fell back, prone, dirt and grit sticking hotly to his back. He brought his right hand to his face, held his knuckles under his nose, and took in a long draft of air. The stench — the thick stink of rotting meat — caused him to gag, bile spilling from between his lips. "Damn," he mumbled. "Damn."

Jake saw himself in his bed at his home, Dr. Turner and his father hovering over him, the physician holding a length of cloth a couple of feet long wrapped around a damp claylike substance that smelled strongly of mustard and salt and lamp oil.

"This is a poultice, Jake," Turner told him. "I'm going to wrap your leg with it. You'll feel some heat but it shouldn't hurt too much. See, what the poultice'll do is draw the poison — the infection — out of you." The doctor drew back the sheet and nodded to Jake's father, who elevated the boy's leg a foot or so above the surface of the bed. Doc Turner worked quickly, dexterously, taking three quick wraps around Jake's lower leg and then securing the poultice with strips of white cloth. The heat — the one he was told wouldn't hurt much — began almost immediately, escalating from mild discomfort to a screaming pain that brought tears to Jake's eyes. He looked away from the doctor and his father and pawed the tears from his face with the back of his hand, ashamed.

"Is it bad, Son?" his father asked.

Jake had to swallow a couple of times before he could trust his voice. "Not so bad, Pa."

Leighton Sinclair nodded, his eyes showing he shared his son's pain. "Sometimes a man has to put up with hurt, Jake. No way around it. Just hold on."

The phrase "Just hold on" twisted its way through Jake's fever-ravaged brain, helping him get to his feet, forcing him to move, to take some action against the infection that, even in his fogged state of mind, he knew could drop him into his grave. He looked at his hand. It was hugely swollen now and the red trailers had become more pronounced, extending beyond his wrist, toward his elbow. He couldn't clasp the hand, couldn't come near forming a fist. His fingers were fat, pasty-white sausages that stretched the skin that covered the bones until it seemed ready to rupture from the pressure. Jake stood, foolishly naked, swaying like a tree in strong wind, doing his best to force himself to think coherently, pushing away images of his father, of Dr. Turner.

"A poultice," he whispered hoarsely. "Gotta make a poultice."

Mud was the only component he could find, but there was plenty of it, thanks to the storm. He stumbled to the bush where he'd spread his shirt and pants and reached to his naked hip for his bowie knife. For a heartbeat, clarity returned. Even so, he had no idea where the knife may have been. He dropped his gun belt to the ground, tore a sleeve from the shirt, and then pulled on the remaining part of it. His face, neck, and forearms were deeply tanned, but the pallid white flesh of his back and abdomen and legs hadn't seen sun in a long time, and he was already beginning to burn. He sat down and hauled on his pants and then his boots. He was able to buckle his gun belt around his waist.

Pockets formed by the roots of trees held the thick black mud Jake sought. Clumsily, using his teeth and his left hand, he tied off the lower part of the sleeve and knelt in the spongy soil in front of a puddle to fill the fabric cylinder with mud. It was soupy at the surface, little more than dirty water, but lower the mud was a composite of soil and decayed leaves, cool to the touch, with an earthy smell that wasn't at all unpleasant. When the sleeve was half-full, Jake eased his right hand into the muck until he felt the knot he'd tied at the end. The cool mud offered some relief from the burning sensation, and that alone made the whole exercise worthwhile.

The exhaustion — the overpowering sense of sick fatigue — struck Jake like a bolt from the sky. He'd been dizzy and disoriented and weak, but now he felt unable to gather the strength to take another step, to check on his horse, to eat a few sticks of jerky. He made it to a patch of shade and collapsed.

It took Sinclair some moments to figure out that it was very early morning and that he'd slept through the balance of the day and the entire night before. His mud poultice had almost but not completely dried during his unconscious hours. His hand throbbed in its soil cast, but the pressure created by the drying muck seemed to force any real pain into the background of sensation. The fever was still with him. He was terribly thirsty, and his gut rumbled with hunger, but the thought of food nauseated him. He gazed around where he'd slept. The early sun made the dew sparkle brightly, like bits of mica randomly strewn about.

If I don't get some help today I'm going to die in these woods. By tomorrow I'll be too weak to climb onto Mare and I'll sit here and boil to death in my own goddamn fever-sweat. He got shakily to his feet. *Ferris said there was a town somewhere around here. A town might have a doctor or at least someone who knows some animal and human medicine. All I need to do is find the town.*

Mare, still securely hobbled, had been able to move freely enough to expand her grazing area to a shaded patch near a sinkhole of tepid water. Jake lumbered up to her, stroked her face while holding on to her neck to keep himself from toppling over, and, after sucking up some of the murky water from what amounted to nothing beyond a stagnant puddle, led her back to his gear. His saddle and rifle were untouched. There was no sign of his knife. Saddling Mare took what seemed like an eternity of hard labor and climbing up onto her back wasn't much easier. Jake nudged the horse with his heels and reined her in a roughly west direction, letting Mare pick her way around trees and through the thick scrub. There was a breeze moving and it was a gift from heaven, drying Sinclair's sweat and cooling his body. He was as at home on a good horse's back as he would have been in a rocking chair. Like a seasoned cowhand riding watch on a quiet night, Jake was more asleep than awake, conscious only of the movement of the horse under him, his body adjusting itself to her easily, naturally. It was a lack of that motion that brought Jake awake. They'd come to a road — or at least a wagon trail — that looked recently used. A pile of horse manure was not more than a half day old. Mare swung her head back to look at Sinclair, her intelligent chestnut eyes all but shouting out to him, "Which way? You're the rider, remember?" Jake squinted against the sun, peering down at the rutted trail. Most of the prints from shod hooves pointed to his left. He reined Mare in that direction, sitting more upright in his saddle now. His horse, too, was more alert, sniffing the air, perhaps catching the scents of civilization.

Jake halted at a sign at the side of the road nailed to a stout post stuck into the ground. The sign was wooden, about two feet by two feet. The lettering was faded but still legible: TOWN OF PENDERTON. The thick wood was riddled with bullet holes, most of which appeared to be from small-caliber weapons. A couple of two-inch-wide gaps indicated the passing of a rifleman with a buffalo gun or similar piece. Sinclair's face broke into a grin in spite of his dried and cracked lips. He recalled that posters for runaway slaves back home had served as targets, too. He and his father had, in fact, sighted in Jake's brand-new birthday gift rifle on such a poster the day he turned fifteen.

Sinclair passed a neat little log-constructed cabin with a couple of toddlers playing with a pair of puppies in front of it. He was about to rein in when he locked eyes with a stout, hatchet-faced woman in a washed-out gray dress. Her mouth was a grim, hard line. She held a 44.40 across her chest with a finger inside the trigger guard. Jake nodded and kept moving. He could feel her eyes following him until he was far down the road. After another mile he passed a house — a frame structure this time — and then another not far beyond it. The road he followed got heavier use here; it was wider and there were few weeds growing up in the ruts and craters. He followed a sweeping arc the road made and then the town of Penderton was laid out before him — what little of it there was. The main street was arrow straight and wide and the wind stirred up dust devils along its length. There were buildings on both sides of the street, some of which had false fronts, making them appear larger and more permanent than they were. No building was taller than two stories. Most were one. Closest to Jake was a stable and blacksmith operation with a corral behind it. There a few rental mounts pushed flakes of hay around listlessly in the sun. Down the street was the largest structure in Penderton: A long, pristinely white, black-lettered sign proclaimed it to be Van-Gelder's Mercantile. A kid of twelve or so was washing one of the large glass display windows at the front of the store. There was a plank sidewalk in front of the mercantile. Next came an empty lot and then a saloon with batwing doors. Three nondescript horses were tied to the rail in front. An alley separated the gin mill and an undertaker's establishment and next to that, a feed mill. At the far end of the street a whitewashed structure with a cross over its large front doors stood like a sentry watching over the town. The opposite side of the street held a restaurant with a hand-painted sign that stated simply EAT HERE, a two-story hotel with a few old gaffers sitting on benches under the front overhang, a sheriff's office, an apparently vacant building with a board nailed across its front door, and a farm tool and carriage store with a shiny phaeton parked in front of it. There was little pedestrian traffic on the street: Two women were looking into one of VanGelder's windows, and a farmer-looking fellow was tying up in front of the saloon. Jake swung Mare over to the man.

"I'm wondering if there's a doc in town," Sinclair said, his voice cracking a bit.

The farmer turned and looked Jake over before he answered. "You sure look like you could use one, all pale and sickly," he observed. "What's that on your arm?"

"A poultice. Look — is there a doctor or anybody who can give —"

"Jus' down beyond where that carriage is parked is Doc's house. I'll tell you this, though, he won't take no farm produce or Reb scrip — only good Union cash. Otherwise, he'll turn you away as sure as chickens don't have no lips. Doc, he's got more money than God. Built kind of a hospital right onto his house is what he done." The fellow paused, as if collecting his thoughts. Jake had already begun turning Mare. The windbag he'd encountered was beginning to fade in his vision and the floating spots were moving in. "Now, was you to stop for a drink here" — the farmer motioned toward the batwings — "ol' Weasel, he'll take damn near anything in trade for a taste of whiskey an' a beer. He's got ice, too — the beer is cold. Every winter, me an' the boys, we go to the river an' cut a full wagonload. Freeze our eggs off too, you can bet on that. Weasel don't pay worth a shit, but we — me an' the boys — sure fancy that cold beer long about this time of . . ."

Jake rode toward the end of the street after mumbling his thanks for the directions. Even through the haze of fever, he asked himself, *Weasel? What the hell kind of name is Weasel? Did I hear that right?*

It seemed like the hitching rail in front of the doctor's office and home was trying to dance away from Jake's left-handed attempts to wrap his reins around it. The buzzing in his ears was back, sawing away inside his head, and he could feel that his face was dripping sweat. "Here," a man's voice said, "let me get that for you." In a moment Jake felt a strong arm around his shoulders, half leading and half carrying him toward the office. "Easy now," the voice said. "Let's get you inside."

The reek of chloroform on the cloth covering Jake's nose and mouth took him back to the battlefield, to a surgeon's tent where he'd hauled a kid with a lower leg

129

wound. The doctor had put the soldier under with chloroform and sawed off the leg at the knee. Early in the war, the anesthetic was available. Now, two years later, neither side had much of it. When the severed limb struck the floor Jake had run from the tent, the vile smell of the chloroform sticking to his hair, his clothes, his skin. Now, drugged and confused, he kicked at the imaginary surgeon with the gleaming saw.

"Easy," the now familiar voice said. "Easy now. There's no need to fight me. Calm down now."

Jake focused on the face of the man leaning over him, pinning his arms and chest to the long wooden table he was stretched out upon. "My leg . . ." Jake mumbled.

"There's nothing wrong with your legs. Your problem is quite a bit higher — in your right hand and arm. I cleaned it out real well. You're going to be all right. Hear? You're going to be all right."

Jake squinted against the sunlight pouring in the surgery window. "Who're . . . what . . . ?"

"I'm Dr. David Oliver. Your legs were turning to rubber outside my office. I brought you in here and took the cataplasm off your hand. I think I got all the infection, and if I didn't, what I poured into the incisions I had to make will take care of it. The cataplasm was a good idea — maybe a very good idea."

"Cataplasm?" Jake croaked.

"You probably call it a poultice. It was drawing pus well. I don't doubt that you saved your hand with it." He smiled ruefully at Jake. "Thank God for chloroform. I had to gouge around in there like a drunken coal miner."

"I've got money — federal gold eagles — in my boots. I can pay . . ."

The doctor grinned, his well-shaved face moving away from Jake. "You must have spoken with Yappy Tolliver. The damned fool wanted me to treat his piles and offered me a mangy-looking duck and a half bushel of potatoes in payment. I told him to shove the duck up his ass and see if that helped. Since then Yappy has been telling anybody who'll listen that I'll only work for cold hard cash on the barrelhead."

Jake began to struggle up to a sitting position, but the doctor put a gentle hand on his chest, easing him back. "Not yet — and I want you in the bed right here for a couple of days. Your right hand and forearm are attached to a board and I want it to stay there for at least forty-eight hours. I'll be checking it until then. Lie back and get some rest. I'll help you over to the bed in an hour or so and get some water in you, too."

The doctor was a compact man of about forty, broad-shouldered and wide-hipped, but with no sign of fat. His dark brown hair showed some gray at his temples and his eyes were clear and piercing. The sleeves of his white shirt were rolled up. Jake's eyes stopped there. The physician's left arm was a short, shriveled appendage, the hand curled in on itself. Oliver caught his gaze. "That's why I'm not in the army surgical corps," he said. "I offered to take any kind of skill and proficiency test they wanted, but those mindless bureaucrats in Washington . . ." He let the sentence die. "What's your name?" he asked after a moment.

"Jake."

"Just Jake? That's a pretty fancy horse out there for a fellow with but one name."

"Jake's enough."

The doctor grinned, showing even white teeth. "Maybe so. I had the mare taken down to the stable — she'll be well cared for." He walked to the door. "Get some rest, Jake. I've got other patients to tend to, and then I'll be back to get you settled in bed. My wife will bring you some water. Drink all she brings."

The doctor's wife was younger than Jake expected her to be. She was a fine-looking woman of about thirty with long black hair and large chestnut eyes. He estimated her to be at least three inches taller than her husband. "I'm Maggie," she said. "Doc's wife and nurse and general handyman and cook, too." Her smile was open and kind and warm. "Doc says you had quite an infection." She handed him a large glass of water.

"I guess I did," Jake said, taking the glass. He raised his head as far as he was able but still dribbled water on his chest as he emptied the glass. Maggie leaned forward with a white cloth and swabbed away the spill. "You rest now," she said.

When Maggie had closed the door behind herself Jake inspected Doc Oliver's work. His arm was secured to a piece of sanded board about a foot and a half long and five inches wide by wraps of thick gauze. Spots of blood seeped through the gauze in places, spotting the whiteness. Jake brought the back of his hand to his nose; the only smell was a pungent, medicinal scent. He lowered his arm down next to his body and closed his eyes, doubting very much that he'd sleep.

The gentle touch of a hand at his shoulder awakened Sinclair, and his eyes popped open. Doc was again looking down at him. Jake blinked several times: The texture of the light had changed from bright afternoon sunlight to almost late dusk. An oil lamp hung from a metal hook across the room. "I guess I slept," he said.

"You did — soundly and for several hours. Let's get you into the infirmary and I'll check my work."

The infirmary was a good-sized room down a hall that contained three vacant beds separated by cloth screens. Next to the head of each bed was a small table, and next to each was a straight-backed chair. Doc supported Jake as he guided him to the last bed in the line. "Lie down and I'll get your boots off," he said. "And your pants, too. Maggie will wash them tomorrow. Looks like you pissed yourself while you slept," he observed. Jake looked away, blushing.

"Nothing to be ashamed of," Doc said. "Shows the plumbing's working as it should." When Jake was prone on the bed minus his boots and pants, the physician drew a light sheet over him. "I have your money from inside your boots," he said. "It'll be safe with me. I'll have Maggie go over to the mercantile and pick up a shirt for you tomorrow. I'll leave water here on the table by your left hand, where you can reach it. No food until tomorrow, though." He brought a lamp closer to Jake and peered at his arm. "Looks like my sutures are holding. Get some sleep." Before Jake could answer, the doctor was walking away from him toward the main part of the house. Both Jake and Doc Oliver flinched as the throaty, percussive boom of a heavy-caliber rifle destroyed the silence of the late evening. "Drunken damned fools," Doc said, turning back to Jake before he could ask a question. "There was a marksmanship contest on the Fourth of July, and a few of the men seem to have stuck around. Every evening it's the same thing. They get liquored up, put their bets on the table, and go out to shoot." Another report rolled through the town, and then, quickly, another. "They'll quit when it's full dark," Doc said. "Then you can sleep."

The sporadic gunfire continued until it was so dark that Jake couldn't see his hand in front of his face. The shooting stopped but it seemed to echo in Jake's ears, in his mind. Instantly, he was back in battle.

It was strange. He could always hear Uriah, even over the furor of battle. *"There — at ten o'clock, that's an officer near the artillery piece — easy shot, Jake . . . His men are loading canister — they're blowing our flank's asses off. . . ." Toole leaned forward and spat on the barrel of Jake's Sharps, up near the front sight. "Still cool enough for a couple rounds, Jake — my spit ain't dancing yet. . . ."*

Then, suddenly, Jake faced his father across the great room in their home.

"You ran, Son. You turned tail on your obligation to protect all this — the way we live, our country, what we believe." The man's face had aged terribly; his eyes were infinitely sad — and tinged with disgust.

"It wasn't like that, Pa. I couldn't watch it anymore, I couldn't do what I'd been doing anymore. All that killing for what, Pa? A god-damn political argument between Abe Lincoln and Jeff Davis? Give them each a bowie and let them fight it out, stop the boys from killing each other."

"You ran, boy. No son of mine runs from a fight."

"Jake? Jake?"

Maggie Oliver's voice tugged Sinclair from sleep. Morning sun cascaded through the window at the end of the infirmary, bright enough to cause a man to squint.

"I have your pants here and a new shirt. Doc says you can get dressed now. You do that and I'll fetch you some breakfast. Hungry, are you?"

Jake considered for a moment. "Ma'am,"

he said. "I could eat one of my boots and get a good start on the second one."

Maggie laughed, the sound as pretty and as fine as good music. She placed the shirt and pants on the chair. "Careful now as you dress. You're likely to be dizzy." Jake sat up clumsily, his right arm and the board it was attached to feeling as big and as awkward as the trunk of a hundred-year-old oak. Maggie was right about the dizziness, but it passed quickly. It felt good to have some clothes on when she came back with a tray of ham and eggs and thick slices of buttered dark bread. The aroma of the large mug of coffee reached out to him. He moved carefully to the chair and balanced the tray in his lap. "Doc's birthing a baby," Maggie told him. "He'll be back before too long. He said you're to eat and then rest. No walking around except to the privy. I'll bring a pitcher of water. Doc says to keep drinking, thirsty or not." She took a folded newspaper from where it'd been tucked under her arm and placed it on the bed. "Here's something to read, if you've a mind to. It's all war news, I'm afraid."

Jake ate everything on the tray before he reached for the paper. Under the masthead of the *Penderton Advisor* the headline was stark, in huge black font across the top of the page:

CONFEDERATES ROUTED IN BLOODY
CONFRONTATION; HEROIC UNION
TROOPS REPEL MASSIVE ASSAULT!

Jake began to read the account and then put the paper aside, realizing that the writer probably hadn't been within a hundred miles of the battle. He had the fighting taking place in the town — from house to house — and mentioned nothing about Pickett or the final charge. The casualty count by the reporter was absolutely insane: He cited over twenty thousand Union men killed, wounded, or missing, and over eighteen thousand for the Confederates. Photographs taken by Matthew Brady, renowned photographer of the Great War, would appear in subsequent editions of the *Advisor,* the text promised. Sinclair sighed and put the newspaper aside.

Doc Oliver was rumpled and tired when he showed up at about midday. He unwrapped the gauze from Jake's arm and inspected his work. Behind Jake's knuckles were a series of perhaps ten or a dozen inch-to two-inch-long series of neatly tied sutures. The swelling was down and there was no stink of infection. The skin, however, was reddened and stretched, particularly between the lines of sutures. "Looks very good," Doc said. He removed the cap from a blue glass jar and spread a thick, sharp-smelling ointment over the injured areas. "Bovine bag balm," he said. "Works better than any of the salves the medical suppliers in Chicago sell — at about a quarter of the price." He rewrapped the hand and arm and secured it, once again, to the board. Noting the disappointment in Jake's eyes, he said, "Look — everything is fine so far. You got off real lucky, Jake. The trauma area needs to be immobilized for at least another day. Today I want you to spend most of your time on your bed. We'll see about tomorrow when it gets here." The doctor stood and wearily put his hands to his lower back. "Like I said, you're very lucky. Don't screw up my good work now."

Waiting to heal was about as interesting to Jake Sinclair as watching moss grow on a damp rock. There was very little pain in his right hand and forearm, but the itching was intense, maddening in a sense, worse than pain. The day dragged. He dozed a few times but dreamed of using a handful of rough straw to scour away the incessant itching. Maggie brought him lunch and then dinner but apparently was too busy in the office with Doc to stop to visit. Late in the afternoon gunfire sounded — at first that of standard-caliber rifles and then the more muscular reports of a Sharps or similar weapon. Every once in a while a whoop or a burst of laughter reached Jake and the tinkling of a honky-tonk piano was just barely audible if the breeze was right. The shooting stopped after dark. The frequency of the yells and braying laughter increased as the night progressed, but it was never quite loud enough to be annoying. In truth, the laughter sounded good to Jake. *Men laugh differently, more quietly, with less joy, before or after a battle. It's nervous laughter then, with none of the release of whiskey and fun behind it. Hell, Uriah and I hadn't really laughed together for a couple of months before Gettysburg — even when we came across some whiskey.*

Jake Sinclair was wide awake, hungry, thirsty, and very surly when Doc Oliver looked in on him the following morning. "This goddamn itching, Doc," Jake greeted the physician, "is going to drive me crazy! It doesn't let up for a second. I didn't sleep a wink all night. . . ."

"Strange." Doc grinned. "The two times I looked in on you, you were sleeping as sound as a federal dollar. And," he added, "the itching is a good sign. It means things are healing up. Let's take a look." He quickly removed the gauze, freeing the arm. "Swelling's way down, no sign the infection has returned. Move your fingers."

Jake complied, feeling some stiffness and some resistance. "Doesn't itch so bad with the dressing off," he said.

"Make a fist," Doc said.

Jake's knuckles smarted and his skin felt tight and hot, but he formed a good fist. He turned his clenched hand over and then back again, gazing down at it as if it were his first newborn son. "Thanks, Doc," he said.

"Sure. Keep it clean and there's no need to wrap it. My services and your stay here are going to cost you six dollars. Maggie will bring you your change from the forty dollars in your boots. You're ready to go, Jake. If you're still in town in a week, come back and I'll remove the stitches. If you're not, cut them and pluck them out yourself. There's nothing to it. Just don't leave them in longer than a week."

Jake stood from the bedside chair. "I won't forget this, Doc."

"Sure you will." Oliver smiled. "In a year or so all you'll remember is the doc with one arm who charged you six dollars for doing next to nothing." He put his hand on Jake's shoulder. "I won't offer to shake with you, Jake No Last Name — at least until the stitches are out. I'll wish you well, though."

The livery stable — Jake's first stop after leaving Doc Oliver's office — smelled of good hay and polished leather and the scent of healthy horses. Jake looked over Mare, asked that her shoes be reset, and checked his saddle. He paid the blacksmith's boarding rate of sixty-five cents per day, and said he'd be by in the morning to get her. As Jake was leaving the barn, the smith was leading Mare to the front work area where his forge and anvil were located.

The sun was strong on Jake's back as he walked from the stables to the Penderton Hotel. He took a room on the second floor, paid his dollar in advance as required, dragged the wooden chair that was, other than the bed, the only piece of furniture in the room to the curtainless window and sat down. Rooms with dressers were ten cents per night extra. "I won't be here long enough to need a dresser," he'd told the clerk.

He watched men go in and out of the saloon for the balance of the afternoon.

Most of the day trade was farmers sneaking off from their fields for a quick drink. Few of them, Jake noticed, carried sidearms. About suppertime a tall, gaunt man in a dark suit dismounted and tied a good-looking roan to the rail in the front of the saloon. He wore a holstered pistol and it rested low on his hip. The holster was tied to his leg with a leather string. Almost immediately another rider tied up outside, this one a squat fellow with flaming red hair and a bushy beard. He carried a long parcel wrapped in cowhide. From its size and configuration, Jake could see that it was a long gun, but it was impossible to determine the caliber or manufacturer. Jake moved from the window and stretched out on the bed. Before long the piano in the saloon began its night's work.

Jake took the holster and pistol from his belt before he left his room, leaving them with the clerk for safekeeping. It was cooler now, although the sun was still sending its harsh light as it approached the western horizon. A fairly stiff breeze was intermittent. Halfway to the saloon Jake crouched as if adjusting his pant leg over his boot and picked up a pinch of dried dirt. He flicked it from his fingers at shoulder height and watched as the grains were whisked away.

Then he moved on to the batwing doors.

It took a few moments for Jake's eyes to adjust to the murky light and haze of tobacco smoke in the saloon and he stood just inside until he could see clearly. The place was interchangeable with every small-town gin mill Jake had ever seen: a long bar behind which was centered the obligatory large seminude painting of a buxom female, breasts bared with a hand coyly covering her groin, a half dozen spittoons spread along the floor in front of the bar, each showing the lack of spitting accuracy of the clientele, oil lamps on hooks throughout the room, damp sawdust, spilled beer, and crushed cigar nubs and cigarette butts on the uneven wooden floor, a few tables with chairs for poker players, and a battered piano at the rear. The saloon smelled of stale beer, cedar sawdust, sweat, and foul breath.

The man who'd left the roan at the hitching rail stood at the bar, his rifle resting on the polished wood. A few other men stood about, schooners of beer in their hands, clustered about the rifleman. Jake eased up to the bar. He immediately understood where the name Weasel had come from: The bartender looked like he'd be more at home raiding a chicken coop than pouring beer and booze. His face was narrow and his nose vulpine, more of a snout than a nose, and his eyes were small and dark and suspicious. His body, too, conveyed the weasel image: It was thin and moved quickly but strangely gracefully — almost sinuously.

"Beer," Jake said, when Weasel nodded at him.

Jake glanced at the rifle on the bar. "Nice weapon," he said casually. "Not many Spencer 56.46s around these days. Longer reach than the arm of God, right?" He turned away and raised the beer Weasel had put in front of him.

"That's a fact." The owner grinned. "Know weapons, do you?" He was tall, probably closer to sixty than to fifty in age, and was dressed in city clothes — white shirt, dark vest, dark pants, and boots. His eyes, Jake noticed, were a pale blue, his gaze unwavering: shooter's eyes. His hair was mostly gray and pushed back from his face, touching his shoulders.

"I've always respected a good rifle like the Spencer and the Sharps." He added, "My name's Jake."

The rifleman nodded. "I'm Will. You shoot, Jake?"

Jake took a long pull at his schooner of icy cold beer. It felt wonderful on his throat and tasted just as good. He wiped foam from his mouth with the back of his hand and smiled. "I'll tell you this, Will — I'd bet that if you give me two practice rounds with your rifle, I can outshoot you with it at any distance under any conditions. So yeah, it's fair to say that I shoot."

Sinclair hadn't spoken loud, but his words had been heard by the men at and around the bar. An uneasy silence followed. The bystanders watched Will carefully for his reaction, trying to appear that they weren't doing so.

"That right?" Will said. "You'll take up my rifle and outshoot me with it?"

"Just as sure as you're standing here," Jake said.

Will chuckled, but the coldness that had set into his eyes made a lie of what his laugh said. "Cocky sumbitch, ain't you?" He paused for a moment and then grinned again. "I guess I might just as well drink for free tonight on you, Jake. Think you can find ten dollars somewhere?"

"I can."

Will removed two cartridges from the side pocket of his coat and put them on the bar in front of Jake. Each was almost three inches long and as thick as a stout man's finger. "Here's how this'll go," he said. "You take your two practice rounds and then I pick a target and we both get but a single round. Best shot wins — no arguments. If it's real close, Weasel here will judge it. He's a crooked-looking sumbitch for true, but he's honest. Agreed?"

Jake picked up the two cartridges. "Agreed," he said. Will handed the Spencer to him, handling it almost reverently. Jake paid the weapon the same respect. The group of men moved out to the street. About a hundred yards from the saloon the road leading to town took a bend around a heifer-sized boulder, its dusty brown crags and surfaces glinting in places as the sun struck bits of mica. Sinclair fed a cartridge into the Spencer's breech, worked the lever action, and raised the butt to his shoulder. The rifle was slightly lighter than the Sharps he'd gotten so accustomed to, but he felt the quality and power of the Spencer as he sighted at the boulder. It was immediately apparent to the group what Jake had selected as a target. The report was like that of a cannon. A geyser of dirt erupted an inch to the right of the rock.

"I'll give you five to one 'gainst Will, mister," an observer offered.

"Me too," another voice said.

Jake ejected the spent cartridge and inserted the second one. "Five dollars each?"

"Five's good."

Jake's second attempt clipped a cigar-sized piece of rock away at the very edge of the boulder and the slug ricocheted into the distance, its high-pitched whine echoing after it.

"Nice shootin'," one of the men said sarcastically. " 'Specially since that li'l rock ain't no bigger'n a goddamn barn." Sinclair ignored the laughter.

Jake handed the rifle to the shooter named Will. "What's your target?" Jake asked.

"Just a couple pieces of board with bull's-eyes painted on them, Jake. Nothin' fancy. We got some already made up inside." Will turned to the group. "Yappy — you go on an' set up a couple of the targets out there about 150 yards or so, will you?"

Yappy hustled back to the saloon almost at a run. "I buy him a drink or two every so often," Will commented.

Yappy grabbed his horse from the rail and rode at a gallop out past the boulder a good distance. There he stopped and turned back, waving to Will. Will returned the wave. Yappy took his horse far off to one side. The two boards he'd stuck in the ground a yard apart were a foot and a half tall and about eight inches wide. Toward the top of each a bright red circle was centered.

"I'll take the right one," Will said. He fed a cartridge into his rifle, cocked it, and raised it to position with the ease and understated skill of a true rifleman, not wasting a motion. He barely appeared to aim before he fired. He handed the smoking Spencer to Jake. "Have at it." He grinned.

Jake accepted the rifle and another round. He loaded and cocked the weapon, brought it to his shoulder, and peered down the sights. He spread his boots apart a few inches wider and squeezed off his shot. Yappy grabbed the two targets, scratched something onto Will's with a pencil, and rode back. He reined in and handed the two boards to Will. The one with the W scratched below the bull showed a good shot. The slug had made a clean hole through the dried wood, very slightly off center.

Jake's shot had been dead on, the hole precisely centered in the red circle.

"Well, shit," Will said. He handed over a ten-dollar bill. The two men who'd offered odds paid twenty-five dollars each, neither of them pleased about it.

"One more time," Will grunted.

Jake nodded. "Sure."

Twenty minutes later they were back in the bar, Weasel sliding beers to them. Jake was better than a hundred dollars richer than he'd been before the contest.

When the group saw that the shooting was finished, they wandered off to poker games or some serious drinking along the bar. Jake and Will stood side by side.

"Strange coincidence," Will said, his voice low.

Jake met his eyes.

"That big battle and then a man showing up here in a nothin' little town a week or so later who can shoot the hairs offa fly's ass without touching the fly, I mean." Will shook his head. "A fella could almost think you're on the run, Jake — a deserter."

"I suppose a fellow could think that. It doesn't mean he'd be right about it."

"No. It wouldn't. Thing is, if I was you I'd get a good night's sleep tonight and go along on my way. Some of the sodbusters and store clerks have blood that's not only red — it's white an' blue, too. If they take to believing you might have run out on ol' General Grant, there'd be trouble."

Jake took a mouthful of beer and swallowed. "What about you? Would I have trouble with you?"

"I'm just giving you a bit of advice, is all. I don't give a good goddamn what you are — but I'll tell you this: I know a sharpshooter when I see one." He paused for a moment. "Like I said, movin' on wouldn't be a bad idea."

Jake finished his beer and set the empty schooner in front of him. "Thanks for the match," he said. Before he turned away, he added quietly, "And the advice."

The next morning Jake was standing outside the mercantile when Horace VanGelder unlocked the front door at six-thirty A.M. A half hour later Jake rode from the stable on Mare to pick up his purchases: a sack of coffee, an open-top holster, a can of fancy peaches in heavy syrup, a hundred rounds of ammunition, six cigars, a Barlow folding knife with a very sharp four-inch blade, a pair of denim pants he put on in the store, discarding his old ones, a good quality hat with a wide Western-style brim, a quart of whiskey, and a peppermint stick. His purchases — except for the peppermint stick, which he kept out — fit nicely into his saddlebags. The knife went into his pocket. It was a sorry replacement for his original bowie, he knew. But it'd do.

Five minutes later he rode out of Penderton, Pennsylvania, headed west, sucking on a stick of candy.

CHAPTER FIVE

Jake rode for seven days without seeing or hearing another human being. He found good grazing for Mare without really having to look for it: The grass in the breaks between the trees and the areas that surrounded the multitudinous spring-fed small ponds seemed to take great delight in pushing itself up from the fertile, loamy soil. He took a few rabbits and got lucky enough to pick a hen pheasant — summer fat and sublimely tasty — out of the air with his pistol.

At his evening camp that seventh day he uncorked the whiskey he'd bought in Penderton, lowered the level in the bottle a couple of inches, and checked over his hand. He'd had no pain nor heat in it since he'd left Doc Oliver's infirmary, and the itching had, for the most part, subsided.

Jake opened the blade of his Barlow knife and tested its edge with his thumb. It was razor-keen and slightly smeared with light grease. He wiped it on his pant leg and slid the very point of the blade under a suture. It took almost no pressure to cut the stitch; he then set the knife aside and plucked out the bit of black thread. Oliver had used individual sutures rather than a running line of them, even on the longer cuts. In fifteen minutes the procedure was completed. Jake sniffed the still slightly reddish wounds. All he smelled was his fresh, healing skin. He grinned and took another long drink from his bottle. He hadn't looked at the label before. He'd asked for a quart of rye and the owner of the mercantile had pulled down a bottle from the shelf behind him and added it to the small pile of purchases on the counter. Jake inspected the label now. It read:

VANGELDER'S PENNSYLVANIA RYE
WHISKEY
THE CHOICE OF SOPHISTICATED
IMBIBERS

· · · · · · · · · · · · · ·

BREWED AND AGED IN THE VANGELDER
DISTILLERY
PENDERTON, PENNSYLVANIA

Sinclair chuckled. "In the mercantile's

basement or maybe a nearby barn," he said aloud. " 'Course a sophisticated imbiber like me knows good whiskey." He laughed again and drank again. Food didn't seem important this evening. The fire he'd already built in a small, hand-dug hole was burned down to white ash — perfect for cooking. Still, hunting for small game was more trouble than it was worth. He filled the empty peach can with water from one of his canteens, dropped in a hefty handful of coffee beans, and set the can on the edge of the fire. When his coffee had brewed he used a pair of sticks to take the can off the fire. After an impatient few minutes he picked the container up, drank a few mouthfuls of coffee that was still much too hot to be comfortable, and brought the level back to the top of the can by adding whiskey. The bottle was considerably more than halfway gone. He corked it tightly and set it aside. *Funny thing about whiskey,* he thought. *It takes the sharp edge off things for me, kind of settles everything down a step or two. Other men I've met get happy or giddy after a few drinks, laugh like schoolkids at a picnic. Whiskey makes some men belligerent, crazy-mad, looking for a fistfight or worse as soon as they down a few. And lots of the soldiers I've met don't find happiness or even fun in drinking. It makes them sad — they go on and on about their mothers or wives or homes or children or dogs or whatever the hell when they have a snootful.* Jake stretched out next to the dying campfire, his head leaning against the seat of his saddle, watching the stars and the skimpy luminescent clouds that drifted past the window in the limbs and leaves far above him.

Pa had his bourbon and branch water at the end of each day. He sometimes had a second, but that was rare. He never showed the effects, although there was always a good four fingers in his tumbler along with the sweet water. The only change in him was the smoky, masculine scent of the bourbon on his breath. He'd sit out on the veranda during the summer months and inside during the cooler or rainy times. Sometimes he'd light his pipe and gray-blue snippets of tobacco smoke hung in the air around him.

Pa would be ashamed of me . . .

"Shit," Jake grunted and sat up. After a moment he reached over and picked up the bottle of Penderton's Best.

I should have run the day after I signed on. I wish I had.

Days no longer seemed to be separate and distinct blocks of time. There was no difference to them beyond the hard facts of day and night. He and Mare covered ground as if that's specifically what they were born to do, but there was no hurry to their travel, no anticipation of arriving somewhere. They were merely moving, and that was good enough for Jake Sinclair.

Jake bought ammunition for his pistol — he practiced with it every day — and coffee and a few cigars and another bottle in a place that was more of a clearing than a town. He had no idea what state the place was located in, and didn't care. The Smith & Wesson .22 had become as much a part of his body as his bowie knife had once been. He'd lubricated the holster he bought in Penderton with the greasy fat of a porcupine he'd killed, stripped the skin from and cooked, and the leather was supple and held the pistol snugly. Jake took to tying the holster lower on his leg than would a cowhand or city denizen or farmer, so that when he stood, the very tips of his fingers grazed the bone grips. That made sense, he thought. When the time came that he needed the .22, he'd need it quickly.

He'd given up shaving long ago, and his hair was well down over his shoulders. He hacked off a few inches of beard with his Barlow knife when its length bothered him, and he did the same with his hair, although cutting the growth in the back of his head was harder than shearing off the growth in front when it reached below his eyebrows. He bathed every so often when he began to smell himself. Jake crossed roads and wagon trails at times but saw no reason to follow them. They'd inevitably lead to people, and he had no need for people just then. He wondered a bit about feeling as he did, but didn't spend a great deal of time worrying about it. He realized that in truth he had no true destination; he believed that eventually he'd get to Texas and meet up with his partner's family, but the mission no longer had the urgency it once possessed. He was riding for the sake of riding, moving vaguely west, eating when he was hungry, sleeping when he was tired, with no plan whatsoever for the next day or week or year.

Jake Sinclair's future had been pretty much locked into place the day he was born, the day his mother died bringing him into the world. Jake would live a structured boyhood, guided by his father. He'd go off to college, come home, find a suitably Southern wife, and take over his father's thousand-acre plantation upon the old man's death. He would be wealthy — rich, actually — just as his father was. His cotton and sugarcane crops would continue to be bountiful, to make him yet richer. He'd hold clear title to over three hundred slaves. He and his suitably Southern wife would start a family and the circle would be repeated, the plantation passed on, the great-grandchildren of slaves now living on the property of Jake's future family after his death. Jake knew all this was true because his father had told him that it was. The War of Northern Aggression never figured into the equation.

Jake's father had meetings at his home long before Sumter. The other plantation owners, sipping whiskey, smoking cigars, and enjoying the Sinclair hospitality, weren't nearly as wrought over the discussions that encompassed state's rights, "those lunatic abolitionists," "Abe Lincoln's perfidy," "and the federal government's desire to crush the Southern way of life," as was Leighton Sinclair.

Jake sighed and did his best to push the memories from his mind. It was better — far easier on the nerves — to simply enjoy the cool, crystalline clarity of the autumn day, the riotous colors of the changing leaves, the pure smells of a season rapidly moving from the heavy doldrums of late summer to the crispness of the fall season.

Mare had begun getting fidgety about midday. After so much time alone with his horse, Jake knew her well, knew when she was content or tired or frisky, when she required a few minutes of stroking along her neck and rubbing between her ears. This afternoon she'd seemed nervous. Her ears were almost constantly in quick, jerky motion, flicking here and then there, pointing at nothing other than the normal things of the woods, snorting frequently. When he came upon a small water hole with some good grazing around it, Jake decided to rein in for the day. His horse's lack of ease had been transmitted to him to a minor degree and he found himself starting at the quick scolding of a bird or an unexpected rustle of a small animal in the brush. It was too fine of a day to argue with Mare. He hobbled her, stripped off her saddle, and left her to graze. He walked out of the clearing breathing deeply of the pristine air, half wondering when he'd come across his nightly meal.

When the cock pheasant erupted from scrub cover five feet in front of Jake, the frantic drumming of the big bird's wings was as loud as a cannon and as unforeseen as a thunderclap on a sunny day. Jake's hand snaked to his side and before the bird was ten feet away two slugs slammed into it, flinging it cartwheeling to the ground. Sinclair grinned as he replaced the two spent cartridges and reholstered his pistol. The draw had been automatic, reflexive, and his shooting damned near perfect. Plus, he had his evening meal — and a fine one, at that. He gathered up the pheasant and carried it by its feet back to where he'd left Mare.

Digging a small fire pit with a stick and his hands and lining it with stones didn't take long. He placed dry wood carefully in the pit, started his fire, and, in the brush, cleaned the pheasant. He washed the meat in the water hole and cut it into chunks that were thick enough to skewer. After doing so he picked up a couple more armfuls of wood; the nights were getting chilly.

Mare was moving about more than she ordinarily did. Jake watched her for a few moments as he roasted the meat over the fire. To salve his own unusual nervousness he drew the Winchester from the saddle scabbard and placed it at his side on dry ground, away from the fire. The bird's meat was sweet and tasty and dripped fat into the flames, turning the outside crisp and sealing in the gamy juices. Jake barely noticed how fine a meal it was and by the time he was flinging the remnants into the brush, he was cursing. Whatever was bothering his horse was now nagging at him. His senses were alert, on guard, and he found himself clenching and unclenching his fists, his eyes every so often swinging to the 44.40. When he heard the sounds far behind him in the direction from which he'd come, it was almost a relief. The bell of a steel horseshoe striking a rock rang clear and true and carried easily through the thick woods. Jake listened intently. There were a few of them, he figured, and they weren't wasting time. As he strained to hear, eyes tightly closed in concentration, the sounds became more distinct: the thud of hooves, a bit of a man's exclamation, the snapping of twigs and small branches. Mare squealed and began to pitch, fighting against the hobbles.

The blow that took Jake down came from behind him as he rushed to his horse. He saw — didn't actually see, but instead, felt — a brilliant flash of light that encompassed everything around him, that was far too screamingly bright to see past or through. He dropped as though lifeless, face first, and didn't move, didn't feel the blood rushing from the tear in the skin on the back of his head.

"If this boy swings, I want first say on his

horse an' saddle, Sheriff." The voice seemed hoarse and sort of far away, but the words were clear. Jake opened his eyes. Ground passed beneath him and there was sweat on the belly of the horse he was draped over, facedown.

"Too late — least about the mare. I already got a pretty good saddle. I'll have to think on that." The answering voice sounded nearer and there was a slight chuckle behind it. "I guess whether or not he'll stretch a rope is up to the judge, ain't it? Come to think on it, that saddle is a good piece of work — better'n what I'm riding."

Jake tested his hands. They were tied tightly together, as were his feet. Another length of rope ran from under his arms across the horse's belly and up the animal's far side to where it was lashed either to the rope holding his feet and legs together or maybe to the saddle horn. Either way it didn't make any difference — the drumlike pounding in Jake's head was his entire world.

"Lots of trees," a new voice said. "Seems we maybe could save some screwin' around and hang Billy right here. We gotta camp tonight an' I don't fancy sittin' watch on these two."

"Keep 'em trussed up, is all. An' hell, it

ain't like the boys in town didn't build up that nice new gallows. They'd be some mad if they didn't get to try out their work."

"Well, that's true enough. 'Course we want them goddamn vigilantes to watch one of their boys swing, too. Thing is, this fella has a bottle of whiskey in his saddlebag. Be a shame not to give 'er a taste later on."

"Later on, my ass. These two ain't goin' nowhere. Break out that bottle. A fine posse like us deserves a drink after runnin' down Billy an' his pal."

Jake sifted the words through the pain in his head, trying to make sense of what he was hearing. *Billy and his pal? Who the hell is Billy? Who are these . . .* He tried to force enough saliva into his mouth to say a few words when the horse he was tied to stumbled over a rock, went to his front knees, recovered, and lurched back upright. Jake saw the blaze of white light again. This time it seemed to last a little longer than it had earlier.

When Jake shuddered back to full consciousness he was tied to a tree, his hands tied behind him, crushed between his back and the rough bark. His legs, extended in front of him from his sitting position, were secured together with several turns of rope. It was past dusk but not fully dark yet. Ten feet away four or five men sat around a fire. He moved his head and felt dried blood crackle on his neck. He groaned without realizing he'd made a sound.

"Sorry I slugged you so hard," a voice said. Jake's eyes followed it. A couple of feet away another man was tied to the huge tree, only his shoulder and the profile of his head visible.

Sinclair had to swallow several times before he could croak an answer. "Who're you? Who're those men?"

"I'm Billy Galvin, not that it matters much, I guess. Those boys are a posse made up of killers, cheats, whoremongers, thieves, and the like — the head man's Sheriff Jason Mott, the worst of the bunch. They're after me 'cause I escaped the jail back in town." After a moment, he added, "They're gonna hang me."

"Why?" was the best response Sinclair could find.

"I shot and killed one of them. He was setting fire to my barn. Two others was inside my house with my wife. They . . . messed with her bad . . . killed her. I was off in town buyin' seed. I stopped in the saloon and sucked down a few beers — more'n a few, if you want the truth. If I'd come right home, I probably coulda saved

Peggy. I didn't, though."

"And the law didn't —" Jake began.

"There ain't no law in Fairplay other'n Mott. He runs the whole show, him and his gun hands. Have for a couple years, now."

"Fairplay?"

"Name of the town."

The men around the fire had given Jake's bottle some use, and from the raucous laughter and curses, they were into a supply of their own. Jake looked more carefully at them. There were five in the posse. A big man, broad-shouldered, bearded, who faced Jake across the fire seemed to be the only one with a badge. None of them paid any attention to Billy or Jake.

"What's your name?" Billy asked after a few minutes.

"Jake."

"Jake what?"

For whatever reason a quick image of the commanding officer of the sharpshooters in Jake's battalion sprang into his mind: Hiram Westlake. Jake could have given his real last name. It wouldn't make any difference. But the lie came easy.

"Westlake," Jake said.

"Well, like I said, I'm sorry I belted you so hard, Jake. I needed your horse and your gun and didn't have no time to discuss it with you. I'd been following you the better part of the day, waitin' for the right moment. Thing is, I seen you draw an' fire at that pheasant an' you damned near changed my mind about what I planned. You're awful fast. Accurate, too. I thought . . . well, shit. It don't matter." Billy lapsed into silence.

One of the men at the fire put a couple of rifle rounds into the air. The muzzle flashes were two feet long, jagged tongues of orange fire. All five of them found the shots terrifically funny. Jake moved his head and shards of pain erupted in it. He gritted his teeth and waited the spasms out. "You tied hand and foot and then tied to the tree, Billy?"

"Yeah. Trussed up like a goddamn Christmas goose. You?"

"Yeah."

"Be good if we could get to the horses," Billy said. "But even if we got loose somehow, that wouldn't happen."

"Why?"

"Only five at the fire gettin' liquored up. There're six of them. One fella is waitin' with the horses and he ain't drunk an' won't be drunk — Mott'd skin the sumbitch alive if he took a drink on guard duty. Mott's as mean as a rattler in a frying pan, but he ain't stupid."

More shots — pistol fire this time — blasted into the night air.

"Damn fools," Billy muttered.

Time passed slowly. Jake's head continued to feel as if his brain were trying to climb out of his skull using a pickax. He attempted to shift his position to see if he could give his hands a little room to work on the rope that held them together, but it was impossible. The rope that held him to the tree must have been applied by a strong man, he thought — he was almost totally unable to move any part of his body from his waist upward. His hands and arms had long since gone numb, as had his lower legs and feet. The boozers quieted; at least two of them passed out. The remaining three sat dumbly, staring into the campfire, past the point of speaking to one another.

"Billy?" Jake said, keeping his voice low.

"Yeah?"

"Who's this judge I heard them talking about?"

Billy's laugh didn't have any humor in it. "He used to be a crooked circuit rider. Now he stays in Fairplay and is crooked there. Mott owns him lock, stock, an' barrel. His trials are a joke. He condemned me without lettin' me say a word in court. Called it murder when I tried to defend my wife and my property."

After a bit, Jake said, "Look, Billy — maybe we can get out of the jail. You already did it once, right? Hell, with two of us —"

"I got out 'cause the jailer was a drunk," Billy interrupted. "He came in so liquored up he could barely stand an' I was able to get him close enough to the bars so I could grab his gun an' make him give me his keys. He ain't the jailer no more, you can bet on that."

"Oh."

Billy's voice dropped lower. "Don't worry about me hangin', Jake. My friends won't let it happen. We've had meetings. There's a good number of us and we're growin'. Come the day — an' soon — an' we won't put up with Mott and his boys. All we need is a few more good men, a few more rifles."

"How will they —"

"You'll see, Jake. Let's let it go for now. But you'll see."

The hours until dawn crawled by. Jake semidozed, nowhere near real sleep, but less conscious of the pain in his head and the icy numbness in his legs, arms, and hands. It was Sheriff Jason Mott who came to the tree where Jake and Billy were tied. He didn't speak as he began working the knots. He was a big man, Jake saw, tall, broad, with huge hands. His features were sharp, chiseled looking. There was what looked like a knife scar on his face, running from in front of his left ear to the corner of his mouth. It was slightly raised but pale rather than livid, indicating that Mott had carried it for a while. Mott's breath reeked of morning-after whiskey fumes. "You have no reason to hold me, Sheriff. I had nothing to do with you, your men, or Billy here."

Mott's voice was deep but not particularly loud as he spoke. "How about murder? You think that gives me a reason to hold you?"

"Murder? You're crazy! I was making camp when —"

"Was either you or Billy who gunned my man," Mott said. "The way I figure it, you lit out and met up with Billy after he escaped, plannin' on runnin' together. Don't matter who pulled the trigger — you're both guilty as sin under law."

"That's horseshit and you know it! You can't arrest me on such ridiculous grounds. No court in the world would convict me — you must know that."

"Can't arrest you?" Mott chuckled. "Seems like I already did, don't it? And don't you worry about a court. You'll get a fair trial." He chuckled again. "Then we'll hang you."

"Damn it, Mott," Billy shouted. "I never seen this man here in my life 'fore last night. If you had half the sense of a goddamn chicken, you'd let him go on his way." He spat on the ground angrily. "You think I'm blind? You're after that fancy mare of Jake's — even if you have to string him up to get her."

Mott turned away from Sinclair and approached Billy, out of Jake's line of vision. The sound of a fist hitting flesh told Jake what was happening.

The sheriff released the rest of the rope holding the two men to the tree and crouched to untie Sinclair's legs and hands. He tossed the ropes aside and stood, pulling Jake to his feet. Jake went down as quickly as he had been jerked up; there was no sensation at all in his legs. He stayed on the ground, trying to mold his hands into fists, pushing blood to them. The coursing of blood to the starved veins and arteries began as electrical pinpricks and quickly escalated to almost excruciating pain in Jake's extremities. He flexed and loosened his hands and kicked out, feebly at first, with his legs. Mott stood back, grinning, watching the two men squirm on the ground, his right hand resting lightly on the grips of his holstered pistol. A glance at the bone grips told Jake his Smith & Wesson was resting in Mott's holster. Anger flashed but Jake kept his mouth shut.

Anger again flared when Mott walked Jake and Billy to the horses. Both men lumbered like semicripples, their steps small and unsure, their legs stiff and not to be trusted. Jake stopped a few feet from the mounted men. Mare was saddled and bridled with another man's tack; his own gear was on an underweight, droopy-lidded gray with almost no chest. Flies clustered around the festering spur marks on the horse's flanks.

"You two can ride sittin' up from here to town," Mott said. "Your hands'll be tied. I won't say this but once: Either of you try anything cute, me an' the boys'll cut you down in a second — shoot so many holes in you the goddamn wind will whistle when it blows through. Now mount up."

The sign a half mile outside town announcing Fairplay was new looking, freshly painted, stark black letters against crisp white paint, and unpocked by bullet holes. The town itself was almost a mirror image of Penderton, with essentially the same stores and businesses, the only difference being that a railroad line ran to the town and there was a shabby depot and some cattle fencing and chutes adjacent to the depot. The mercantile was smaller and there were two saloons, one at either end of town, but beyond those differences, Fairplay had nothing new to offer. The sheriff, his posse, and their two prisoners didn't draw much attention as they rode down the street. A couple of old men sitting in front of the mercantile watched as the riders went by, but both averted their eyes when Jake glanced at them.

The sheriff's desk occupied space in the front room of the office. In the rear, accessed through a narrow corridor, were two barred cells across from one another. Mott shoved Billy and Jake into the one facing the back of the building, slammed the door, and locked it. Jake took the three steps it required to get him across the cell to the barred window. Outside, not fifty feet away, stood the gallows, the lumber looking bright and fresh, not yet bleached and dried by the sun. Jake turned away. There was no cot. A tattered and thin blanket was bunched in one corner. Next to the blanket was a slop bucket. It was hot in the jail and the smell of old sweat and bodily odors of past prisoners seemed to have permeated the bars and the walls. The air hung in the cell like a dank fog, motionless.

Mott brought their dinner — the only meal they were to get that day — shortly before dark. The two prisoners had to stand against the back wall by the window as the sheriff unlocked the door and slid the tray across the floor. There was a single large plate with a little pile of fatty beef and two pieces of stale, crumbling bread. There were no utensils of any kind. "No coffee?" Billy complained. "Can't you at least bring us some coffee?"

"Sure," Mott said. "I'll bring it with your pie and ice cream, when I come later to tuck you boys in for the night."

Jake choked down a couple of slices of the beef and gnawed at a piece of the bread. "You might as well eat something, Billy," he suggested. "No sense in starving yourself."

"I ain't real hungry. Seems like it's about this time every night the thoughts about my wife come floodin' in on me. Peggy was her name. She was a good woman."

Jake nodded. "I'm sure she was," he said. "I'm real sorry you lost her, Billy."

The darkness thickened in the cell, the only light a very faint glow from the front of the office. Even that was extinguished, and the prisoners heard the office door close. A train rattled by, just out of sight, neither slowing nor stopping at the Fairplay station.

"Mott's gone out whorin' and drinkin' like usual," Billy said. "Just like every night when I was here before I escaped." He lowered his voice. "I guess you're wonderin' why I don't seem too awful worried about being hanged."

"The thought crossed my mind."

"Well, don't you worry. It ain't gonna happen. The Night Riders won't let it. They'll either spring me outta here or grab me up when Mott and his men bring me out to the gallows. One way or the other, Jake. But I ain't gonna hang."

"That's real good, Billy. I hope your boys can pull it off."

"No doubt about it. You watch an' see. I'm thinkin' they'll be in the crowd comin' to gawk at the hanging, all armed up good, an' cut loose at them sons-a-bitches an' be rid of them for goddamn good." After a moment, he added, "Simple plans are the best ones, ya know?"

"Sure they are, Billy," Jake said.

Sure they are, Billy. Could be you're right — maybe simple plans are the best ones. I'd sure hate to put my life in the hands of a bunch called Night Riders, though — 'specially if they're store clerks and farmers and ranch-

ers who've probably never fired a shot at a man. It'd make more sense to blow the window right out of the wall than attack at the gallows. 'Course the explosion would probably kill Billy and me. Or maybe these Riders can overpower Mott somehow.

Gunfire and then a burst of laughter sounded from the street. A woman's voice, high pitched and strident, screamed, "You dirty son of a bitch!" followed by more laughter. Jake adjusted his position on the floor, his back against the wall. His legs, feet, and hands still tingled, but the pain was long since gone. The back of his head was tender and his hair matted with crusted blood, but the worst of the throbbing ache had dissipated. Billy's breathing from the corner was slow and even, interrupted every so often by a mumbled, indistinguishable few words.

At least when he's asleep he doesn't have to think about his wife and what happened to her. Awful thing — purely awful: wife raped and murdered, property burned, life torn apart so bad it could never be put together again by Mott and his crew. Jake shook his head slowly back and forth, imagining how he himself would react to the same events. He closed his eyes and lowered his chin to his chest. *There's Mott, Uriah said. At about five o'clock.*

175

See him? The sheriff's head appeared with the sights of his Sharps on his forehead. Jake set the first trigger and eased light pressure onto the second . . .

It was well into the morning before Mott strode into the cell area from his office. "Over against the wall so I can get your grub to you," he said. "And look here, boys — there's even some coffee with this fine meal." The prisoners moved to the wall. Mott unlocked the cell door, slid in the tray, and relocked the door. "Your trial is comin' up," he said to Jake. "The judge asked your last name. What is it?"

Jake stepped to the tray on the floor, crouched, and picked up a thick ceramic mug filled with barely warm coffee. "What difference does it make, Mott? The judge is in your pocket, right? He'll do what you tell him to do."

Mott laughed. "Ol' Judge Konrick ain't in nobody's pocket," he said. "Funny though how him an' me agree on sentences most times."

"Yeah," Jake said. "Funny."

"Jas?" a woman's voice, morning scratchy, called from the office. "You back there?"

"One of your raggedy-assed whores?" Billy asked. To Jake he said, "The sheriff here pimps out a herd of saloon heifers. Ain't one of them less ugly than a goat's ass."

Mott's face flushed as he glared at Billy. "You talk a whole lot for a dead man," he said. "You'll look good at the end of the rope, boy." Mott's eyes flicked to Jake before he turned away toward the office. They glistened like those of a snake, seething from the inside, promising pain, promising death. "You too," the sheriff said. Jake held the glare.

When Mott was gone Billy took the second mug from the tray and picked up a piece of moldy bread. He peered at it and then tossed it back onto the tray. "Things are gonna be way different here, Jake," he said. "When the Riders come after me, Mott is gonna be the first man down. We'll have our town back. Fairplay was a good little burg, at one time. Nice place. It will be again."

Jake moved to the window and looked out past the gallows. "How'd he take control? Wasn't there any law?"

"Sure there was — an old coot named Cyrus Riordan. He hired Mott on as a deputy when the railroad started the town growin'. Mott started bringing in his men right off — gunmen and gamblers an' outlaws. Then one day Cyrus was gone an' Mott was wearing the sheriff's badge an' that was it."

"How many men does he have?" Jake asked.

"Maybe forty or so — maybe a few more. New hardcases show up every so often, join up."

Jake finished his coffee. The thick dregs in the bottom of the mug made him grimace. "How many of your Night Riders are there?"

" 'Bout thirty. All good men. We didn't really get together until a few months ago. Had to be careful about our meetings. That's what brought Mott's men to my place — I'd had a couple meetings there."

"The Riders — they fighting men?"

Billy looked away almost sheepishly. "Any man can be a fighting man when his home an' his family is being threatened. An' we don't look for pitched battles, Jake. Our plan is to snipe them sons-a-bitches, break them that way. Pick 'em off one to a time."

Jake nodded.

There was sudden heat in Billy's voice. "Don't you go thinkin' because the Riders ain't gunfighters they can't do what they need to do. I've known most — hell, all — of them my whole life, an' you couldn't find a better group of men. When they come for me they'll end Jason Mott. If the rest of that trash don't run then, we'll keep right on takin' 'em down one by one."

"Whoa, Billy — seems like you're hearing something I'm not saying. I'm sure your Night Riders are a strong group of good men."

"You betcher ass, Jake. They are. We all of us want the same thing: We want our town back, and things back to the way they was before Mott. Once we have that, we'll shut down the Riders. Disband, like they say in the army."

"I see," Jake said, not seeing at all. *They'll gun down a band of outlaws and killers and then go back to selling ribbons and nostrums or following a mule's ass behind a plow?*

Jake glanced down the hall before speaking. "Your men will come when you're taken out to the gallows, then?"

"No — they'll be there already, in the crowd, waitin', with their guns up under their coats."

"Crowd?"

"Sure enough. A hangin' is a big thing in these parts. Folks come from all over, bringin' their whole families to watch. The whole town'll turn out, too. They used to use a big oak jus' past where the church was before it burned, but now Mott had this gallows outside put up."

Jake walked back to the window, looking away from his cellmate. It was difficult for him to meet Billy's eyes, to see the confidence in them, the sure awareness that he'd walk away from the whole episode.

"Maybe you never had friends like I have in the Night Riders," Billy said to Jake's back. "These boys, hell, I'd trust them with my life, Jake."

That's precisely what you're doing, Billy.

Sometime after noon, Mott and an old fellow dressed in grimy and tattered clothes that, from the way they failed to fit him, were obviously castoffs appeared at the cell door. The sheriff's face was grim and his hand rested on the grips of what had once been Sinclair's Smith & Wesson .22. "Put the slops bucket up here and then stand facing the back wall," Mott said.

Jake carefully picked up the almost over-flowing bucket, brought it to the front of the cell, and joined Billy at the wall. After Mott unlocked the door the old man shuffled forward and fetched the foul-smelling bucket. Before he turned away with it, he whispered, "Sattiday." Jake's head snapped around: The old coot's hoarse whisper was loud enough for Mott to over-hear. Nevertheless, the sheriff stood where he'd been, apparently unaware of the hurried and brief communication. Jake glanced over at Billy. He was standing with his face to the wall, but Sinclair could see his grin. When they heard the office door close, Jake moved closer to Billy. "Can you get a message to the Riders? We need to get you out of here, Billy — as soon as possible. Like tonight."

"That ol' boy who looked like a bar rag is named Howie," Billy said. "He's older'n God an' does odd jobs like swampin' the saloons an' such for booze money. We kinda use him to carry messages now an' again. Howie, he whispered to me. They're plannin' on hangin' me Saturday. The Riders will be there."

"Damn it, Billy . . . look, today's what?"

"What what?"

"Day of the week. I gave up trying to keep them straight a long time ago. What's the day of the week?"

"Today's Thursday, Jake. Will be all the live-long day," he added, grinning.

"Billy," Jake said. "This isn't right. You've got to get a message to your men. Mott's all the things you've said he is — but he isn't stupid. There's something that —"

"Ya know," Billy cut in, "I'm gettin' tired of your bad-mouthin' the Riders. Mott ain't stupid? Well, neither are we — an' you can take that to the bank. Jason Mott don't know it, but he's gonna catch a bullet — maybe a lot more than one — Saturday morning. An' you can take that to the bank, too, Jake."

Sinclair broke eye contact without speaking.

The heat grew as the day slid languorously on, time moving like molasses in the coldest part of the winter. It was deep autumn — it shouldn't have been hot. But it was. They got their meal sometime late in the afternoon, again on a single tray: fat, greasy beef that'd been too long in the heat, and ragged chunks of stale bread. Again, there were no utensils. It was either pick up the meat with their hands or do without eating. Both men opted to eat. The bread was hard enough to crack teeth.

At dusk the noise from the saloons started. Billy and Jake listened to what sounded like a horse race on the main street followed by gunfire, yells, and drunken laughter.

"Jake, I been thinkin'," Billy said. "I owe you. It's my fault you're sittin' in this goddamn cell right now. If I hadn't slammed you with that branch, you'd be ridin' that pretty mare off to wherever it was you were goin'."

"I guess I'd have done the same thing, I

was running for my life. It wasn't me in particular you wanted to drop, Billy, I know that. You needed my horse, my gun, and you did what any man would do."

"That don't matter," Billy said. Then, resolutely, "Like I said, I owe you, an' I pay my debts. You ask anyone if that ain't true. So here's what I'm sayin', Jake — me an' the Riders will bust you out of this jail one way or another. It don't matter if Konrick says you gotta swing, which is what he'll say, sure as you're born. All that drunken ol' fool knows is condemnin' men to the rope. But don't you worry. We'll pop you outta here like we was yankin' a cork outta a bottle."

"I . . . I appreciate that, Billy."

"Sure. An' I'm hopin' you'll join on with the Riders after we get you out. Seems to me you'd be a real good man to have with us, a man who knows some about fighting."

"I've seen some fighting," Jake said.

The night moved in slowly. When the meager light that made it to the cells from under the door of the office was extinguished and the prisoners heard the front door slam, they sat in the steamy, still blackness. Neither had much to say.

Sleep didn't come to Jake Sinclair. He sat with his back against the wall under the window, listening to the night. At first the racket from the saloons gave him something to hear, but eventually that died and Jake was left with the summer crickets and the screech, almost too high to hear, of the bats that swooped in on the flying insects outside. Billy breathed deeply and snored sibilantly when he exhaled.

They came before dawn, Mott carrying one lamp, one of the other men another. The boot heels of the four men sounded very loud as they came from the office. The light was harsh in the cell, making shadows sharp-edged, pushing the soft darkness away. Jake stood. One of the men fit a key to the door and swung it open. "You go on and get against the far wall," Mott said to Jake. He set the lamp on the floor and hefted the shotgun he carried in his right hand across his chest, finger within the trigger guard, the steel of the barrel sending back glints of lamplight.

"Billy," he said.

Billy sat up and knuckled his eyes, beginning a yawn before he saw Mott and the others, before he realized what was happening. "Ahh, Jesus," he gasped. His face went white. "Ah, Jesus," he said again. Jake took a step forward and the twin maws of the shotgun swung to his chest. "Go on," Mott growled to the cluster of men standing around him, "bring him out. Let's get this done."

Billy tried to push himself to his feet but couldn't get his legs under himself. He flopped back down on the floor. His hands fluttered about his chest and then moved to cover his face, as if attempting to hide himself. Mott stepped into the cell, shotgun still leveled at Jake. Two of the others stepped past the sheriff and hauled Billy to his feet, grabbing him under his armpits. "This ain't right," Billy said in a child's voice, almost too quiet to hear. "This ain't Saturday — this ain't right." He jerked his body toward Jake, his face corpse white, his eyes beseeching, begging.

They half carried, half dragged Billy from the cell. Mott pulled the door closed and the man with the key locked it. Two men pulled Billy along, trying to keep him erect between them. Two others picked up the lanterns. The sheriff stood back, shotgun hanging loosely from his hand. Jake found Mott's eyes. "You'd best pull the trigger on me right now," he said. "Otherwise I'm going to kill you one day." His voice was low but it carried to Mott and to his four men.

The gallows was a dark blur, indistinct in the moonless, cloudy night. It was a long time before Jake saw the men outside, saw them dragging Billy, saw them carrying Billy up the stairs to the platform. Jake couldn't see the rope and the noose, but he knew it was there. One of the men carrying a lantern mounted the stairs to the killing floor and set his light down. Then Jake could see the noose.

Billy couldn't stand. The two men who'd carried him up the stairs held him upright. Another fit the noose over Billy's head, tightening it around his neck. Mott stood back, holding his shotgun. "Stand back offa the trap," he said. "Hold him up until it drops." The men shifted their positions, reaching out to hold Billy where he needed to be.

Jake's nails were gouging into his palms, his eyes not on his friend but on Jason Mott and the lever that protruded up through the floor next to him. Mott lifted the shotgun up over his shoulder with his left hand and reached out his right to the lever. For a long moment he looked at Billy's face. Then he grasped the lever, hesitated for a heartbeat, and jerked it back. Billy dropped. There was a loud snap — like that of a breaking stick — and then no sound at all.

Sinclair turned away from the window, from the execution tableau. He stood for a long time in the center of the cell, almost at attention, back straight. The weight on the gallows caused the fresh nailing to creak slightly as Billy's body turned below the trapdoor. Jake stepped back to the window.

Mott followed the other three men down the stairs to the ground. Jake watched him in the same manner a snake watches a cornered mouse.

CHAPTER SIX

Time didn't actually pass for Jake Sinclair in his cage. Instead, things around him changed: daybreak into midday into night, night silence to daylight city life to the revelry and off-key music at night, often interrupted by gunshots, the passing of a train that seemed to be on no particular schedule as to Fairplay. There was a thick-witted rhythm to his life that Jake was forced to accept, and he felt himself becoming as dull and as mindless as the events — or nonevents — of the sheriff's office.

Jake slept too much. He realized that, but sleep was safe, and it used up parts of the days and nights. He was losing weight. His pants hung loosely around his waist and he felt fatigued almost all of the time, regardless of the fact that he moved little in the course of a day. Even thinking came to be more trouble than it was worth. Staring at the brick back wall of his cell with a blank mind was easier.

Much of that changed late one night about ten days or two weeks after Billy's hanging.

"You! Jake!" The raspy whisper cut through Sinclair's light sleep, bringing him immediately to full consciousness. He stood and moved to the barred window. It was raining lightly, he saw, and there was little light. The whisper — louder now — drew him closer.

"Jake, goddammit! Wake up. I ain't got the night to spend out here."

A wrinkled, wide-brimmed hat with rain running from it came into Jake's line of vision, followed by a wave of whiskey breath. There was a creaking sound from outside, a muffled curse, and another exhalation of booze.

"I'm here," Jake whispered. "Who're —"

"We're gonna spring you out. We got it all figured. You just set tight till Friday night an' then be ready to haul ass. We'll have a horse for you. We'll —" The speech was interrupted by the creaking sound and then a sharp crack followed by a dull, wet thump. "Son of a bitch!" the outside voice cursed. "The goddamn crate busted. Hellfire! I cain't . . ."

The next thing Jake heard was boots splashing through mud and water. He could barely pick out a hunched form running in a weaving path away from the jail. All that remained was the fog that smelled like a saloon. *A drunk flapping his mouth, playing some kind of stupid prank? Or — one of Billy's Night Riders with a plan?*

Tendrils of hope gathered around Sinclair. He tried to convince himself the chance of rescue was a real one — that the messenger had been chosen for his ineptitude, so that if he were caught, his drunkenness could explain his actions. "Jus' tryin' to cheer up this poor feller, Sheriff."

Jake shook his head. *Nah. Who the hell would send a stumblebum with a message that important? Too drunk even to find a damn crate that'd hold his weight. It doesn't make sense.* He sat, back against the wall, under the window, pondering. His bit of hope didn't last long. *Still . . . stranger things have happened.*

Mott made an appearance at Jake's cell door late the next day. "We'll be taking you to trial tomorrow night, all nice an' legal," he said. Jake noticed that his bone-gripped Smith & Wesson rode in the sheriff's holster.

"Why not just go right to the gallows — save the time of a crooked trial?"

Mott chuckled. "Still porky, I see. That's good, I guess. A man can get tired of prisoners that act like aunties."

"You enjoying my horse?"

The sheriff laughed again. "Ain't a bad mare, all in all. I had to take her down a couple of pegs, but she's behavin' now." His eyes met Jake's. "That bother you? That I took a whip to that horse?"

Jake spoke slowly, controlling his voice, holding Mott's eyes. "You better make real sure you get me killed one way or another, Mott, because if you don't, I'll watch the light go out of your eyes. I'll watch you die like the snake you are. You hear?"

The laugh seemed slightly exaggerated this time. "I'm gonna like watchin' you swing, boy," he said as he turned away. "Gonna enjoy pullin' the lever."

The rest of that day passed, and so did the next.

Mott came for him after dark accompanied by one of his men, a young fellow who looked barely twenty, with a twitch in his left eyelid and canine teeth that were far too long for his face. He held a double-barreled shotgun across his chest with his finger inside the trigger guard. Mott held a lantern.

"Come up close here and put your hands where I can reach 'em," Mott told Jake. "Try anything an' Wolfie here'll put you outta bidness." Jake stood a foot from the cell door and held out his hands. Mott reached through the bars and applied the heavy steel shackle-handcuffs. Then he keyed the door and swung it open. "You walk in front," he said. "Wolfie an' me will follow. Go on up to my office."

Jake stepped out of the cell. Wolfie jabbed the barrels into his back to start him moving down the aisle. Lantern light showed at the end of the corridor and the illumination from Mott's lamp stretched a long, narrow shadow of Jake on the rough wooden floor in front of him. He stopped at the partially open office door. Wolfie jabbed him again. "Move," he said. "Over by the desk."

The door was a heavy one, solid wood hung on large brass hinges. Jake eyed it quickly. *A full inch of good wood. It'll stop the shotgun and Mott's .44. If I can get in front of it and then slam it closed . . .*

He tensed his shoulders and shifted his body weight to his left foot, which was a half stride behind his right. The shotgun barrels hit him in the back of the head this time, and they hit him hard. Jake stumbled forward, the starburst of white light from the blow blinding him for a moment, weakening his knees. He lurched into the office, dazed. Amazingly, inexplicably, the sheriff's big wooden desk lifted itself a good two inches off the floor and then crashed back down. A wrenching, screeching sound, like a good saw blade striking a nail, was followed by an explosion that was louder than anything Sinclair had heard during the war. A ceiling beam twisted free and slammed downward, striking Wolfie across the shoulders, jamming him to the floor, the weight and power behind the beam crushing Wolfie's head like a stomped-on cockroach. Dazed, Jake instinctively covered his face as a whirling cloud of flame and dust and shattered boards rolled down the aisle like a stampeding herd of buffalo. Mott, taken down as Wolfie fell, screamed just as the concussion hurled Jake across the office floor and bounced him off the wall.

Jake picked himself up from the floor. He could hear Mott still screaming, even over the shrill screeching in his ears. The lantern that had sat on the desk lay shattered on the floor, and flames were already tonguing the scattered papers and the upended chair. Jake gaped dumbly at the door — it seemed to be dancing in its frame. Then it swung open.

"Jesus, boy, I'm glad to see you!" a sheet-draped figure shouted. "We kinda figured we buried you under the jail."

Another hooded head appeared in the

doorway. "Mighta gone a little heavy on the dynamite," he said. "But come on — we got you a horse right outside." The words cleared the clouds from Jake's mind and put the strength back in his limbs. He was through the door in a heartbeat. Eight or ten hooded and robed men on horseback were clustered in front of the sheriff's office, the barrels of their rifles and pistols sweeping the street. One held the reins to a saddled horse. Even with his hands restrained in front of him, Jake was in the saddle in a second, grabbing at the reins the other tossed over the horse's head. Some gunfire sounded. Jake didn't know if it came from the weapons of the Night Riders or from Mott's men — and he didn't much care. He banged his heels into his mount's sides and galloped after the already fleeing group. When he reached the end of Main Street he dared a glance over his shoulder — and immediately hauled his horse around in a sliding turn at the full gallop. Before the dust from the turn had begun to settle, Jake was racing back toward the jail.

The scene was chaos: The sheriff's office was afire and the jail area was gone — disappeared, transformed into a low pile of smashed bricks, broken boards, and twisted steel bars. The front of the office remained standing, but perilously so — the whole of it listing back toward where the jail had been. The saloon had emptied and men and women clogged the street. Two men dragged a man — or a body — out of the front door.

Mare, a length of broken hitching rail flailing from the end of her reins, reared again, eyes wild, chest glistening with panic sweat. It was the same image Jake had seen seconds ago, the same one that had brought him back at a gallop. He dragged his mount to a sliding stop, cringing at how roughly he was forced to use the reins. He was off the horse and in front of Mare in a second. In another moment he'd freed her reins and hauled himself onto her back. Mare had every bit of the speed he remembered. Within a few minutes he'd caught up with the Night Riders.

Sweat glistened on the arms of the blacksmith, even though the fire in his forge scattered red-orange coals and he'd not yet swung his hammer. Jake's eyes went to the man's forearms: they looked like they'd been carved from hardwood to represent the strength of some mythical god. "Look away — turn your head," the smithy said.

"I'm not afraid you're going to miss and hit me instead."

"That ain't the point. These hand shackles are made from good steel. When I lay my cold chisel to it, there might could be splinters. Lance your eye like an Injun tossed a spear."

Jake turned his head and the blacksmith positioned the sharp edge of his chisel on the thick chain that held the two handcuffs together. He struck twice and each time Jake felt air move against him and heard its quiet *whoosh.*

"Now you gotta stand and rest the edge of the parts round your hands on the anvil." This time Jake felt the cold steel ever so slightly touching the outside of his right hand as the smith positioned his chisel. A single stroke freed Jake's hand, and a moment later, his left was free also.

"Thank you," Jake said. "You're Burdett, right?"

"Burgess. Most call me Bull. I didn't think you got the name when Billy's pa was introducin' everyone." He held out a ham-sized hand. Jake took it and they shook hands. Burgess's grasp was light — he had no need to prove his strength in a handshake. "Let's go on in, have a drink with the other boys. One thing, though — I seen you go back and grab up your horse. That took a fair set of nuts, Jake. Seems like you'll be good for the Riders."

Jake nodded.

Bull's big face broke into a grin. "You ain't said you'd join up yet. I know that. Here's the thing, though: We sprung you outta jail an' no doubt cheated the hangman. I'd think you kinda owe us some time. No?"

"That's the way I see it, Bull. Now — about that drink you mentioned . . ."

Jake rarely felt short, but walking next to Bull from the barn to the house he was dwarfed by the sheer magnitude — the muscular immensity — of the blacksmith. Bull caught the curiosity in Jake's eyes. "I'm six feet an' seven inches tall, an' the last time I weighed myself on a stock scale at the train yard, I went 331 pounds." He grinned. "I like to get that outta the way. It's only natural folks wonder, and it don't bother me none. Hell, I'm right proud of being what I am."

"No reason not to be, Bull. I was you, I'd feel the same way."

That seemed to please the big man. His smile broadened. He cuffed Jake lightly on the shoulder, almost knocking him over.

There were nine men in the living room of the house. Three lanterns provided more than enough light to see the small table in the middle of the room with the half dozen bottles and several glasses on it. The bottles were getting hard use. There was a celebratory giddiness to the conversations that struck Jake as odd. The Night Riders seemed more like a bunch of drunken college boys who'd just come back from their first sally to a whorehouse than a band of vigilantes who'd just destroyed a sheriff's office, killed a deputy for sure and maybe the sheriff, too, and freed a prisoner, to boot.

One of the men stood and walked to Jake, extending his hand. "I'm Billy's father," he said. "My friends call me Lou. We're all glad you're here."

Sinclair shook the man's hand. "Sorry about your son, Mr. Galvin. I didn't know him a long time, but I liked him."

"Everyone did. He was a good, honest man." Lou motioned toward the table. "Pour yourself a drink and I'll introduce you around to the Riders and we'll talk."

The whiskey, Jake noticed from its color and its scent, wasn't the 'shine or rotgut he'd been buying in the towns he crossed. He poured five fingers into a heavy glass and sipped at it. "My name's Jake," he said to the room.

Lou Galvin introduced his colleagues one by one. Each stepped forward to shake

Jake's hand.

Introductions completed, the men returned to their seats. Jake and Lou Galvin remained standing by the table. "It's our understanding that Billy told you about what has been going on in Fairplay — about Mott and his crew. It's also our understanding that you're a fighting man, Jake."

Sinclair kept his face impassive and didn't respond.

"You're wondering how we came to that information," Galvin said, as a statement rather than a question. "The Night Riders are not without resources. One of our sympathizers is — well — the town drunk, actually. He spends a good deal of his time just outside the jail, in the shade, back by the cell window. He's always around. He's like a street dog. No one really notices him. He listens well, and he's not quite as drunk as he's perceived to be. He heard conversations between you and my son."

"I'm not sure . . ." Jake began.

Galvin held up his hand. "Where you came from is none of our business. What is our business is that you possess certain skills that we lack. We're farmers and drovers and store owners and clerks, Jake. Our town has been taken over, our church burned, our women abused, our men shamed. The war has taken up the army and the state law — those we'd logically have gone to for help. There is no help for us, frankly. So we formed the Riders. We're not a fighting unit, but we've made our point to Mott a few times. And," he added, "we managed to get you out of jail."

"There's that," Jake said. "Of course, if I'd been in the cell, I'd be dead now."

"An oversight in the quantity of dynamite. Nevertheless, you aren't dead and you're free. But that incident serves to make my point, Jake. We're in need of a man who knows things we don't know, who can direct our efforts."

"Mr. Galvin," Jake said, "I'm not a leader, and if you think I am, you're mistaken. And it seems to me that you men are doing pretty well just as you are. Even with blowing hell out of the jail you got me out without any casualties, and —"

"One of our boys was wounded in the foot and we lost a horse," a heavyset gent interrupted.

Galvin nodded. "You see — that's the problem. Our man was shot by another of our men, as was the horse. In the furor out front after the explosion . . . well . . . as I said, we're not used to armed conflict. There was no real plan beyond getting you out of that cell." He lifted a bottle from the table and refilled Jake's glass.

Galvin met Jake's eyes. "There's nothing stopping you from mounting up and riding on. We can't demand anything from you. But you've seen what's going on in Fairplay. You saw my son hanged. We need your help. It's as simple as that. What do you say?"

Jake took a long drink from his glass. *I don't need this. I just left a war. I'd be a fool to jump into the middle of another one. Mott's men are gunmen, used to fighting, used to killing. These clerks and farmers can't win this thing. What they're trying to do is right and just, but good intentions never stopped a bullet.* He took another sip of whiskey. His father floated before his eyes, face stern. *Damn it, Pa — this is the kind of thing I'm trying to get away from.*

Jake sighed and looked around the room, his glance stopping for a quick moment on each of the men. "I won't have my men shooting each other or shooting our horses," he said. "If we're going to do this, we're going to do it right."

Sleeping in a regular bed — one with a shuck mattress and a blanket that hadn't covered a horse's back all day — took some getting used to. Jake was used to the forest sounds of the night, the tiny scufflings in the brush, the cries of owls and other night birds, the quiet whisper of the wind through the trees. Those were gone, replaced by the shifting of horses in their stalls, the yip of a dog, the creaking and settling of the old house in which Jake slept — or attempted to sleep. It was an easy enough transition, though. By his third night of Lou Galvin's hospitality, Jake slept through the night.

The Fairplay Night Riders was far from a tight operation. Jake had realized going in that the men knew nothing of combat or surveillance or military-type planning. They were brave and committed, but those two qualities didn't make a man's aim any better. And a trained coward was much more likely to survive a battle than a heroic amateur.

The morning of his fourth day at Lou Galvin's farm Jake was up and at his bedroom window before the sunrise had really gotten under way. He watched as the muted pastels of dawn grew into splashes — and then blazes — of vivid color. He heard the impatient scraping of the draft horses' heavy steel shoes on the floors of their stalls as they awaited their morning rations of grain and hay, the lowing of a half dozen penned cattle near the barn, the subdued, cigarette-raspy voices of the hired hands as they walked to the kitchen of the house where they'd have their breakfasts before starting work. Jake heard the first laughter of the day from the hands as their coffee chased the final vestiges of sleep.

Not too different from home, he thought. *The accents and words of the workers are different — no Georgia Negro drawl, no women's voices calling to children, none of Pa's hounds clamoring for their table scraps. It feels the same, though.* A sobering thought intruded on the pastoral scene and his memories. *But it's different. Pa's plantation wasn't under siege by a slew of gun hands and outlaws, and Pa's son hadn't been hanged like a common criminal in a lawless town controlled — owned — by a band of men to whom the lives and property of others mean nothing.*

The sharp crack that had ended Billy Galvin's life sounded again in Jake's mind, so real he was almost surprised that the hired hands passing under his window didn't hear it. He saw the tautness of the rope, saw the rope twist slowly with the deadweight it carried. He saw Jason Mott pulling the wooden lever.

Jake turned away from the window, un-clenching tight and sweaty fists he didn't recall forming. *Tonight's meeting,* he thought, *will be the beginning of the end of the siege of Fairplay.*

There were better than twenty Night Riders gathered in Lou Galvin's barn for the meeting. It was a calm, late September night, and a full moon cast almost enough light to read a newspaper by. The scent of fall was redolent in the crisp, fragrant air. In the barn, in the hay storage area that'd been cleared for the gathering, cigarette and cigar smoke drifted in bluish clouds to the loft above. Lanterns hung about the room sputtered, their light harsh. Men drank coffee from thick mugs or whiskey from glasses, their eyes wandering from one another to Jake. Sinclair stood at a side window gazing out. When he felt the group had finished with their greetings and were ready to settle down, he turned from the window.

"I'd like you boys to gather up here by me for a minute," he said. "I want to show you one of the reasons why you need to listen to me and need to do what I say if you want to get out from under Mott. Come on up here."

They clustered around the window and Jake stepped away, giving them a clear view of the outside. "What do you see?" he asked.

A few voices ventured opinions: "Lou's west pasture, couple outbuildings . . ." "Ain't nothin' out there *to* see." "A pretty night, is all." "Hiram, one of our lookouts," one said.

"Right," Jake said. "Hiram — one of our lookouts. And what's the idiot doing? See that little red glow? The damned fool's smoking a cigarette!" He shook his head in slightly exaggerated disgust. "He's smoking a goddamn cigarette. Tell me this: Why not wave a lantern for Mott's men to pick up on?" The Riders moved sheepishly away from the window as Jake strode to the front of the room.

"Mott's not stupid," Jake said. "I'm sure he has men out checking on these meetings, checking on the places they're held. If he was of a mind to pull a sneak attack, the only protection we'd have would be an early warning from our lookouts." He paused for a moment. "If that happened right now, Hiram would be dead and we'd be sitting ducks."

Jake met the eyes of several of his audience. "You boys wanted me here. OK — I'm here, and I'll be here until this whole mess is over. Or I'll be here as long as my orders are followed." He waited while the word "orders" sank in. "I said orders and that's exactly what I meant. I'm not some military genius, but it's damned clear that I know a whole lot more about this stuff than you men do. We can't afford to act like a bunch of bumpkins and clerks, not if we want to get the town back."

Jake paused again. "I want each of you to take a long look at the fellow next to him. Go ahead — do it." Each man, somewhat self-consciously, looked over the friend and neighbor standing closet to him. Jake gave them a long moment.

"Some of us are going to die as this thing goes on. It could be the man you just looked at. It could be you. I got to make this very clear: Some of us are going to die. Anybody here is free to leave right now with nothing further said. But if you stay, you stay to the end. Clear?" Feet shuffled and throats were cleared, but no one moved toward the door.

Jake walked to the stack of hay bales where the bottles and glasses rested. He poured and drank a couple of inches of whiskey, allowing some of the tension to dissipate. Then he took his place again at the front of the room.

"Anyone heard how bad Mott was hurt in the explosion at the jail?" he asked.

"Banged him up some an' burned off a good bit of his hair," a clerk from the mercantile said. "Didn't do him no permanent harm, from what I heard."

"He was drinkin' at the saloon a couple days after we sprung you, Jake," another said.

Sinclair nodded. "OK. I don't think he's gonna just let it pass. We moved into his territory, wrecked his property. He can't allow that — not an' keep the respect of the vermin he has working for him. So — he's planning something, some sort of attack."

A buzz of hurried, semiwhispered discussion arose from the men. Jake cut through it.

"We're not going to let that happen. Late Saturday night the Night Riders are going to Fairplay." There was an eternity of silence. This was the moment Sinclair had both anticipated and dreaded. The reaction of the men to what he'd just said would determine the entire course of the battle against Jason Mott. Jake's face remained hard, without expression, his hands casually at his sides. He looked as if he were waiting to make a purchase at the mercantile — and an insignificant little purchase at that.

His palms moistened and drops of sweat began under his arms and started down his sides. His stomach tightened as if he awaited a punch.

The " 'Bout time" that was the first re-action from the Riders brought a grin to Jake's face. The "You betcha"s and "Damn right"s that followed rose in volume and enthusiasm. Jake let it roll — it was precisely what he wanted to hear. He moved to the bottles and glasses and poured himself another drink. When he had the attention of the men once again, he went on.

"Today's Wednesday. By the end of the day Friday I want each of you boys — in bunches of two or three — to come on by here with the weapons you're gonna be carrying. We'll need some things from the mercantile, too. Who can help me there?"

A large gent, clean-shaven and well dressed, raised his hand. "I can, Jake," he said.

"You work there?" Jake asked.

"I do. My name's Moses Terpin — Moe — and I own the sumbitch, as well."

Jake grinned. "Good. That helps. Let's talk after the meeting. Now," he said to the group, "we need a way to get in touch with one another, warn each other of problems, call ourselves together. We're too far apart for men on horseback to spread an alarm or a call for help. I've got an idea about that. Now, let's talk a bit about how we're going to post lookouts and what those lookouts are going to do. . . ."

Mare seemed to have suffered no ill effects from her time away from Jake. There were a few spur scrapes on her flanks that were healing well, and some abrasions on the sides of her neck, probably from Mott quirting her, but those, too, were healing. Jake ran the tips of his fingers over the slightly elevated flesh and then had to stop. The anger that flooded over him was too much to handle just then.

He'd worked two coats of a bear fat and light oil solution into all the parts of his saddle and left it draped over a fence in the direct sun for a couple of days. The saddle showed no abuse from Mott's use of it, but Jake cleaned and oiled it almost obsessively in order to claim it back from the outlaw.

The fact that the saddle — and Mare — were never actually his own to begin with didn't occur to Jake Sinclair.

Lou Galvin had brought a gun belt, open holster, five hundred rounds of ammunition, and a new Colt from the mercantile on the third day Jake had been with him. The Colt felt unwieldy in Jake's hand after the smaller Smith & Wesson at first and the wooden grips somehow too large and cold to his palm. A few hours of practice draws and dry-aiming and firing of the new weapon made the equipment begin to feel familiar. The holster was a bit stiff and Jake needed to file the front sight of the pistol so that it cleared leather smoothly, but those were very minor and easily remedied problems. Galvin replaced Jake's Henry rifle with one of his own, and Jake was anxious to sight in the rifle. It wasn't that he didn't trust Lou's eye, but that he trusted his own more.

Mare took to the fall mornings. She snorted as soon as Jake swung into the saddle and pitched a few feelin' good crow-hops to show her feistiness and tugged at the reins after Jake brought her under control. She wanted to run, and on the long wagon road that led from Galvin's hay barn to his main pasture, Jake let her do just that. She wasn't the fastest horse Sinclair had ever ridden, but she wasn't far off that mark. The rush that always accompanied a ride on a galloping horse took over all of Jake's senses as Mare rocketed down the long, gently curved road. The rhythm of the shod hooves that seemed paradoxically slow given the speed with which the ground was being covered, the taste and cool touch of the autumn air, the scent of the last cutting of hay for the year, and the visual panorama of the unsullied countryside combined, and the individual parts became larger than the whole — it was an *experience* rather than a fast ride on a good horse.

Jake left the wagon road and pointed Mare into the pine forest that surrounded Lou Galvin's home and ranch. Galvin's acreage was small by Southern plantation standards — a few over four hundred — but encompassed fertile, loamy soil, many acres of never-harvested tall timber, several year-round streams, a small lake, and some of the most scenic vistas Jake had ever encountered. Billy's place and the two hundred acres his father had given him when he married were beyond the forest. The new house and barn were blackened piles of scrap lumber now, and the land went untended. Lou rarely spoke of his only son, but his eyes conveyed the terrible scope of his loss. A widower for over twenty years, Lou had never remarried. Instead, he'd devoted his life to his and his wife's only child. Billy, friends told Jake, had been a quick learner, a good and intelligent farmer, and a man who was looking forward to raising a herd of children. The entire Galvin holdings would have, of course, gone to Billy upon Lou's death.

Not too different a situation. One place here,

one in the South. Different crops, different ways of working the land, but two strong men who'd built lives for their families and themselves. Now neither has a son to carry on the tradition — Billy killed by outlaws. And me . . . in a sense, killed at Gettysburg, at least as far as my pa and my people will ever know. He shook his head to dismiss the thought.

Rocks were always good targets: They shattered satisfyingly when hit directly head-on, offered up stingy chips and shards when the bullet was off-center. They skipped about when hit, giving the shooter a moving target. And they were plentiful. Jake hobbled Mare, placed a melon-sized rock thirty paces out, and fit six cartridges into the cylinder of the Colt. The weapon was still brand-new, still smelled of the light oil that'd been applied to it for shipping in Hartford, Connecticut. Jake had immediately converted it to take cartridges. He dropped the pistol into his holster, allowing it to settle itself. His draw was automatic and unhurried but clean; his palm found the grips and his right index finger slid into the trigger guard as if the weapon were custom made for him. He fired the six rounds rapidly, his body slightly hunched, boots parted, left foot several inches behind his right, Colt held about two feet out from his body, slightly over waist height. Only two of the slugs hit the rock and neither impact accomplished much. He reloaded, realizing that the slight weight difference between the Smith & Wesson .22 and the Colt he now held had thrown off his aim. The adjustment he made in how he directed his fire was minute — but it worked. His target zipped away as the first round struck it and split in half when the second hit. Of the four remaining bullets, three further reduced the size of the half rock Jake was concentrating on. He swung the barrel of the Colt to the second piece of rock and grinned as it disintegrated when his final bullet smashed into it.

He sighted the rifle for distance at about seventy-five yards, firing at a rock in which specks of mica glittered under the bright sun. He adjusted the front sight, fired several more shots, and nodded. He ran through the same process at fifty yards and then at twenty-five. *Anything closer,* he told himself, *and I can hit them by swinging the rifle instead of shooting it.*

Jake rode slowly back to the ranch, enjoying the feel of the afternoon. The talks he planned to have with the Night Rider members ostensibly to check over their weapons were more planned to familiarize himself with the personalities of each man. It was an even bet that at least a couple of them would be useless in a battle; he wanted to know which men he could count on and which he couldn't. The Night Riders were to begin coming that afternoon, depending on how readily they could leave their jobs or farms without drawing attention to themselves.

Moe Terpin, owner of the Fairplay Mercantile, brought a clerk in a delivery wagon with some tarp-covered supplies. Terpin presented a fine-looking engraved twelve-gauge shotgun for inspection. "This isn't going to be of much use at any distance," Jake told him. "I'll tell you what: Let's you and me trade my rifle for your scattergun." The clerk, Hy Strong, carried a Colt under his white apron, stuck in the waist of his pants behind his belt. "Gonna shoot your eggs off, Hy," Sinclair observed. "Make sure there isn't a round under the hammer." It was clear from the look on the clerk's face that he'd not thought of that precaution.

Men wandered in on no particular schedule. Jake met them, discussed their weapons with them, felt them out about any experience they may have had. He was disturbed to find that most of the men had wives and young children — the reason they weren't serving in the army. Jake carefully avoided asking the sympathies of any of the Riders in the ongoing war. He didn't care — and it didn't matter.

By Friday evening Jake had met each one of the vigilantes. After dinner he sat with Lou Galvin on the front porch. "They're good men," Jake said. "But it bothers me a whole lot that not a single one of them has ever fired a shot in anger, Lou."

"They were all friends of my son."

"I don't doubt that, and I don't doubt that they're hot to avenge Billy's death. The thing is, a man acts differently in the heat of battle when he's being shot at — when there's another human being in his own sights and he needs to pull the trigger."

"These boys'll be fighting for their homes, their families, too. That should make a difference. This isn't a political conflict like the goddamn war our country is in now — this is as personal as a man's son or daughter. Or his wife and his home."

Jake nodded. "I'm counting on that, Lou. But I've got Saturday night pretty much planned out as a hit-and-run — a quick skirmish that'll do some damage and let Mott know we mean business."

"Care to go over the plan with me?"

Jake shook his head. "Like I told the boys,

I'll tell them everything they need to know on Saturday night when they get here. I'm not being evasive with you, Lou. The fact is, I'm not completely straight on all the details at this point."

Galvin chuckled in the darkness. "You're a diplomat, Jake. I don't doubt that you've got ever' second of this little soiree mapped out in your mind. No?"

"Maybe," Jake admitted. "But what remains up for grabs is if any of it'll work."

"If it's not too complicated, it'll work." Galvin struck a match to light his pipe, and for a moment his face was illuminated by the orangish flare, brightly enough so that Jake could see the man's eyes were hot and intense. "I thought over what you said the other night," Galvin said, shaking out the match, "and I posted some lookouts — three of them, full-time, day and night."

"Good. I was going to suggest something like that. I'm certain Mott has already figured out that your farm is the Night Riders's headquarters. Why he hasn't attacked yet I can't explain. But he will, Lou, and we need to be ready for him."

"He hasn't attacked because he's a damned coward!" Galvin snapped vehemently. "If it wasn't for that gang of cutthroats he keeps around himself, he'd be nothing — less than nothing."

Jake let a moment pass, listening to Galvin suck angrily on the stem of his pipe. "Maybe so," he said. "But we can't underestimate him. That'd be a real big mistake."

Galvin was silent for a long moment. "I suppose so," he finally agreed. "I hope we can do some damage Saturday, Jake. We need to show Mott that we have some teeth. And we need our boys to come to believe that, too."

Saturday dawned cool and rainy and the rain continued throughout the day. Thick gray clouds made the daylight hours seem like evening, and when night finally fell, the darkness was almost impenetrable. The moon, barely at a quarter phase, was obscured by slow-moving dark clouds that blocked what little illumination it offered.

Jake paced in front of the eighteen men assembled once again in Lou Galvin's barn. The Night Riders did their best to cover their apprehension, to hide it from one another. Laughter was often too loud, and the outbursts were frequently followed by periods of an empty silence that seemed louder than the forced hilarity. Sinclair had seen it before, the tightness of the faces, the quick movements of eyes that seemed a bit too bright, the white knuckles on the hand that clutched a rifle, the jaws working as fast as pistons as a chaw of cut plug or a bit of straw was reduced to pulp between gnashing teeth.

"This'll be a skirmish, men, not a pitched battle," Jake said, his voice level. "We'll get in, hit, and get the hell out. There'll be resistance, but it won't be concentrated. What we have going for us is surprise. After this, Mott will be looking for us, be more ready for us. But for tonight the advantage is ours." He looked into the eyes of his troops and then went on. "This is war, gentlemen. Wars are won by killing the enemy. It's as simple as that. If you get a shot at an outlaw, take it and make it count." He paused. "Keep this in mind: You're fighting for your family, your friends, your town and home. All those are worth the risks you're taking.

"OK. We're going to split into two groups. Lou will lead one, I'll head up the other. Here's how it's going to go. . . ."

Fairplay that night seemed like a stretch of desolate and abandoned buildings anchored by the light and noise from the saloons at either end of the street. A locomotive, hauling a single passenger car and three empty flatbeds, wheezed away from the depot. Rain, swept by a wind that had freshened and become sharp, kept pedestrian traffic to a minimum. The horses tied in the front of the saloons hung their heads, stoically enduring the rain and the chill.

Inside the batwings of both places the bars and beer- and tobacco-juice-sodden poker tables were jammed with drunk and semi-drunk men cursing, laughing, slugging down shots of rotgut and schooners of beer, slapping at the asses of the whores parading by them. The piano players, sweating with exertion, pounded out attempts at music that could barely be heard over the alcohol-fueled revelry. A cloud of tobacco and lantern smoke hung just below the ceilings, as thick as the rainclouds that moved sluggishly about the night sky. Fistfights started and ended quickly, with one or more of the combatants dazed and bleeding on the sawdust that was spread on the rough plank floors, sodden with booze, tobacco juice, and blood.

Jake, well outside the splash of light from the saloon, sat on Mare with the butt of Galvin's shotgun protruding from the scabbard at his right knee. He focused the small scope on the sheriff's office and jail in the middle of the block of buildings. It was as dark as its neighbors. Even in the murky light and the misting of rain, he could see that a good deal of work had gone into the building since the Riders had blown it up. The rear — the jail — was studded with framing but not yet enclosed. The office itself had been essentially rebuilt and the raw lumber looked naked in the rain. Mare, at Sinclair's cue, started ahead, walking, her hooves sucking at the mud with each stride. Jake looked back over his shoulder twenty or so yards behind him, where his men were waiting in their robes and hoods. He saw nothing. *Good.* He peered beyond the sheriff's office toward the other end of the street and again saw nothing but rain. *Good.* He took a fat stogie from inside his slicker, clenched it between his teeth, and after using three matches, got the tip glowing a cheery red, in spite of the rain. The acrid smoke, as bitter as the smell of burning skunkweed, constricted his chest and made him cough wrackingly. He spat a flake of tobacco to his side, grimacing. "Nothing like a good smoke," he grumbled. He drew on the stogie again, being extremely careful not to inhale any of the smoke.

Jake reined in across from the sheriff's office and sat for a moment, sucking on the vile cigar. Then he reached back into his saddlebag, took out a pair of sticks of dynamite, and wrapped the fuses together tightly. He touched the joined fuses to the end of the stogie and jerked back as bits of powder sputtered from the point of ignition, reminding him of the sensation of blowback after firing his Sharps. Mare jerked her head around at the hissing sound, watched for a second, and turned back, uninterested. Jake stood in the stirrups and hefted the two foot-long sticks. He leaned back a bit and then swung his arm in a fast, looping arc. The sparking whiteness of the fuse material marked the travel of the explosives to the building. Jake's throw was right on; the dynamite punched a jagged hole through the front window of the office and thumped to the floor. He brought Mare's reins up tighter, keeping control of her head.

Jake had expected the blast to sound like that of a cannon — deep, rolling, powerful, the throaty roar of a mighty weapon. Instead, the dynamite exploded with a sharp, ringing, almost high-pitched *craaaaack* that was stunning in its attack on the relative quiet of Fairplay. The burst of hot white light that preceded the report by the briefest part of a second was lightninglike, searing, etching itself on the eyes of anyone seeing it. Sinclair shook his head and blinked rapidly to clear his vision. Spots still floated in front of him as he watched the new roof of the sheriff's office rise up as a single piece, almost in a sort of slow motion, twisting slightly in the air, and then, suddenly, shattering as if it were made of glass rather than lumber. Torn boards and fractured beams whirled out of the structure like lava spewing from a volcano. Flames were there almost immediately, licking at what was left of the structure before most of its components had struck the ground. Jake's eyes had been on the front door after he tossed the dynamite, and he'd have sworn that the door seemed to be sucked far inward and then catapulted away, part of the heavy frame dangling from it, to where it skidded through the mire of the street and came to a stop ten feet or so from him.

"Hot damn," he breathed appreciatively.

Both saloons emptied and men, guns in hand, gaped at the smoldering scraps of lumber that had moments before been Mott's headquarters. A slug whistled past Jake's head, and then another. The crowds from both of the saloons rushed on foot, slogging through the mud, firing without aiming, rushing toward the only enemy they could see at the moment: Jake Sinclair.

Two waves of Night Riders, one from each direction, in ragged lines that stretched the width of the street, swept toward the outlaws, rifles and pistols blazing. Jake wheeled Mare, his hand already in his saddlebag, and pointed her at the glut of men to his right, sucking on his cigar. The outlaws, most of them drunk, stumbled into one another, unsure whether the lone man charging toward them or the Night Riders presented the greatest danger. Jake hunched low in his saddle, single stick of dynamite clenched in his hand with its fuse touching the ember of the cigar, saw the clerk from the mercantile fire at an outlaw who was swinging his pistol toward the clerk. The outlaw snapped forward at the waist as if he'd taken an unexpected punch, and then pitched forward into the mud, hands clutching at his belly, his pistol dropping from his fingers.

Jake powered through the mass of men, Mare's broad chest and striking forelegs taking down any stupid enough or slow enough to fail to get out of her way. The two bands of Night Riders swept past the crowd and one another and continued down the street and out of town.

Sinclair felt Mare slipping but touched her with his spurs to ask that she give him all the speed she possibly could, regardless of the footing. There was barely an inch of fuse left when Jake raced past the saloon and hurled the dynamite. Mare had gone two strides before it blew and both horse and man felt the force and the heat of the explosion.

CHAPTER SEVEN

The original plan had been for Jake to loop back behind the buildings along Main Street, dynamite the second saloon, and then follow his men as they galloped toward the Galvin Ranch. Mare was struggling, though, working two or three times as hard as she would on normal ground, her hooves sinking deep into the glutinous mud, making each stride a battle. She'd broken a frothy sweat and her breathing was becoming labored.

Jake swung his horse out of the quagmire of Main Street, Fairplay, and rode into the rainy darkness, the sounds of his men ahead barely reaching him. The footing was a bit better outside town; the prairie grass and scrub roots held the soil together more effectively than the churned slop in and around the town. The Night Riders, Jake knew, would be peeling off from the group toward their individual farms, ranches, and homes, those who lived in and near Fairplay swinging back when it was safe to do so.

A good raid, Jake thought. *A damned good raid.*

He hadn't seen a single Rider go down and at least a couple of Mott's men were wounded or killed. The roof lifting off the sheriff's office played again in his mind like the pictures from a stereopticon presentation and the *crump!* of the explosion in the saloon sounded again in his ears. The barrels of whiskey went up like kerosene, the flames pawing at the sky, the lanterns inside smashed and spewing their fuel to the hungry fire.

He reined in atop a small rise. Behind him the fires put a pale glow into the night. Ahead was wind and rain-swept darkness. Near the town the railroad tracks glinted wetly in the orange-yellow light of the blazes. He listened for a full five minutes but heard none of the sounds of horses and riders coming toward him from town, and the balance of the Night Riders headed to Galvin's ranch were far ahead. He stroked Mare's neck. Her breathing was more regular now, and she danced a bit in place, wanting Sinclair to cue her to do something other than standing still in the cold rain, looking at and listening to nothing, knowing there was a dry stall, fresh water, and good hay awaiting her at the end of her night's work.

One of the lookouts the Night Riders had posted stepped out from behind a set of young pines, rifle over his shoulder, appearing ghostlike in the darkness. Mare had caught his scent before Jake saw the man, but his Colt was in his hand by the time the nighthawk showed himself.

"The boys say it went real good, Jake. They tol' me you're quite a hand with that dynamite." His face wasn't completely distinct but the whiteness of his teeth in a broad grin was clear.

"It went well," Jake said. "Far as I could tell, all of us who went out came back, and we hit Mott pretty hard."

"Lou said that new sheriff's office purely went up like a Fourth of July rocket. I wish't I could have been there to see it. Next time out, I'll be ridin' with you, Jake."

"Anybody mention if they saw Mott?"

"Nobody did. The boys, they figure he was servicin' one of them whores of his an' everything was over by the time he got his drawers up."

"Could be," Jake said. "You watch careful now. That crew isn't going to take real

227

kindly to what happened tonight."

"I'll do that, Jake." The lookout grinned. He offered a casual salute. Jake's right hand began to rise automatically, without conscious command, to return the salute. He stopped it halfway and made an unnecessary adjustment to his slicker.

First salute I've seen since just before Pickett's charge.

There was a nonmilitary joviality in the Galvin barn that reached Jake on the far side of the structure, in Mare's stall, where he was rubbing her down with an empty grain sack, cleaning away rain, sweat, and mud from her coat. There was a tad too much laughter, a little too much hilarity for the men to share, considering it wasn't a battle they'd just won, but a quick skirmish without the intense engagement that he knew would come later on in the conflict. *Still,* he chided himself, *these fellows aren't trained fighters and they did well. They drew some blood, followed orders, got the thing done. What's the harm in them letting off the tension with a few too many hits at the bourbon bottle and telling one another how brave they are?*

Jake tugged a short-bristled brush from the collection of grooming tools Galvin and his men had assembled in a tattered four-quart basket and used it on Mare's legs. He was just finishing up when Lou Galvin walked down the aisle carrying a lantern.

"The boys are wondering where you are, Jake," he said. The whiskey on the man's breath reached Sinclair a moment after the words did. "They did a good job tonight, didn't they? I think they'd like to hear that from you, though. Tellin' each other gets old after a couple of times."

"They did fine. I was planning on coming right over, Lou," Jake said. "Soon as I looked after Mare."

Jake placed the basket next to a pair of grain barrels and the two men walked toward the gathering. "Do you think we accomplished much of anything with this raid?" Galvin asked. "Anything that'll make any difference?"

"We kind of declared war, Lou — joined the battle. Everything is going to go faster now. I can guarantee you that Mott isn't going to swallow his jail being blown to hell again, and a couple of his men wounded or killed." He stopped walking and Galvin did too, turning to face him. A wave of laughter ebbed and then receded.

"I need to make clear to the Riders that things have changed, that they need to watch themselves and their families. A little too much booze has flowed tonight for me to get through to them right now, but I want to bring them back in a day or so. And if Mott starts attacking farms and ranches, I want the men to come here, to bring their families and be ready for a siege."

"I don't know how you'll convince them to leave their homes, their land, their stock, Jake."

"If this gets real bad — and I think it will — they won't have a choice. There aren't more than a few hundred men within thirty or so miles of Fairplay, Lou. It won't be hard for Mott to figure who's a Night Rider. And if he burns a couple places and kills a few innocent men, it won't bother him. You've got to realize —"

Two distant reports — a shotgun from the sound of them — stopped the conversation. Sinclair's and Galvin's eyes met in the harsh light of Lou's lantern. "That ain't good," the older man said. Jake held up his hand for silence. A moment passed during which the wind-driven rain outside and the laughter and carousing of the Night Riders were the only sounds.

"No answering fire," Jake said. They waited another full minute. There was no further gunfire.

"Might be one of the boys maybe heard

an animal in the brush and let his imagination get the best of him — fired before he thought it over."

"Yeah, I suppose," Jake answered dubiously. "Even so, I'm going to saddle up and go out and take a —"

A voice reached them, and even in the distance and over the wind and rain, the note of fear — of panic — was clear, although the words were indistinct, more of a wail than a sentence or statement. The voice sounded again, this time closer. "Mr. Galvin! Jake! We got bad trouble!"

The group heard that even over their celebration. Their drinks and tales forgotten, they rushed out the front door of the barn to where Jake and Galvin stood, Lou still holding his lantern. The splashing of a horse at speed reached them a heartbeat before they saw the rider — one of the three lookouts who'd been posted, his rain slicker whipping about him, his horse's chest frothy in spite of the rain. "Those bastards strung up Archie an' Todd!" he shouted, voice breaking. "They hung 'em from an oak an' they're both dead!"

Jake hustled to the rider and grabbed at his reins. "Tell us what happened," he demanded. "Calm down and tell us what happened — come on, climb down. We need to know exactly what happened out there, Jim. Get hold of yourself!"

The rider swung down from the saddle, his double-barreled shotgun still clutched in his hand. He drew air in shuddering gasps, his eyes wide with panic, sweeping over Sinclair and the other men but not focusing. Jake took the shotgun from his hand and checked the breech. Both barrels had been fired. Lou Galvin stepped forward and put his arm over the rider's shoulder. "Tell, us, Jim," he said. "This isn't the time to lose control. Just tell us what you saw, what happened."

Jim struggled with his fear, his Adam's apple bobbing in his throat as if he were gulping water after a long thirst. "Yessir," he croaked. He swallowed hard a couple of times, his hands dancing in front of him almost spastically, as if trying to pull words from the rain that fell on the group. Galvin took his arm and led him into the shelter of the barn. The others followed silently, their faces now pale, the hilarity of a few moments ago swept away by the rider's fear.

"Me an' Archie an' Todd was posted out just like we was supposed to be, maybe a hundred or so yards apart, keepin' a good watch — or as good as we could on a night like this. We'd talked it over earlier, and we was goin' to keep in touch with each other, give a owl hoot every so often jus' to let each other know we was OK an' awake an' all." He gulped some air and swept rain from his face with a hand. "Go on," Jake said quietly.

"Yessir. Well, it seemed like I hadn't heard no owl hoots from either of those boys in some good time. I hooted myself a few times but didn't get no answer. I got a little worried an' decided I'd work myself over to where Archie was, off to my right. See, I was kinda in the middle of the three of us. I got to where Arch had been — as close as I could figure, anyway. He wasn't there. That scared me some and I started over to Todd's position. It was darker'n a son of a bitch and still raining hard, but my eyes was pretty used to it. I went on by my position and then I come upon a big oak maybe halfway between me an' Todd an' there they was, hangin', dead, twistin' at the end of ropes when the wind hit them. Their hands was tied behind them and they was gagged with cloths. Even in the dark an' rain I seen there was nothin' I could do for either of them boys. I guess I kinda . . . I run off, then, run to my horse an' fired off my shotgun for a warning an' rode on back here at a gallop. It's a goddamn wonder I didn't kill my horse an' me, both." He sucked some more air and then looked away from Sinclair and Galvin and the group of Night Riders, focusing on the hard-packed dirt floor in front of him at his feet. His voice took on a defensive tone. "Wasn't nothin' I could do — nothin' at all, 'cept get back here an' give the alarm."

"Of course there wasn't anything you could do, Jim," Lou said. "I'm just glad they didn't . . . glad you got back here safely."

Jake stepped back from the other men and clapped his hands to get their attention. "We don't have time to talk right now," he said, his voice hard. "I want armed men in a ring around Lou's house and barn. If there's any trouble — if you see anything — fire twice." Without questioning him, the men started for where they'd left their rifles and shotguns.

"Wait," Jake said, stopping them. "If you hear the alarm — the two shots — don't leave your post. You hear? *Don't leave your post.* I'll be there to tell you what needs to be done." He paused for a second, meeting the eyes of several of the Riders. When he continued, his voice was quieter but still tight and emphatic. "I know many of you have families you're worried about. They'll be OK for tonight. Tomorrow we'll bring your people into Lou's house and barn. The women can sleep in the house with the youngest children. Men and boys will bunk in the barn."

A quick buzz of conversation — questions — began. Jake held up his hand. "We don't have time to discuss anything just now. Get out there and take your positions. We'll talk at first light. Now move!"

If they were going to question Jake, he figured it would be now. The men with wives and kids unprotected wouldn't like the idea of leaving their people alone overnight. *Hell, I wouldn't like it either,* he thought. *Would I obey the order?* He watched the men, not quite realizing he was holding his breath. When they turned away and hustled to fetch their weapons, Jake exhaled. *No,* he thought, *I'd be riding hard for my home and the hell with Galvin, Sinclair, and the Night Riders.* He glanced at Lou, who met his eyes and nodded almost imperceptibly. "I'll be riding inside our line through the night. I'll call out and identify myself every so often," he called to the backs of the men.

"Make sure you sing out loud and clear, Jake," Lou warned. "Those fellas are primed and ready to fire."

Jake nodded. "I didn't see Moe Terpin here tonight," he said. "Why's that? He seems like one of our biggest supporters in all this."

"He is. Thing is, his wife — Ivy — took sick a couple of months ago and she's in a bad way. Could be Moe couldn't leave her. In fact, I'd bet on it, Jake. Nothing else would keep him away from riding with us."

"I see." Jake started back into the barn. "Come on along with me while I saddle my horse. Tell me," he said as they began walking, "is there an undertaker in Fairplay? And more importantly, is he with us?"

"Sure — Isaac Wells is our undertaker. Has a parlor and a furniture store right down Main Street. Ike's too old to ride with us, but he's dead set against Mott and with us every inch of the way. I've known him for a slew of years."

"Good," Jake said, hefting Mare's saddle, blanket, and bridle he'd set next to her stall. "That's real good. Can someone get a note from me to Moe first thing tomorrow?"

"Well — sure. What do you have in mind?"

"Just an idea now. I'll stop at the house after first light to write my note, OK?"

Jake considered borrowing a horse from Galvin's string, but Mare seemed to have recovered completely from her earlier work. He arranged the blanket, set his saddle, and pulled the cinches. As Lou walked to his house, Jake stepped into a stirrup and reined Mare toward the woods to the east of the Galvin spread. The rain had slowed to a light drizzle, at times more of a mist than a rainfall. The footing remained poor, but scudding clouds frequently allowed illumination from the moon and stars — a break that hadn't occurred earlier in the night. There was a stiff, swirling breeze that smelled more of snow than rain, and that cut twisting paths through the mist.

Jake called out and a Night Rider answered. Jake jogged his horse up to the man and drew rein. "I'm going outside the circle," he said. He turned in his saddle and gazed through the damp darkness. Galvin's house was a hulking mass with the dimmest of lights showing in a couple of windows. He turned back to the guard. "I'll try to come straight back in and I'll be shouting out to you." He grinned. "Do your best not to shoot me."

The Night Rider's face didn't change. He remained grim. "Archie and Todd were my friends, Jake — 'specially Archie. We been fishin' and huntin' together since we was sprouts. I'll tell you this: Somebody's gonna die for stringin' him an' Todd up."

Sinclair nodded. "And Billy Galvin, too. We'll see to that," he said. He nudged his horse ahead toward the woods, using the breaks in the mist and fog to attempt to determine where the executions took place. Finding the two men wasn't something Jake looked forward to, but he wanted to cut them down before their friends saw them. The thirst for revenge would run hot enough and high enough without the Night Riders seeing two of their number with their necks broken, dangling from the end of some outlaw's frayed ropes.

There was an eerie stillness to the woods, as if the moisture in the air somehow drowned out the natural, normal sounds. Mare's hooves sucking at the mud with each stride seemed far louder than they should. Jake squinted his eyes, peering into the woods from the periphery, where he rode. The breeze freshened, clearing some of the mist.

The two men weren't far into the woods. The huge oak they hung from was at the edge of the forest. Mare huffed and danced as the scent of death reached her. Sinclair calmed her by talking to her, stroking her neck. The branch — a thick one, perhaps a foot in diameter — was eight or nine feet above the ground. The men, side by side with their hands bound behind them, moved slightly as the wind touched them. The ropes creaked against the bark of the branch. Jake took his pocketknife from his pants and urged Mare to the corpses. She argued a bit, shying from the dead men, but Jake was able to goad her into position. Their boots were about three feet or so off the ground. Jake, in the saddle, had an easy reach to sever the ropes above the stretched necks. He moved his knife toward the nearest rope and then stopped. *If I cut them down now I'll have to leave them on the ground until I get back with a cart. If I do that they'll be fair game to the coyotes, the foxes, the bears — any meat-eater. A bear any larger than a yearling could still pull them down, but those boys are better off where they are for now.* As grotesque as the thought was of leaving the corpses hanging, the alternative was worse. He'd seen many dead men — and parts and limbs and heads — of dead men in the past two years. Death — violent death — was no longer a stranger to him, no longer carried that same shock, the quick sense of revulsion, it once had. Men who fought in the battles a war generated were sometimes killed. So were men who fought against outlaws. That was a fact of life. All this Jake Sinclair knew to be true. *Why, then,* he asked himself, *am I sitting here on my horse staring at these two corpses as if they were going to come back to life and explain whatever it is I'm feeling to me?*

Jake pocketed his knife and swung his horse away from the scene of the murders, back toward Galvin's spread.

By the time he'd situated Mare back in her stall and hitched one of Galvin's cart geldings to the traces of a small farm wagon, the first colors of day were chasing off the melancholy of the night, and with it, the rain.

There was a light on in the kitchen of Lou's house and Jake drove the wagon to it, tying the gelding to the hitching rail outside. Galvin heard him and opened the door before Jake could knock.

"Coffee's ready," the older man said. "Come on in and sit down." He glanced beyond Sinclair and saw the wagon. "I guess you're going out to bring in Archie and Todd," he said. "That's a sad piece of work. I was planning on doing it this morning. You want me to ride out with you, give you a hand?"

"It's a one-man job, Lou. I can handle it." Jake sat at the big kitchen table and Lou brought two mugs of coffee from the stove. He sat across from Sinclair.

"The boys will be bringing their families in today," Lou said.

"How's the food situation?" Jake asked. "There's no way to tell how long the folks will be holed up here."

"Food's the least of our problems. We have plenty stored and we can slaughter a beef whenever we need to. I've already stockpiled flour, salt, canned goods, coffee, and the like for the winter. Moe always puts together a big order for me about this time of year — enough staples to get me and my men through until spring."

"Good. After we finish our coffee I'll ask for a pen and paper to write that note I mentioned to Moe at the mercantile. I'll ask him to arrange for the undertaker — Wells, Ike Wells, right? — to come out, too."

"You don't need to write a message, Jake. I can have one of my men ride into town and talk with Moe and Ike."

Sinclair shook his head. "I know that, Lou. And I know your men are loyal to you." He hesitated for a moment. "But starting today, we have to play everything real close to the vest. The less Mott knows about what we're doing, the better off we'll be."

Galvin drank from his mug. "Yeah. I suppose." After a moment he asked, "What do you suppose Mott's going to do now, Jake? He can't shut down the town — he still doesn't know how many Night Riders there are or who they are."

"He'll figure that the men close to you are members and he'll be watching those who work and live in town. And he'll obviously know about what's going on here. See, the battle lines were drawn last night, Lou. I know hauling the men and their people to your place is a big move, and a hard one for the families. There's no way around it, though. They'd be as vulnerable as newborn babes out there on their farms and ranches."

"Good thing most of the harvest is in. I guess most of the stock out on pasture will survive until this is over." Lou sighed. "Won't be all bad having some kids and women around again. Been lots of years since my Billy was a boy and even more years since his mother died. A ranch becomes too much like one of those factories back East without some young life on it, Jake. I was planning on a passel of grand-children. I wanted Billy to stay on here — build himself a house and start to take over the ranch for himself and his family. He was too independent for that. He bought that piece of land of his and he and his wife lived in a damned log shack while he was building their home. Wouldn't even accept materials from me. He was into Moe real big on credit, but Moe knew he was good for it.

Now . . . well . . ." He didn't finish the thought.

In the silence Jake finished his coffee and set down the empty mug. "If you'd get that pen and paper for me," he said, "I'll get on with things."

"I'll put you at my desk, Jake, let you pen your note there." He met Jake's eyes. "I've got a stick of sealing wax around somewhere, too. I'll find it and bring it in to you." He stood from the table. "Might as well get to it," he said.

The big rolltop, littered with bills and invoices and the other paperwork of a working ranch, was set in a small room — once a nursery when Billy was a newborn, probably — had a single window that allowed the burgeoning morning light into it. The lamp Lou carried along was almost unnecessary. Jake cleared an area on the surface of the desk, dipped the pen into the ink pot, and began to write. As he did so, Galvin placed an unused stick of red wax and a few lucifers and an envelope on the desk and left Jake alone. Within ten minutes the note was written and the envelope sealed. Jake carried it and the lamp downstairs.

"I'll have this carried to Moe right away," Lou said.

"Good. Will you take care of changing the guards?"

"You want lookouts during the day, too?"

"There's no choice in the matter, Lou. None. You need to keep in mind we're at war here, and we're under siege. In fact, let's get a few extra men out riding between the guards — make sure we're covered everywhere, all the time." His voice sounded even to himself harder and more stringent than he intended, but he didn't soften his words.

Galvin nodded wearily. "I guess you're right. I'll see to it."

Jake extended his hand to the older man. Now his voice was lower, calmer. "Keep in mind we're at war here, Lou. We don't want any more surprises like we had with the two men out in the woods."

"No. We don't." They shook hands.

Jake rattled and banged the wagon across the pastureland toward the woods. He stopped at the first guard he reached. "You'll be relieved before long. Nothing going on here?"

"Nope. All's been quiet. Coffee'll taste good. Maybe tonight the fellas posted out here could get breaks — have someone spell them for a bit, let them ride in to the house and drink some coffee. What do you think?"

"We'll do just that," Jake said. "Good idea. I should have thought of it last night."

The nightguard grinned. "I'll tell you what, Jake — you just keep on thinkin' on how to kick Mott's ass for good, an' the rest of us will take care of stuff like givin' guards a break."

"Fair enough," Jake said. He slapped the reins lightly on the gelding's back, starting the horse forward.

The day was promising to be a fine one — cool, clear, the air tinged with the scent of fall. The bird sounds from the forest reached Jake as he slouched on the wooden slab seat of the wagon, directing the horse every so often to avoid the deepest ruts and largest rocks in their path. A quick rustle of branches straight ahead caused Jake's right hand to drop to the grips of his Colt. A flash of the gray-white tail of a squirrel as it leaped to another perch quieted Jake's pulse.

The harsh reality — the brutal starkness — of the pair of corpses hanging from the branch of the oak, their faces now a pale, ghastly, fish-belly hue, the flesh of their necks a good several inches longer than normal due to the bodyweight stressing the dead flesh — sapped the beauty from the day. Jake stopped the gelding ten feet away from the oak. The image of Jason Mott appeared in his brain, and Sinclair's fists closed tightly. He tried to shake off the picture, but it didn't work. His body tensed and the tension in his jaw locked his teeth together hard enough to cause pain. Hatred was a new sensation to Jake, but one he recognized immediately. It surged through him, powerful, encompassing, demanding. "I won't forget what I'm seeing right now, boys," he whispered hoarsely. "When I take Mott down I'll see all this again." He took a long, deep breath, let it out, and urged the horse forward. *Did I hate the blue bellies I killed? No — hell no. They were the enemy, but I didn't hate them. They were men just like me who were on the wrong side of what we both considered a just battle. This* — he looked again at the hanged men — *is different. There's no justice in what Mott and his men are doing, no good in it at all. It's pure pain and evil. That's where the difference is, and that's why it has to be stopped in any way I can stop it.*

The gelding shied from the corpses, eyes wide, the scent of death heavy in his flared nostrils. Jake pulled against the bit hard enough to give the horse something to concentrate on and wrapped the reins around the brake handle. The air around the bodies was fetid and rank. Their bowels and bladders had long since released and their skin gave off the smell of raw meat. Birds, Jake saw, had already gotten to the men's eyes, but not much damage had yet been done. He stood on the bed of the wagon and sawed through the rope of the man closest to him. When the rope parted Jake caught the weight of the body and eased it down on its back. He placed the second man next to the first. The corpses had stiffened during the night and they looked strangely artificial stretched out on their backs, as unnatural as men standing at strict attention in a nonmilitary situation. Jake tried without success to close their eyes. Then he pulled the tarp he'd brought over the two cadavers, climbed back onto the driver's seat, and turned the wagon away from the oak tree.

The lookout, standing on a knoll a hundred yards away as Jake drove past, took off his hat and held it over his heart until the wagon lumbered by his post.

There was a large hay wagon backed up to the front of the barn as Jake drove in. Three boys, all blond and dressed pretty much alike in denim pants and flannel shirts, ripped around the corner of the house yipping like Indians on the warpath.

The oldest looked to be seven or eight years old, the other two a year or so younger. Jake's gelding started a bit as the youngsters raced past and then he settled down. A girl of twelve stood by alternately watching the boys and eying Sinclair. Jake tipped his hat to her. The girl blushed prettily and smiled at him. When she turned away to rush after the boys he noticed that her auburn hair was tied into a neat braid that reached below her waist.

Jake guided his wagon to the back of the barn. He was about to leave the driver's seat to slide open the door when one of the Riders — a fellow named Zeb — pulled it open from the inside. "I seen you coming, Jake," he said. "I cleared out some space in the tack room for Archie an' Todd till Ike gets here. Pull the wagon right on in." Three blond heads peeked around the edge of the barn. "Get outta here, ya whelps, or I'll take a switch to ya!" Zeb hollered. "Ain't notin' to concern you boys here. Go on, now!" The heads disappeared. "Grandkids," Zeb explained.

"Nice-looking boys," Jake said, simply for something to say.

"Damned if they don't get into everything, though," Zeb said, the pride in his voice obvious. "Good boys, though. That's their sister out front — the girl with the braid. She's supposed to be keepin' watch on her brothers."

"Looks like a big job." Jake eased the gelding and wagon through the door and Zeb closed it behind him. Jake wrapped the reins around the brake handle and stepped down. Zeb nodded toward a doorway. "Right in there," he said. "I guess we'll have to put 'em on the floor, but I swept it out real good." They carried the corpses one at a time into the tack room and covered them, once again, with the tarp. "Hell of a thing," Zeb observed. "I'm sorry you had to go out alone to fetch 'em in, Jake. I didn't know you'd left till you was gone. I'da come along and give you a hand."

"Not necessary, Zeb. Thanks anyway." Jake backed the wagon out of the barn, pleased with the good training of the gelding. Some — many — farm horses knew as much about backing a cart or wagon as they did about Egyptian history. Zeb pulled the sliding door shut. Sinclair drove around to the side of the barn, parked the wagon, set the brake, and freed the gelding from the reins and tack. He took the horse into a stall, gave him half a bucket of water, and rubbed him down. The gelding grunted with pleasure as Jake worked on him, bringing a small smile to the man's face. Jake left the horse with a thick flake of hay and a stroke of thanks on his neck.

Jake watched the activity at the front of the barn. Another freighter-sized wagon had pulled in, the four draft horses that had pulled it snorting, sniffing the air, catching the scent of other horses. The wagon was apparently a two-family venture; a pair of women ordered a herd of children of various ages about while two men unloaded barrels of salted pork, flour, and dried beans. The aroma of brewing coffee drew Sinclair to the Galvin kitchen. He was surprised only for a moment when he found four women in the kitchen, a large pot simmering over a hot fire on the stove, and a vat of eggs cooking in a large black spider next to it. A chuck wagon–sized coffeepot rested on the warming grate of the stove. He stood, hat in hands, watching the activity. One of the women, a stout, pretty lady of about forty, glanced over at him, a smile beginning on her face. "Help you with somethin'?" she asked.

Jake nodded at the coffee. "May I?" he asked.

The woman laughed. "*May* I? Last time I heard a man say the word *may,* it was old Doc Richards jus' before he lowered my drawers to check my plumbing, when my Calvin was about to be birthed. I swear that man had fingers as big as tree trunks. Jammed one up my little back passage and I near hit the ceiling."

"Rosey," another of the women said, "you're gonna scare this poor fella talkin' like that. Lookit him — he's blushin' already."

Jake forced a smile, feeling heat in his face. "I . . . uhh . . ." he stuttered.

"Git your coffee an' clear out," Rosey ordered. "We got people to feed an' no time to admire a stud horse jus' now." The women tittered at Jake's discomfort as he poured himself a mug of coffee and carried it back to the door. "Thank you, ladies," he said. For some reason that phrase brought on more laughter. He was glad to put the kitchen behind him.

His sleepless night and the somber task this morning began to catch up with Sinclair as he stood in the sun sipping his coffee. His eyes were gritty and a sort of general fatigue, like a weighty blanket, settled over him. Lou approached from behind and Jake started as Galvin greeted him.

"The fellow I sent to Fairplay with the message should be back before long, Jake. I told him to stop in and drink a beer at the saloon — see what the talk was about, try to get a feeling for what's going on with Mott." He looked more closely at Sinclair's face. "You look like you need sleep," he said.

"Yeah — I do. I'm going to my room. Would you send somebody for me as soon as the rider gets in? I want to talk with him as soon as he gets here. Same thing applies if the undertaker pulls in, too. OK?"

"I'll see to it, Jake. It's Rip Daniels I sent. He's a sensible fellow — a good friend of my Billy, and about Billy's age. Rip will learn what he can without being obvious. You go on and get some shut-eye."

The room Jake had been using was small and sunny. He stretched out on the bed, listening to the corn shucks complaining under his weight. He didn't expect deep sleep; instead, he planned to doze for an hour — perhaps two at the outside — and then to go down and await both the message carrier and Isaac Wells, the undertaker. If the messenger had gotten to Moe Terpin at the mercantile as Jake planned it, the undertaker would be hauling a pair of coffins in his hearse to Lou's place very soon. Jake closed his eyes. The fall sunlight streaming through the window was like a loving mother's touch on his face. It was midafternoon when Lou Galvin touched Sinclair's shoulder, bringing him instantly awake.

"Jake? Ike Wells is here. I sent him around to the back of the barn, told him where the bodies are. You wanted to talk to him, right?"

Jake swung his legs off the bed and stood. "Yeah, I do. Thanks, Lou. Maybe you should come along, too." They hurried down the stairs and through the kitchen to the barn. Wells had pulled into the barn through the back door, and his hearse now stood outside the tack room.

Ike Wells didn't look like any undertaker Jake had ever seen. Wells was portly, dressed in a good business suit that looked tailored to his rather rotund form, and he was ruddy cheeked and smiling as he extended his hand to Sinclair. His gray hair was neatly parted in the middle and pomaded to the contours of his skull. His eyes, a deep chestnut, looked like he was coming to a birthday party rather than to haul off two unjustly hanged men. Jake took his hand. The grasp was firm, warm, and dry. Wells's smile broadened.

"You look a little incredulous, Jake," he said. His voice was pleasant, masculine, without the darkly somber tones undertakers tended to employ. "I'm apparently not at all what you expected?"

"That's for sure, Mr. Wells," Jake admitted. "No disrespect, but you don't fit the image of your profession."

Wells laughed delightedly. "I hope not, young man. Because I tend to the dead doesn't mean I'm in constant mourning — and call me Ike."

A cluster of three or four Night Riders opened the back door and started toward the hearse. Wells stepped forward to meet them. "Gentlemen," he said, "out of respect for Archie and Todd, I'm going to have to insist that only Jake and Lou here assist me. You'll soon see your friends after I've done my work. I'd appreciate it if you'd keep the others out, too."

Jake nodded as the men shuffled back out and pulled the door shut after themselves. "Thanks for that, Ike," he said. "Moe reached you?"

"Oh yes. He sure did. Shall we unload?"

The coffins, constructed of pine and stained black, rested on the floor of the hearse side by side, their brass fittings catching the light. Jake hopped into the hearse and shoved at the rear of a coffin; Ike stood at the back gate and took the weight as Jake eased the box and himself out of the hearse.

Galvin raised his eyebrows, a grin starting on his face. "Sure seems to be a heavy coffin," he observed. " 'Specially since it's empty an' all." They placed the first coffin on the floor of the tack room and the second next to it. Ike took a narrow, flat tool from the hearse and used it to pop the four nails holding each of the coffin tops in place. He and Jake lifted the first top and set it against the wall. Lou looked inside the box and whistled. Four small wooden cases — each labeled

DANGER
Masters & Thomas Explosives, Inc.
Warren, New Jersey
mining load dynamite — 60 sticks
DANGER

rested in a snug line inside. The second coffin contained four similar cases, along with a long parcel wrapped in several turns of oilcloth. "Moe sent this along," Ike said, grabbing the parcel. "Said he'd had the damned thing for over a year with not a single customer showing the least bit of interest in buying it." He handed the package to Jake.

Jake had handled such parcels before. That it was a rifle was no surprise. But as he felt the weight of it, he drew a breath. When he broke the twine holding the oil-cloth and unwrapped the weapon, he drew another breath. "Holy God," he said quietly. "An 1859 Berdan Sharps .54-caliber carbine." His voice was reverent, as if he held a sacred icon. The cherry wood of the stock and forepiece was rich and polished and without blemish, smooth to the touch, but not featureless, like glass. Rather, the wood was warm, almost like the flesh of a living creature, a natural feel to it. The blued barrel, breech, and trigger guard were coated with thick shipping grease that smelled a bit like lantern fuel.

"You've seen one of these before," Galvin said. It was a statement, not a question.

Jake nodded, not taking his eyes from the rifle he held in his hands. It wasn't exactly the weapon he was used to, the one he'd carried and used up until Gettysburg. That Sharps was the 1862 model, with the dual trigger system. This 1859 version was a bit more basic, but it was the same stunningly powerful caliber: .54. And, like the '62, it was completely capable of firing a thumb-sized slug that would carry unerringly to its point of kill for a mile.

"Moe sent along a sack of ammunition for that buffalo gun, too," Lou said. "It was tucked next to a dynamite case." He hefted the cloth bag. "Feels like a sack of rocks," he said. "I guess you need a hell of a load to take down an animal that big." He paused for a moment. "Jake? Jake? What's . . . you OK? You look —"

"Yeah. I'm OK," Sinclair said, rewrapping the rifle. He tied the twine over the oilcloth carefully and set the Sharps outside the tack room, on a stack of bales of hay. "Let's get the men into the coffins and onto the hearse. No offense, Ike, but the sooner the bodies are off the place and headed for town and your parlor, the better the morale around here will be."

The bodies had gone past the stiff, un-yielding rigor state and were now flaccid, loose jointed. Ike and Sinclair completed their grim task quickly and the undertaker placed the tops on the coffins. "No need to nail them down till after the viewing in town," he said. "I'm not carrying anything but dead men this next trip."

Lou and Jake watched as the undertaker wheeled away from the barn. The men unloading wagons in the yard paused and put their hats over their hearts, watching the hearse until it followed a curve in the trail and was out of sight.

"Well," Galvin said, replacing his hat, "I'm

real ready for a drink. Join me, Jake?"

"No — no, thanks, Lou. I'll take you up on that offer a little later. I'm going to go out for a ride, maybe put a few rounds through that rifle Moe sent. Kinda see what it'll do."

Lou took a half step, putting himself in front of Sinclair. Their eyes met and locked. "Something tells me you already know what a Sharps can do, Jake. The way you reacted to that weapon — well — it was strange, my friend. But look, it's none of my business. I won't mention it again, to you or anyone else."

"I appreciate that, Lou. If you'll let the others know to expect hearing some gunfire in a little while, I'll go saddle my horse. Catch you for that drink when I get back."

Galvin watched Jake as he strode back to the barn. After a moment, he went to a group of Night Riders to tell them to expect some shooting out beyond the guards, and to spread the word to the other men.

The light was still strong, the sky cloudless, as Jake, wrapped rifle over his shoulder, pointed Mare to the periphery of the forest at a jog. When the ground became level and relatively clear, he extended her gait to a lope. When he reined to a stop he was about five miles from the Galvin Ranch, in a broad, sweeping field that was broken here and there with boulder-sized and smaller rocks. He tied Mare to a low branch of an oak, took a piece of cloth and a canning jar of whitewash Lou had found for him from his saddlebag, unwrapped the rifle, tied the sack of ammunition to his belt, and began walking. The butt of the Sharps felt good in the palm of his right hand, and the forged steel of the barrel over his shoulder warmed quickly in the sun. He'd wiped the metal parts of the weapon clean of the protective grease before rewrapping the rifle. The warmth of the direct sun would take care of the rest of the slightly oily feel to the metal.

The sound of boots in the dirt and low brush and the heft of the Sharps took Sinclair back to the battlegrounds he'd seen since he signed on with the Confederacy. The sense of his partner and spotter, Uriah Toole, walking next to him, was all but palpable. He shook the image of Gettysburg away before he had to relive Uriah's death during the final charge. *Here I am again in another war with another Sharps rifle. When I left the army I never thought I'd be in this position again — but here I am.* The thought depressed him. *But this is different,* he told himself. *This isn't a political war controlled by bureaucrats and profiteers on both sides. This is good against bad — it's that damned simple. Jason Mott has no more right to do what he's been doing than a rattlesnake has to attend church services.* Mott pulled the lever on Billy Galvin again in Sinclair's mind, and this was a memory he couldn't shake away, chase away, by concentrating on something else. *I'm doing the right thing by stopping Mott. Without someone who knows something about fighting, those Night Riders would be easy prey for Mott and his killers.*

Jake stopped next to a rock protruding through the soil and worked the wire catch on the canning jar. He tipped some of the sluggishly flowing whitewash onto the face of the rock and walked on. He noticed that his hand was trembling as he poured. He didn't like that at all. He walked on a hundred yards, stepping around other rocks that would make good targets, until he stopped next to one that showed a few inches of a narrow face above the surface of the ground and dabbed some whitewash on it, using the cloth this time. He picked his way through brush and scrub that was becoming thicker and higher and poured the rest of his whitewash on the face of a foot-high rock. Then he balanced the empty jar on top of the rock and started back to where he'd decided to fire from, where he'd be able to sight in the Sharps with the targets he'd created.

Jake fed a cartridge into the rifle and eased the bolt forward, the quiet *snick* of the operation an indication of the craftsmanship that was a part of everything Christian Sharps and his partner William Hawkins made in Hartford, Connecticut. He brought the butt of the weapon to his shoulder and tucked his cheek against the stock. His finger at first reached for the second trigger he'd become accustomed to, and then settled against the sole trigger of the 1859 model. The pull required was heavier than Jake would have liked, but the action — the progression of the trigger as he squeezed it home — was smooth. The rock Jake had dumped whitewash on disappeared into a mist of dust and tiny chips before the bass thunder of the report even began to carry away from where he stood. There was a nub of rock left when the air cleared, pointing straight up toward the sky, no more than an inch or so wide and a couple of inches high. Jake loaded and fired again. A geyser of dirt leaped out of the ground an inch to the right of the little stone spire. *Wind? Nah — there's no wind at all. Either my poor shooting or this brand-new rifle needs a tad of sight adjustment.* He reloaded, found a target in a tiny blue wildflower a foot from where the rock had been, corrected his aim the slightest bit, and fired. The stalk didn't move at all, but the little flower was suddenly gone. Jake drew a breath and then exhaled, not quite aware that he was smiling.

The second target, out another two hundred yards beyond the first one, shattered in a most satisfying fashion. The third target he estimated to be out at over a quarter of a mile. It wasn't a terribly long reach for a Sharps, Jake knew. He loaded the rifle and brought the butt to his shoulder. It felt like it belonged there. He eased the trigger back. The slug trimmed off the top two inches of the boulder. He ejected the spent cartridge and sat down, cradling the rifle in his lap. He touched the barrel at midpoint between the rear and front sights. It was barely warmer than the sun had made it as he carried the weapon over his shoulder.

There was a very slight rise a half mile outside Fairplay, Jake recalled, that would give him a clear line of fire to the front of the saloon closest to the end of Main Street. It wouldn't be a hard shot — he'd dropped Union officers at twice the distance under conditions he had to accept, regardless of what they were.

This time around, he could choose the day he'd kill Jason Mott — and if that one didn't work out, there was always the next.

CHAPTER EIGHT

Jake was finishing rubbing down Mare when one of the blond boys he'd seen playing earlier rushed up to him in the barn. "I'm a courier," he said quite seriously, standing at attention outside Mare's stall. Jake swallowed his smile. "I can see that," he said. "What's your message, son?"

"Mr. Galvin's in the kitchen with Rip Daniels. Mr. Galvin, he says for you to come on over to talk with Rip. He also said he shagged the women outta the kitchen for a few minutes. An' that's the end of my message." The boy saluted but didn't make a move to leave.

"OK, son. Thanks."

The boy held his salute. Sinclair looked at him quizzically. "You're supposeda dismiss me," he said.

"Oh. Sorry. You're dismissed, courier. Good job."

The courier grinned proudly at Jake. "It's

a right good thing for them Rebs I ain't old enough to go off an' fight. I'd have them slavers and see-sessionists runnin' home or dyin' like the dogs they are on the battle-field."

Sinclair's smile disappeared. "Maybe so." When the boy looked like he was going to speak again, Jake said a little more force-fully, "Dismissed, soldier." The boy picked up on Jake's tone of voice and scurried to the front of the barn. The boy's words hit him like a dark blanket being dropped over him. *"Slavers and see-sessionists dyin' like the dogs . . ." I saw enough of the dying. And I caused enough of it.* He stood silently in the stall for a minute, staring into a jumble of battle scenes, hearing the unrestrained roar of cannonades, the sharp pops of muskets and rifles, the screams of men hit with bullets, with shrapnel — and those be-ing run through by bayonets. They screamed the loudest. It took another minute to get rid of the images and the thoughts.

The light was fading as Jake crossed between the barn and the house. Several of the women he'd seen earlier in the kitchen were clustered about a long table, serving supper to men and boys seated there. There was no sign yet of a siege mentality. Laugh-ter rolled around the table and spirits seemed high. Jake noticed one fellow at the table surreptitiously pour from a pocket flask into his coffee cup. The scent of the food — beef stew, from the savory smell of it — reached Sinclair as he opened the kitchen door.

Lou Galvin and Rip Daniels both swung their eyes to Jake as he came in. The two men were seated at the table, glasses in front of them and an empty glass in front of a vacant chair, a bottle center-table. Galvin nodded toward the empty place. "Sit down, Jake — but first, shake hands with Rip Daniels. He's a good man and one I'd trust like I'd trust my own son." Jake stepped toward Daniels and extended his hand. Daniels stood and they shook, silently appraising one another. Daniels was a man of average height, with that whipcord-lean look that farmers and ranchers tend to have. His skin was deeply tanned, his dark hair, obviously cut by someone other than a barber, long, covering his ears and his collar in the back. His eyes were chestnut, a compelling, attention-demanding glint to them. He looked like a man who would laugh easily.

Sinclair pulled up a chair and Galvin poured two inches of whiskey into the glass in front of Jake. "How'd that buffalo gun work out, Jake?" he asked.

"It's a good weapon. Reaches way out there."

"Buffalo gun?" Daniels asked.

"Moe sent the gun along to Jake today," Lou said. "Thought maybe he could use it."

"Can you?" Daniels asked.

"Maybe," Jake said. "Thing is, for close fighting it isn't much good 'cause it's a single shot. Uses cartridges, but still, loading up takes time. Powerful, though." He looked over at Daniels. "What did you find out in town?" he asked.

"Well, not a whole lot. I drank some beer at the saloon and listened to what was going on. Mott came in after I did. He ran his mouth about hanging the Night Riders one at a time — those he couldn't gun down. His boys liked that."

"Was there much talk about our raid?"

"Yeah — you bet. Mott's crazy mad about the damned jail being blown up again. Seems like they're all hot to saddle up, but there doesn't seem to be any plan yet. Some of them were grousin' about that but shut up when Mott came in." He drank from his glass and wiped his mouth with the back of his hand. "Most of those outlaws couldn't find their asses usin' both hands if it wasn't for Mott. I'd say that killing him would be like chopping a rattler's head off — what's left can't do anybody harm."

"Most them are pretty hard cases," Galvin said. "I'm not real sure they'd slink away if Mott went down. Jake? What do you think?"

"Hard to say," Sinclair answered noncommittally. "Could go either way, I suppose. I tend to agree with Rip, though — unless there's one or two within the gang who're looking to take over from Mott, maybe even plotting against him. If that's the case, killing Mott wouldn't accomplish anything but putting another killer in command."

"Jason Mott would be dead, though," Lou pointed out. "There's a lot of good done right there."

"I can't argue with that," Jake said. He looked again at Daniels. "Did you get any feel for where Mott is staying now that the jail is wrecked again?"

"Yeah. He's got a couple of rooms at the saloon down the street — on the other side from the one where I was today. He's had whores in the rooms for some time. I guess he just had a couple of them double up. He goes back an' forth during the day, one saloon to the other."

"He walks?"

"Sure. Not worth climbin' on a horse for that little bit of distance." Daniels grinned. "Anyway, you took his horse. He was carrying on about that."

"Oh?"

"Yessir. He said he's goin' to take you down himself. Kind of promised that to the whole gang."

Sinclair considered for a moment. "You say Mott goes back and forth between the two saloons, right?"

"Yessir. Least he did a few times when I was there. I can't swear he does it every day."

"What about the rest of them? What do they do all day? Are there assigned duties, anything like that?"

Rip grinned. "Don't seem like it. They drink, play cards, jump on a whore, argue with each other 'bout who's faster with a gun or better with his fists, an' that's about it. 'Cept for the lookouts they have posted — maybe four or five of them, it's hard to tell — it doesn't seem like they do much of anything."

"Any idea where the lookouts are posted?" Jake asked.

"There's one at each end of the street. I seen both of them. The others, I don't know. They're not out real far from town, though. They changed shifts about noon or so and it wasn't five, maybe ten minutes before the men coming off were lined up at the bar."

Jake thought for a moment. "They didn't bother you? Didn't they know you and Billy Galvin were tight friends?"

"I suppose they knew. Thing is, Billy had lots of friends. They had no reason to get after me. I sat there an' drank my beer, is all. They figured I was just another sod-buster gettin' drunk rather than following a mule's ass."

Sinclair stood. "OK. Good, Rip." He extended his hand. "I'd like you to oversee our lookouts — make sure they're out there and wide awake, decide who you want in what position, all that. Will you do it?"

Rip Daniels stood and shook Jake's hand. "Yeah, I'll do it," he said. " 'Course I'll do it. You can count on me."

"I know I can. That's why I gave you the job. Thanks, Rip." He nodded to Galvin. "I've got some things to do. Let's get together later and talk, Lou." He turned back to Daniels. "Let your men know I'll be going out a couple of hours before dawn tomorrow, Rip. Tell 'em not to use me for a target."

"Yessir. I'll do that. Which way you goin' out?"

"I'll be headed for Fairplay," Sinclair said. "Be back maybe midday or so."

Jake left the kitchen and headed for the

main barn and the blacksmith's enclosure adjacent to it. The ringing of a hammer against steel indicated that the smith, the man called Bull, was at work. Sinclair stopped under the large oak near the house, watching the activity around him. A woman stood before a churn, pumping away at it, her almost waist-length auburn hair floating up and down on her back in rhythm with her arms as she worked the plunger. A toddler sat on the ground off to the side a couple of feet, playing with a rag doll almost as large as the child herself. Several other women stood together in any angry cluster, glaring at the kitchen Jake had just left, their postures and the quick motions of their hands as they spoke indicating that they'd not again be shagged out of their rightful territory. A man on a strong-looking bay gelding rode in, a rifle over his shoulder. He nodded to Jake and continued on to the corral at the side of the barn, his horse's hooves snapping up smartly, almost before they touched ground, with each stride. It was a good, peaceful country scene and it took Jake, for a few moments, back to his home. There, the women and children would have been black, but that made no difference. The sounds were the same — the *chunk-swish* of the churn, the quiet thunk of the hooves, the clear, melodic note of struck steel, were the same. Only the rifle over the fellow's shoulder was discordant. Firearms were a part of life on Jake's plantation, but his father didn't allow them to be flaunted, to be carried so brazenly. At home the rifle would have been in a saddle scabbard, readily at hand, but not blatantly exposed. Sinclair sighed and walked out of the shade to the smith's anvil and forge where the big man worked.

Bull, bare-chested, with a leather apron tied at his waist, set aside his hammer to shake hands. His grip, Jake noticed, was dry, although his face was running sweat, and the pelt of fur across his chest and abdomen was dripping wet.

"I've got a little piece of work for you," Jake said. "It shouldn't take you long. Here's what I need." He crouched, brushed the dirt smooth with his hand, and scribed the project. "These two," he said, "want to be two and a half feet. This one needs to be three feet because it sticks out here. . . ."

Jake had never needed reveille in the army. He and his father both had the unusual — and inexplicable — skill of waking exactly when they'd desired to when they went to sleep. This morning Jake awoke at three hours past midnight. He'd slept in his clothes on top of the covers. He stretched, yawned, and picked up his boots, carrying them down the stairs and through the kitchen to the outside to avoid waking the others who slept in the Galvin house. He carried the Sharps in his right hand. He took a lantern from the counter in the kitchen under the window and lit it as he stood outside the kitchen. The moon was full, impossibly huge, close enough for a tall man to reach up and touch. It was almost light enough to read a newspaper without other illumination, but Jake knew the darkness would be thicker and more pervasive inside the barn.

Several of the horses nickered at Jake as he walked by their stalls with the lantern, anticipating their morning feed. Others slept soundly in the awkward-looking standing position a sleeping horse often assumes. A couple were down in their stalls, on their sides, in the acutely vulnerable position very few horses in the wild dared to attempt. The air in the barn was redolent of hay, horse-flesh, and well-cared-for leather. Jake inhaled it as if it were a fine perfume.

Mare nosed at him, seeking a treat, which he provided, as he stepped into her stall with his saddle. She crunched the apple wetly, thoroughly enjoying it. Sinclair blanketed and saddled the mare and let her finish chewing before he placed the bit into her mouth. As ever, Mare was ready to go — energetic, curious, happy to be outside. She crow-hopped a couple of times, simply showing her spirit, and Jake grinned as he easily rode to the light bucking. Jake swung her toward Fairplay, setting the pace at a slow lope, the bright moonlight making the way clear. He didn't see the lookouts he passed, which was good — they were keeping out of plain sight. That they were there and on the job, Jake didn't doubt for a moment. The men knew that both Jake and now Rip Daniels would have their asses for shirking the job or sleeping at a post.

It was cool out — brisk, actually — and there was no wind, no breeze. Sinclair shifted in his saddle, the Sharps across the tops of his thighs, the metal of the barrel cold, even through the denim of his pants. He shifted his weight slightly again and felt the slightest stutter-step in Mare's gait. She wasn't used to nervous movement from Jake in the saddle.

This isn't right, he thought. *Something's wrong here. I don't know what it is, but something's wrong.* Mare's ears flicked to the side where some small night creature rustled in the scrub brush and then quickly returned to their forward-pointing position. Jake felt the sensation of dampness in the hand that rested against the forepiece of the rifle — his palm was sweating. *What the hell? This is just another assignment — it's taking down an officer. How many times have I done it — and done it well, quickly, surgically — in the past? Too many to count — too many kills to remember.* He shook his head angrily. *They weren't kills. They were . . . what? Excisions. I was excising men who could — would — give the orders that would kill me, kill the men around me. War is war.*

The very first vestiges of light began to hint at themselves in the east. There was no color and no real light yet, but a faint, ephemeral glow almost too vague to discern was indicating that the night was beginning to draw to an end. Jake rode on, his horse working smoothly under him, the steady, rhythmic drumming of her hooves the only sound in the universe. Pictures flickered in his mind, passing and changing so quickly that he couldn't completely see one before the next replaced it: blue-coated men swept from the backs of their horses, faint red mists hanging in the air for a part of a heartbeat in the space they'd just occupied, a sweating, bare-chested fellow directing

Union cannon fire, a longhaired, bearded officer who seemed to be gazing straight at Sinclair through a spyglass from a half mile away, a courier at a full gallop on a good horse, plucked from his saddle. Jake fought the images, fought whatever was going on in his head. *I told Lou Galvin this was war and that's what it is. I signed on to help here. I'm a sharpshooter. The Night Riders need me. I won't let them down.*

The colors and the light at the eastern horizon were stronger, more vivid now. The shadows placed by the bright moonlight were being swept away and the land becoming more distinct. Jake reined in at a small sinkhole and dismounted. There was, he noticed, a parchment-thin glaze of ice over the surface of the water. He led Mare to it and she poked her nose through it, sucking water. When he mounted and rode on he could see fingers of smoke rising from a couple of places in Fairplay, reaching up toward the sky before being dissipated by the wind.

Jake's vantage point was pretty much as he recalled it. The hill was a low one, but tall enough for his purposes. The slope was thickly covered with dead prairie grass and scarred here and there with sizable rocks protruding from the soil. The breeze passing stirred the brownish yellow stalks of grass and weeds slightly, creating random patterns before moving on. Jake hobbled Mare on the far side of the hill, untied the tripod Bull had crafted for him the day before from behind his saddle where he'd carried it, and walked with it in his left hand and the Sharps in his right, to the top of the hill.

The day had broken crystalline clear, the air sharp and sweet. Main Street of Fairplay lay, by Jake's estimate, three hundred yards away, slightly below him, the road a dusty rectangular line between the buildings on either side of it. A mule-pulled farm wagon driven by a man in a heavy gray coat was the only traffic, and as Jake watched, the driver swung his rig down an alley and out of sight. Jake set up the tripod, the longer leg extended in front, and rested the rifle on the plate Bull had fitted to it. The device was solid, sturdy, the half-inch round stock it was made from heavier than necessary to do what little it needed to do. Jake placed melon-sized rocks at the base of each of the three legs. He pushed against the tripod lightly. It didn't move. He pressed harder and it remained in place. "Good," he said aloud.

Jake cleared the dead grass and bits of

rock from the ground at the stock of the Sharps and lowered himself to the ground, a boot on each side of the steel triangle in front of him. He dug his heels into the soil a bit and shifted his butt back and forth until he was settled and stable. Only then did he peer down the sights.

The view of the farther saloon was marginally better than that of the closer one, simply because of his perspective from the hill. The whitened rack from a longhorn steer mounted on the wall over the batwing doors on the farther gin mill winked bits of the morning sunlight back at him. The glass of the two lanterns, one hung on each side of the doors at about head-height on a tall man, glinted light back at him. He had an unobstructed view of the front of the closer bar. Smoke from the chimney of that one indicated the place was coming awake.

The calm — the period of thoughtless inactivity — that Jake always experienced as he waited on a stand settled over him, and he welcomed it. This state of being totally aware of what was happening in the target area but detached from everything else, as if nothing or no one existed other than the target, was a prerequisite of any truly effective sniper. Sinclair had begun to learn it many years ago in tree stands while wild boar hunting with his father. "Just go away, Son," his father had told him. "Don't be here in any physical way. Only your eyes should move and your mind should be as quiet and calm as your body. . . ."

Early morning traffic in Fairplay was moving. A swamper emptied a bucket in the street in front of the farther saloon. Some hammering — greatly reduced by the distance — reached Jake from inside the wrecked sheriff's office. Five men rode out of the livery stable corral, each in separate directions. Within fifteen minutes, five others rode into town, tied their horses to the rail in front of the bar with the steer horns, and pushed their way through the batwings.

Sinclair sat, watching, his eyes the only part of his body that moved.

There was more traffic on Main Street now, both pedestrian and mounted. Men, in twos and threes, strolled back and forth between the saloons. A couple of workers used a draft horse and a chain to wrestle lengths of board from the front of the sheriff's office. Amazingly, the tinkling of a piano reached Jake at a time when most people would barely be finishing breakfast.

When Jason Mott and one of his cohorts stepped out and stood in the sun under the steer horns, Jake's hands moved slowly. His left went out to the stock of the rifle resting on the tripod plate made to accept it. His right hand moved to the breech and his index finger curled within the trigger guard. Only after his hands were in place did he lean slightly forward at the waist, easing the right side of his face against the walnut stock. What breeze there had been had dwindled to nothing as the sun rose higher; now the air was dead still. Jake found Mott's face in his sights and lowered the rifle a hair, sighted on Mott's chest. A head shot at four hundred yards was too risky — the chest was a broader target and actually, a slug from a Sharps placed pretty much anywhere on the upper body would kill a man just as dead as the same round would entering the target's forehead. Jake drew a long breath. The barrel of his weapon was perfectly steady. *This isn't right.*

This doesn't feel right. Jake released the breath. Mott was waving one arm, making some sort of emphatic point to the outlaw he was speaking to. He moved his body slightly and Jake had to adjust his rifle accordingly. *He's going to start walking in a few seconds. A still shot is always more sure than one at a moving target. This is the time.*

Sinclair took in another long breath. His finger quivered the slightest bit against the smooth, highly polished curve of the trigger. *What the hell? I've never trembled before when I was on a target.* Never.

It was a matter of a slow, steady squeeze and his job would be finished. He could ride back to Galvin's place and tell Lou and the men that he'd cut the head off the rattlesnake. Then he could move on.

Beads of sweat started from his hairline and wandered down to his eyebrows, the liquid quickly turning cold on its journey. He swallowed hard. *This isn't a war. I can't kill like this, a sniper in a civilian world. I'll face Mott and take him down, but I can't do this. Mott deserves to die, but . . .*

Faster than he liked to move while aiming, Jake adjusted the position of the Sharps slightly and tugged the trigger. Mott, his hands stopped in midgesture, stood for the briefest part of a moment and then dropped to the wooden sidewalk. So did the man he was talking to. Another, who'd just begun pushing through the batwings from the saloon, hit the floor and rolled to the side. The dried, bleached bovine skull between the long sweep of the horns exploded in a puff of grayish smoke, scattering shards and splinters of the thick bone in all directions. Mott scrambled to his knees and dove into the saloon, a half heartbeat ahead of his cohort. The report, a deep, flat crack to Sinclair, rolled over the prairie and the town with the heavy resonance of an artillery round.

Jake stood, ejected the spent cartridge, and slid another into the breech. He raised the Sharps to his shoulder. This time, he noticed, there was no quiver as his finger touched the trigger. The lantern above and to the left of the batwings shattered, the metal base and tank ruptured and twisted, spun away. A blue flame appeared immediately, lapping at the dark stain of kerosene on the wood. Jake reloaded and took out the lantern on the right. It too spewed fire. Three men rushed out of the nearer saloon, two shouldering rifles, followed almost immediately by another pair of outlaws armed only with pistols. A rifle barrel appeared from behind the batwings, between the escalating fires on either side of the swinging doors. Sinclair put a round into the center of one door, tearing it from its moorings and hurling it back into the saloon. A livery wagon sagging on its steel springs from the weight of the six barrels of beer it carried had emerged from an alley a moment before Jake had fired his first shot. The driver scrambled for safety and the confused and weary pair of draft horse stood in the traces, heads hanging, apparently familiar with the sounds of gunfire. Jake swung the rifle to a barrel and squeezed off a round. Beer arced in a delicate, glistening stream to the ground. Sinclair was a man with a long-established fondness for beer and ale. He licked his lips as he watched the amber fountain, his mouth moving in swallowing motions without his being conscious of it. Loading, aiming, and firing had already become an almost instinctive procedure — without thought, his hands steady and sure. He created two more beer geysers, shooting at points low on the barrels.

Jake grinned as a pair of old rummies — bar hounds who spent their days running errands or emptying spittoons in exchange for a shot of red-eye or a schooner of beer — lumbered out of the saloon waving bar rags as peace flags, hustling to the beer wagon. They sat in the growing puddles at the barrels, filling their hats and drinking them dry, hurrying frantically to repeat the process before the sources ran out.

Buckets of water were being hurled at the flames from the lamps on either side of the batwings, killing the fire before it could entrench itself and begin to do some real damage. A pair of rifle barrels poked through the flimsy glass of the front windows of the saloon, quickly joined by another, and then another. The reports sounded to Jake like the Chinese firecrackers kids shot off on the Fourth of July — puny, insignificant when compared to the crashing roar of his Sharps. He stood, arrogantly, waving to the riflemen, knowing full well the rounds from their rifles, even with a sharpshooter behind the trigger, couldn't reach him. He smiled broadly and was considering hauling the red bandana from his pocket and waving that when a slug whistled past his head, slicing through the air with a screeching hiss long before the resonant bellow of a Sharps or a similar caliber weapon reached him. "Holy shit," he grunted, dropping to the ground.

Jake knew that there was an enclosure behind the sheriff's office and adjacent to the railroad depot where several of the outlaws' horses were kept, and he knew that it wouldn't be long until those horses were saddled and bringing their riders into the reach of rifles. As attractive as the thought of further shooting up of the town was, Sinclair crab-crawled backward, dragging his tripod with him, the Sharps cradled in his arms, until the top of the hill was between himself and Fairplay.

Mare was ready to travel. As accustomed to gunfire as she'd become, the percussive blast of the buffalo gun was a bit much for her nerves. She danced when Sinclair mounted, and she wanted to run. He gave her all the rein she wanted. Within moments, Jake heard the sharp crackle of gunfire behind him. The sound brought a grim smile to his face. The range, he knew, was too long for the standard rifles, and he'd yet to meet a man who could shoot at a moving target from the back of a galloping horse with even a cannon such as a Sharps and hit anything smaller than a good-sized barn.

Jake had started up a gradual rise when blood erupted from the left side of Mare's neck and spurted into the breeze generated by her gallop. The horse stumbled half a step, shook her head violently from side to side, but recovered her gait, blood still flowing freely. It was then that the deep, hollow boom of the high-powered weapon reached Sinclair. He spurred Mare over the top of the rise and dragged her to a sliding stop, out of the saddle and on the ground at her head before she was fully halted. It was a flesh wound, he saw — a furrow about four inches long dug into Mare's neck muscle a half foot below her ear. She'd bleed a bit, but it didn't look like the major artery that ran through the set of neck muscles had been hit. He grabbed the hobbles from his saddlebag, fastened them onto Mare's front legs and shoved her a bit more down the grade. Then, hauling the Sharps from the back of his saddle, he threw himself to the ground, crawled ten feet or so, and peered back at the riders pursuing him.

Ten or a dozen men rode in a foolishly tight cluster, firing even though now they had no visible target. One rider sat his still horse fifty yards behind the group. The sun sparkled off the breech of his rifle as he raised it to his shoulder. Jake fed a bullet into his Sharps, aimed, and plucked the marksman out of his saddle with a hole in his chest the size of a large man's palm. The outlaw's rifle spun up and away from him and raised a puff of grit when it struck the ground. Jake reloaded. The knot of men had spread out and one of them had pulled ahead of the others, reins in his teeth, riding hell-for-leather, cranking the lever on his rifle and shooting at the gun smoke that rose from Jake's last shot. Sinclair fed his Sharps with steady fingers, quickly but not hurriedly. The leading, hard-riding outlaw's horse — a shiny bay with a good long stride, continued on for several yards before he realized that he no longer had a rider and then broke sharply to the side, shaking his head, reins flailing, keeping pace with the other riders for a few moments and then slowing to a stop, sides heaving. The man was a crumpled figure facedown in the dirt, the back of his shirt already saturated with blood.

Sinclair reloaded and set his sights on the buffalo gun in the dirt and grass a couple of hundred yards away and fired. Dirt, rock, bits of gleaming metal, and shards of wood burst from the ground and a second report followed the bellow of Sinclair's round. Again, the grim smile appeared. There must have been a round in the chamber and that's what Jake's shot had found. He no longer had to worry about the big gun, nor the man who'd fired it at him.

Jake got the hobbles off Mare's legs, barely avoiding a slashing hoof as the horse, now almost frantic with the pain from the gash in her neck and the heavy smell of her own blood, reared, squealing, eyes wide. He scrambled as close to Mare's side as he could get, rifle clenched in his right hand, saddle horn and reins in his left, and danced a clumsy, unbalanced two-step with her until a misplaced hoof and a half stumble gave him the momentum he needed to haul himself into the saddle. He used his heels against Mare's sides to urge her into a gallop, letting her drain off her panic through exertion. He held the gallop for a mile or so and when he checked the mare to a lope, she responded as always, her fright left behind. He turned in the saddle to check on his pursuers. They were stopped, clustered again, over a mile behind him. He rode on at the lope, letting Mare pick her way through the scrub.

Why did they rein in? There was still a good bit of ground to cover before he reached Galvin's place. The outlaws couldn't catch him, not unless his horse went down — which was certainly a possibility, given the terrain. Why, then — why didn't the outlaws push him, hoping a rock or woodchuck hole would grab a hoof, snap a pastern or a leg? It didn't figure. Jake rode on and when he began to hear his mount's breathing become heavier, he reined her down to a canter. The furrow on her neck was still weeping blood, but the wound had already begun to form a crust along its length, the blood clotting well.

He scanned a line of trees ahead and picked out a watchman in a tree. He waved and watched the lookout's hat wave back. Jake swung Mare toward him and stopped under the tree. "Something caught my eye," he called up into the branches. "A bit of light."

The lookout shifted his position on the branch he sat on, leg on either side, and looked down at himself. "I don't see what . . . son of a bitch!" His eyes — and Jake's — came to rest on the guard's belt buckle, a fancy, Sears catalog-ordered model in silver, embossed with the Union Eagle, the size of a twenty-dollar gold piece. "Damn," he said. "My wife give this to me a couple years ago for Christmas." He nodded to Sinclair. "You got a good eye on you, Jake." He set his rifle carefully across his thighs, released the buckle, and began hauling the belt through the loops in his pants. "I'll jus' put this away till this whole deal is over."

"You do that," Jake said. "Fine-looking buckle, though." He rode on, holding Mare at a walk.

When Sinclair reached the Galvin barn he was hungry, very thirsty, and his Sharps needed cleaning before the acids released by the firing could set into the rifling of the barrel, but Mare put all that into the background. He rubbed her down, avoiding the wound, checked the set of all four of her shoes, and offered her a half bucket of fresh water, which she sucked at enthusiastically.

He left her stall as she munched a scoop of crimped oats from her feed box and returned a few minutes later with a bottle of alcohol, a tin can of bag balm, a pan of hot water, and some strips of clean white cloth provided by the ladies in the kitchen. One of them — the woman who had embarrassed him so thoroughly several days ago with her comment about Doc, stood on her tiptoes and used a washcloth to clean the stippling of burnt powder from his face, commenting that "you need a wife to keep you tidy an' keep your rooster crowin'," again bringing a bright rush of blood to his face.

Mare crunched half an apple as Jake wet a strip of cloth with alcohol and gently but very thoroughly cleaned the wound. She shied away from the burning, but the other half of the apple calmed her down. The wound was less serious than it had looked when it was bleeding freely. The separation of the edges of flesh wasn't wide enough to warrant sutures. There'd be a scar — proud flesh would form — but that would happen with or without stitches. He spread the viscous, medicinal-smelling bag balm the length of the furrow, considered wrapping Mare's neck, and decided against doing that. Fresh air was often the best medicine for horsehide cuts, and the cloth wrapping would cause the horse to rub her neck against any surface she could find in her stall or out in the pasture.

Lou Galvin met Jake as Sinclair was leaving the barn, a mug of steaming coffee in each hand. Jake accepted one gratefully, blew over its surface for a moment, and took a mouthful. It was better, just then, than the finest Kentucky bourbon, fragrant, rich, and strong enough to dissolve a musket ball. He drank again, nodding his thanks.

"Let's go inside, talk a bit," Galvin said.

Sinclair noticed how drawn the older man looked, how the dark half-moons under his eyes sagged, the tight set of his mouth. They walked side by side silently, around to the front of the house and into the parlor. The room was a formal one, Jake saw, probably used only on holidays when neighbors visited, to lay out corpses for mourners who called, and when the preacher came by for a meal. The furniture was ponderous, stuffed to an almost rock-hard firmness, the surface of the fabric as scratchy as dried straw. A symmetrically neat arrangement of logs was set in the fireplace, kindling in place, awaiting a match. The hearth was immaculate; there hadn't been a fire in the room in a long time. Lou sighed as he settled into an armchair facing the couch where Jake sat.

"How'd it go?" Galvin asked.

Jake considered for a long moment before answering. "Not bad. I dropped a couple outlaws. One had a buffalo gun. I got lucky and blew up the rifle."

"I doubt much luck was involved, Jake. Seems to me you handle that big Sharps awful well." He paused for a moment. "What about Mott?"

Jake held his friend's eyes. "I had a shot — a clear one. I didn't take it."

Lou's face hardened. "He pulled the lever that ended my son's life, Jake."

"I know that."

"Let me get this straight," Galvin said, setting his coffee cup on the floor in front of him. "You had Mott in your sights and didn't pull the trigger? Why the hell not?"

Jake shook his head. "It would have been an execution, Lou — not something done in a battle. I've done more than enough of . . ." He let the sentence die, unfinished.

Galvin's voice rose. "An *execution?* Jesus Christ, didn't that animal execute Billy? Tell me the difference, Jake — go ahead and do that."

Sinclair looked down at his boots. "I can't, Lou. There wouldn't have been any difference. But I couldn't do it." After a moment, he added, "I'm sorry, Lou."

Galvin shook his head in disgust. "You could have ended the whole thing today and you say you couldn't take the shot." He made the word "couldn't" sound like a vile disease. "Shit!"

The peace that the formal parlor offered earlier had been sucked out of the air by Lou Galvin's words, by his anger. Both men sat in the stifling quiet. From outside, the only sound that reached them was a quick burst of childish laughter.

Galvin drew a breath. "Look," he said, "maybe you have some sort of strategy in mind, something I don't understand. Is that it?"

Sinclair shook his head in the negative.

"Look," Galvin said again, "I didn't figure you were a virgin when you came to us. You're a fighter — I could see that in you. You've killed before — I can see it in your eyes, Jake. You might as well have a sign around your neck saying 'Killer.' "

Jake began to rise to his feet.

"Sit, damn it," Galvin snapped. "I'm not through yet. You think I didn't know you weren't the usual saddle tramp or drifter? You're military, Jake — probably Reb, but definitely military. The way you take care of your gear, your horse, carry yourself, take command — all that tells a story." Lou sat back in his chair. "You showed up not long after the bloodbath at Gettysburg. I figure you're a deserter."

Again, Jake started to rise, but Galvin went on. "That doesn't mean anything to me. Why you walked away isn't my concern. I can't judge you or any other man. I doubt I could have stayed with either side after the carnage you boys had seen." His voice became a whisper. "Thing is, you had that son of a bitch in your sights and you didn't —"

"I was a sharpshooter in the army of the Confederate States of America," Jake said. "You're right about me being military." On his feet now, Sinclair looked down at the older man. "I had lots of men in my sights, just like I did Mott. I killed those other men. Today I killed a couple of outlaws who were chasing me, shooting at me. That's what made all the difference. That's why I rode away from Gettysburg on a horse I salvaged — stole, I guess. I couldn't be an executioner any longer. I'll protect myself and I'll protect people who are important to me, but I won't be like Mott, the man who pulls the lever — not for you or your Night Riders, not for anyone or anything."

He took a step toward the door.

"Sit down, Jake," Galvin said quietly. "Give me a minute."

Jake stopped and, after more than a couple of seconds, turned back and took his seat on the couch once again.

"What you've done in the war and who you've done it for doesn't matter a hoot to me. Reb or Union, it seems to me that we have a whole generation of good men killing each other over bullshit an' politics. I read in *Harper's Illustrated* that a boy — a Union private — put a bayonet through his own brother's chest — a Reb private — at Manassas. That was . . . well, hell, Jake — I'm wandering here. Point is, without you, those outlaws would go on doing what they were doing as long as they wanted to. I got to thank you for that." He shook his head a bit. "Passing on the opportunity to drop the man who hanged my son won't ever set right with me, Jake. I guess you can understand that, and you'll understand it even more if you ever become a father. But I know you had your reasons, and I guess that'll have to be good enough for me."

"Thanks, Lou," Sinclair said quietly.

The silence returned to room, this time almost funereal rather than tense, as if neither man quite knew what to say or how to end the meeting.

"One more thing," Galvin finally said. "You mentioned Mott's men were chasing you. What stopped them? Seems like your gunning a couple of them would have heated them up so they'd ride hard to get you."

"I wondered about that. Then I thought about it as I rode back here. What's happening is this, I'm pretty sure: Mott gave his men orders to chase me a bit but not to follow me here for a fight. He's not a fool. He's thinking he has the town in his hand and fighting a pitched battle here would only cost him some men and some time. Hell, why not just sit back and keep running Fairplay exactly as he has been? It's worked for him for several years. There's no reason it won't keep working. Sit tight, run whores, swill booze, and be the goddamn king of Fairplay is a fine way to go, at least in his mind. Why bother with a bunch of farmers holed up on a ranch miles away from town?

"He knows the men can't stay here forever, Lou — that eventually they'll have to go back to their homes, their own spreads. That's when he'll hit them. Here, they're like an armed and guarded encampment, but separately they're easy prey for Mott's gang of cutthroats. They can wipe out your boys one by one, family by family, attacking whenever Mott cares to."

Galvin leaned forward and picked up the now cool cup of coffee he'd set on the floor earlier. He sipped from it and grimaced. "Cold," he said. "I'm going to the kitchen to freshen this. Give me your cup — you can use a refill, I'm thinking."

Jake handed over the mug. He rose and walked to the window. The blond young girl raced around the edge of the house, screeching, running for all she was worth, clutching at her dress to keep from stepping on the hem and tumbling. A few feet behind her one of her brothers was in pursuit, a yard-long milk snake writhing from his fist, his smile broad enough and bright enough to outshine the sun. Jake smiled at the children and then was suddenly disoriented, almost dizzy. The images of him and his friend Apollo, the son of his family's cook, chasing Apollo's sister, Aphrodite, across the pasture grass with a fat swamp toad, washed away the scene outside the window of Galvin's house. Neither black had a last name; most slave owners named children born on their plantations whimsically, with about as much forethought as they'd give to naming a litter of mongrel puppies. Aphrodite and Apollo had been Jake's best friends through his childhood, and their mother's sister had been his nanny. They'd still been with his father when Jake left for war. He had no idea where they were now — if they'd abandoned the plantation after the Emancipation Proclamation or opted to stay with the elder Sinclair. Abraham Lincoln's five pages of handwritten words, declaring "that all persons held as slaves are, and henceforth shall be, free," tolled the end of the Southern livelihood and way of life, according to Confederacy sympathizers.

Jake had never felt that his friends were chattel — property — and, actually, hadn't given the idea much thought until very recently. It was simply the way things were in the South — perhaps as things were supposed to be. Now he wasn't at all sure about the institution of African slavery. It was difficult for him to imagine his father's slaves taking care of themselves outside the plantation, away from a master who provided them with everything they had — food, housing, medical care, even clothing. But, still, didn't a black man deserve a shot at freedom? And what about the Negro babies being birthed now? Should they grow up under the lifetime yoke of —

"Jake? Where are you? Here's your coffee.

You look dazed, son."

Jake took the mug. "Drifting a bit, I guess," he said. He sipped at his cup. The heady scent of whiskey reached him even before the aroma of the coffee in which it was mixed. "Just the thing," he said, following Galvin back to their seats.

Lou lit a cigar and drew on it until clouds of fragrant bluish smoke surrounded him. "Cigar, Jake?" he asked.

"No — no, thanks. This Irish coffee'll do me just fine."

Lou settled more comfortably in his armchair. "So," he said after a long moment, "what can we do — from a military standpoint, I mean?"

Jake didn't need to think before speaking. The answer to that question had been in his mind ever since his ride back from the gunfight that morning. "I don't see that we have but a single option, Lou, unless all of you want things to stay just as they've been since Mott took over."

"You know we don't want that, Jake. That's why all of us are here, armed, posting guards and all. What's your plan?"

Jake drank half his coffee and lowered the cup. "It's not much of a plan quite yet," he said, "but I think I have an idea."

"And that idea is what?"

"I'm approaching the whole thing from — like you said — a military standpoint. If two armies were in the same basic situation we have here, the one feeling the pressure would act quickly and decisively."

"Oh?"

"Yeah," Jake said. "I say we attack Fairplay and shoot Mott's ass off right there in town."

Chapter Nine

The whole goddamn operation was coming apart.

Mott had the entire town of Fairplay tucked securely behind bulwarks of huge, fantastically long tree trunks that ran, unbroken and straight as a schoolmarm's ruler, the full length of the town. The cannons — four-inchers and some with maws double that — were firing canisters and grapeshot, tearing gaping holes in both men and the attack line Jake had formed. Now the outlaws were jamming long lengths of heavy chain into the barrels of their artillery, the chains twisting sinuously, strangely slowly and gracefully in the air, cutting men in half as easily as a sharp scythe shears ripe wheat. The horrible whine of the chains through the air was just as Sinclair had heard it at the bloodbath at Antietam — an eerie, high-pitched tone that was far more frightening than the reports of the cannons themselves.

301

A hot-air observation balloon drifted in the wind currents above Fairplay, a flagman directing Mott's artillery. Jake squinted at it carefully through the smoke and then fell back, stunned, aghast. Uriah Toole, still headless from Pickett's charge at Gettysburg but somehow clearly identifiable, pointed his red flag directly at Sinclair. Billy Galvin, a noose snug around his neck, trailing a short length of rope, was jacking rounds into his rifle, firing nonstop. One of his slugs took Lou Galvin in the forehead and Lou's lifeless body spun — cartwheeled — off into the prairie like a tumbleweed in a stiff wind.

Jake fed a cartridge into the breech of his Sharps, drew a breath, and placed his sights on the chest of an outlaw behind the crank of a Gattling gun. Jake eased back on the trigger and tiny bits of blowback gunpowder stung his forehead and cheek. The slug lumbered out of the end of the octagonal barrel, hesitated for a long moment in the air, and then made an abrupt turn, picked up speed and velocity, and blew a massive hole into the chest of the little boy who'd been chasing his sister with the milk snake. The outlaws were using what looked like a medieval catapult of some sort, hurling liquid sheets of white-hot molten . . .

Sinclair writhed in his bed, the light cover

wrapped around him as tightly as a leather restraint, his face, his chest drenched in sweat. He fought to a sitting position, gasping, the narrow bed rocking crazily as he battled against the horrors of his nightmare. A gentle shaft of moonlight opaquely lighting the room brought Jake to his senses. His breath rasped in his throat as if he'd run full-out far too long and his heart banged frantically in his chest. Sucking in air, almost sobbing, he unwrapped the sodden sheet from his upper body, tossed it aside, and made his way on trembling legs to the window. He leaned forward, nose touching the cold glass, supporting his upper body with his hands on the sill. He didn't know how long he'd been asleep, but the night was still deep-dark and there was no hint of light at the eastern horizon, not even the vague pastels of false dawn.

A single lantern shone from window to window in the barn as the man carrying it moved about inside the structure. As Sinclair watched, another light moved from the far side of the barn to join the one he'd seen first. A horse in one of the stalls nickered and, in a moment, another stomped steel-shod hooves on the wooden floor and answered with a low whinny. A pair of men moved from the darkness into the scant light in front of the barn, slid the overhead door open, and went inside, leaving the gap open. Both men had rifles over their shoulders.

Jake took his hands from the sill and stood straight before the window. His breathing was regular now — almost normal — and the light-headed trembling sensation was gone. It was chilly in the room and his sweat became a clammy blanket. He used the shaving towel from the hook on the side of the dresser to rub his chest and face dry, scratched a lucifer, and lit his lamp. The water in the basin was cold as he slapped it on his face and neck. He whipped thick suds in the saving cup and worked the Ohio Brand razor a few sweeping strokes against the buffalo-leather strop Lou had provided. Jake had missed the morning ritual of shaving during the time he was drifting, although at the time he hadn't realized it. Since being at Galvin's place he'd been shaving daily. It was a good way to start a day. As he was wiping away lather from his neck his hand brushed against locks of hair that now reached damned near his shoulders. He gathered a thick clump and sheared off a good three inches, and then worked his way around the back of his head, the Swedish steel blade parting the hair cleanly, effortlessly. He pulled on his denim pants and then his boots. He buttoned his shirt and shrugged on his vest. Last, he buckled on his holster and Colt, tying the holster low on his right leg. His fingers moved around his gun belt, assuring himself that each loop contained a fresh cartridge, although he'd checked at least once the night before. There was a seam of yellowish light at the horizon the next time Sinclair glanced out the window. His Sharps had been leaning against the wall next to his bed. He picked up the sack of .54-caliber cartridges from the floor next to the stock of the rifle and distributed them among his vest and pants pockets, checked to be positive that there was a round in the chamber and the safety lock in place, and left his room carrying his rifle in one hand and his lantern in the other. The light created sharp-edged shadows in the hall in front of him. As he passed Lou's bedroom he saw that the door was open and that the room was empty.

The cheerful aroma of brewing coffee reached Sinclair before he started down the stairs, as did the hazy light from the kitchen, which grew stronger as he walked through the parlor. Lou Galvin sat at the table, a mug of coffee in his hand. He nodded toward the pot on the woodstove. "Help yourself," he said. "But be careful an' drink it slow — otherwise it'll melt your teeth down to nubs." He grinned. "I may have made it the slightest bit strong."

Sinclair took a mug from the sideboard and filled it. He sipped. "No stronger than, say, a cup of lye and catamount piss — but it tastes just fine." He sat across from Lou.

"So," Galvin said. "Today's the day." He shook his head. "To be honest, I'm not sure if I've been dreading or anticipating this — maybe a bit of both."

"The men are ready, Lou. They're spoiling for a brawl."

"I know that. But I always come back to this: They're not soldiers, not fighters. Before you got here, it was the rare man among them who'd fired a single shot in anger. They don't know what a real battle is, don't know any more about tactics or strategy than a newborn kitten."

"They don't need to. It's a simple, straightforward plan. All they have to do is shoot outlaws from the wagons. Those slabs of hardwood we muscled into place will stop pretty much anything Mott has to throw at us."

"Maybe. I sure hope so." He paused. "I'm still not sure about cutting the horses loose, Jake. Seems like burning bridges behind us. If we do need to turn tail . . . well . . . I just don't know."

Sinclair stood from the table and refilled his coffee. He carried the pot from the stove and topped off Galvin's mug, then returned the pot. "It's just like I've been saying, Lou — it takes four good horses to haul each of those three freighters. There's going to be a whole lot of lead flying and at the end of the battle — no matter who wins — we'd have twelve horses bleeding out on Main Street. Those animals are trained and trusted, Lou, and the men need them on their farms and in their businesses. They'd be awful hard to replace."

"I suppose that's true. Still . . . I just don't . . ." Galvin let the phrase die.

"There's another point, Lou, and I think you know it as well as I do. Turning back isn't an option. We either kill damn near all of Mott's gang or we die trying. If we lose, those scum won't leave a single man breathing. They'll finish off every last one of us just like the blue bellies did at . . ." Sinclair stopped himself and stared into his coffee.

"At Shiloh? Second Manasas?" Galvin asked quietly. After a moment he said, "Your allegiance — where you came from before you showed up here — hasn't been much of a mystery to me, Jake. It doesn't make a damned bit of difference. You threw in with us and that's what counts."

Nervous, quick laughter sounded from the yard. Sinclair stood and walked to the window. The barn was lit up now and clusters of men stood about in front of the wide-open front doors. Inside Jake could see the first of the three freighters with the board-length slabs of two-inch-thick hardwood with the bark still in place serving as armor. The cigar box–sized gun slots were like undersized portholes on a passenger ship. Jake turned back to his friend. "The ten men who rode out last night were the best we have," he said. "The element of surprise will make a big difference. You can count on that."

"I am counting on that. We're all counting on that." He sighed and stood. "Let's get to it, Jake." He held out his hand. Jake took it. They shook hands as if they were sealing a business deal neither of them was particularly pleased about.

". . . enough ammunition in each of the wagons to put twenty rounds into each of those outlaws and still have lots left over. Just keep what we've discussed and planned for in mind and we'll win this thing. Questions? Anybody have something to say?" Jake strode back and forth in front of the group of men in the barn, holding the eyes of one and then another, and another. The fact that they were in a group rather than clusters of three or four or five men boded well, Sinclair thought. Whether or not they realized it, the men had come together as a united force. Their determination to crush the enemy was all but palpable in the air.

One of the farmers raised a hand. "Got me a question an' something to say all at once," he called to Jake. "Y'all gonna have your good friend with you this morning?"

Sinclair's confusion showed on his face. "Good friend? I . . ."

"Sure — your good friend Mr. Sharps! If'n you will, we ain't got a thing to worry about." The laughter and hooting that rolled through the men was far more than the lame joke called for, more of a function of nervousness than actual humor. Jake played along with it, encouraging the release of some of the tension. "I'll tell you boys what," he said. "You'll hear my good friend talking today — his voice is some louder than those peashooters you're carrying." He waited until his troops settled down. "One more thing," he called to them. "Take a good look at me and what I'm wearing. I'll be out and on foot a good bit of the time, between the wagons and so forth. Try not to shoot me, OK? It'd ruin my whole damned day." The men laughed again, shifting on their feet, cuffing one another on the shoulder, their eyes gleaming in the lantern light with a combination of bloodlust and trepidation. Jake waited for complete quiet and then raised his Sharps over his head as if it were a command sword.

There's no possible way to sneak three heavily loaded freighters carrying a total of about fifty armed men and four trussed-up outlaw lookouts who weren't looking out quite sharply enough into a small town like Fairplay, and the Night Riders didn't attempt to do so. The first wagon, ahead of the others by three or four minutes, pulled to a stop midblock, in the center of the street, across from the sheriff's office. Jake stepped over the planks at the rear of the wagon and walked forward. He unbuckled the traces and the reins of the four snorting horses and whacked the lead horse on the rump, sending him on his way. At either end of the street men jumped from their wagons and did the same thing. In moments the two mares and the other gelding Jake had set free were followed by eight other horses, the small herd of them instinctively turning back toward their home at a shuffling lope.

Jake, rifle shouldered, stepped toward the sheriff's office. Repair work, he noticed, was pretty much complete and the wreckage resulting from the past raid was all but invisible. A couple of men stepped out of the saloon and watched dumbly as Jake scratched a lucifer to fire with his thumbnail and touched the flame to the twined fuses of a pair of sticks of dynamite. At any other time the smooth, sparking arc — which flowed up from Sinclair's hand, rose quickly, and then flashed like a shooting star in the darkness — would have been pretty, even celebratory.

This morning it was a signal that a battle to the death had begun.

An eye-searing burst of white light preceded the roar of the explosion by the briefest part of a second. The front window and frame, along with the roller shade attached to the inside, catapulted past Sinclair, a single pane of glass amazingly unbroken and reflecting the already hungry flames in the office behind it. The as yet only partially shingled roof caved in gracefully, slowly, feeding the fire below. The door hung awkwardly from its top hinge for a moment before the entire doorway fell in, belching smoke and fire into the street.

Lanterns blinked on the length of Main

Street and hurriedly dressed men, some bootless, most with unbuttoned shirts or no shirts at all, began pumping pistol and rifle fire into the three freighters. Slugs made a hollow sound — much like that of a knuckle thunked against a ripe melon — as they struck the thick slabs of wood. The wagons, Jake knew, were able to absorb whatever gunfire Mott could send them. They were vulnerable to dynamite, but that had been part of the gamble that's part of any engagement. It was a good bet that the outlaws simply didn't have any of the explosive: Moe had cleaned out his mercantile of dynamite — as well as most of his stock of weapons and ammunition — at night with midnight loads to Lou Galvin's ranch.

A bullet whined by Jake's head too close for comfort and several more dug up spates of dirt at his feet. He scrambled toward the back of the freighter he'd ridden in on just as Lou Galvin leaned out to give him a hand up. Jake reached for the hand but never touched it. Almost magically a fountain of blood shot out from Galvin's wrist and arced to the grit of the street. The entrance wound was small — a jagged little tear the size of a five-cent piece, but as the slug exited it carried with it a flap of flesh and bits of bone and cartilage. Sinclair used his momentum to heft himself over the back of the freighter's rear ramp, slamming into Galvin and taking the stunned man crashing to the floor. Two Night Riders dropped their rifles and rushed to help the older man. "No, damn it!" Jake yelled. "Stay at your posts and keep firing — I can handle this!" He snatched a handful of cloth strips and a bottle of grain alcohol from the wooden packing case nailed to the center of the wagon floor. The blood that had been a fountain was now a steady flow, its metallic scent even stronger in the wagon than that of the acrid gun smoke. Galvin was already in shock, skin chalk-pale, eyes beginning to roll back in his head. Jake slapped his friend across the face — hard. Galvin's eyes began to focus. He yelped when Sinclair poured alcohol into the exit wound, turned the wrist over, and did the same to the smaller entry puncture. He wound a length of cloth around the wrist, but within seconds blood was dripping from the underside of Lou's wrist. Jake rigged a tourniquet just above the elbow, pulled it snug, and tied off the cloth. For a moment, the eyes of the two men met. There was nothing to say and they both knew it. Sinclair turned away to pick up the deer hide covering his Sharps, unwrapped the rifle, and slid a cartridge into it.

Light was coming on fast. Although the sun hadn't yet cleared the horizon, the long splashes of color to the east had been chased away by the break of day. Jake hunkered in front of a gun port and scanned the row of buildings across from him. The sheriff's office was burning nicely and flames had propagated to the empty storefront next to it. Down the block a trio of riflemen on the saloon roof were silhouetted against the sky, their muzzle flashes further establishing them as targets. Jake drew a bead on the middle outlaw and eased back on his trigger. The man simply disappeared, the velocity of the big Sharps slug at that minor distance such that the rifleman was hurled the length of the roof and off the back before the report reached his partners. One of the outlaws dropped behind the cover of the roof's low parapet; the other hesitated a moment too long. The bullet struck him at his belt line and his face met his shins as he folded like a pocketknife being snapped shut, leaving a thick arrow-straight streak of blood to the rear edge of the roof and a reddish mist in the air as he was pitched off and dropped to the ground near his equally dead partner.

After the first twenty-five or so minutes of the battle the barrages of gunfire from both sides diminished to an ongoing, more logically paced crackle. Jake had warned his men this would happen. "In a fight where both sides have fairly good cover, after first hot and heavy exchanges, the battle slows way down. Men pick their shots — they aim rather than spraying lead toward the enemy. Some men get sloppy for a moment, show too much of themselves, don't keep as tight a watch. Those fellows end up dead. I want you boys to stay alert and stay alive. This showdown isn't going to be over in an hour or even a couple of hours. I guarantee that. If we let up, we lose. It's as simple as that. We've got more ammunition than we need, and we're not outnumbered by more than a few men. Stay sharp and we can win in Fairplay and take back your town." In a second, he'd amended his statement. "*Can* win?" he questioned himself. "Hell, we *will* win! And look: If anyone sees Mott, let me know. He's got a bill that's due to be paid to me."

"I'm pretty sure I seen him haul his ass into the hotel from the saloon, Jake — maybe ten or fifteen minutes ago — carryin' a rifle in one hand and a pistol in the other," one of the men responded.

"Yeah — I seen that, too," another agreed.

Jake nodded and hunkered next to Lou Galvin. The older man's wrist was weeping some blood, but the tourniquet seemed to be holding well. "Your hand's looking good, Lou," Sinclair said. "You'll be grabbing the ladies by the ass in no time."

Galvin forced a smile that was more of a grimace. He forced some words Sinclair had to lean closer to him to hear. "My ass-grabbin' days were over a decade ago, Jake. Tell me — how are the boys doing?"

"They're doing fine — real good. I figure Mott has about forty-five men in play, spread along both sides of the street. We've dropped at least four of them and yours is the only bad wound we've taken." He waited out a volley from their wagon and then spoke again. "No deaths on our side, Lou, and we're doing our best to keep it that —"

The young farmer at the gun port a yard away from Galvin and Sinclair ratcheted a round into his rifle and drew a bead. Before he could fire his head snapped back like that of a condemned man hitting the end of a gallows rope and a fist-sized chunk of his temple and a spatter of gray matter slapped against the canvas on the other side of the wagon. The man at the next port dropped his rifle and vomited, choking, gasping. Two others set down their rifles to rush to their fallen comrade. "No! Goddammit, no!" Jake bellowed angrily. "Get back to your posts and keep firing! There's nothing you can do for this boy now except to keep fighting!" He eased the body past Galvin and to the rear of the wagon. He took a blanket from the stack of three or four and spread it over the corpse. When he'd asked the women to supply each wagon with a few blankets, no one had asked him what they were for — they knew. It was easier — safer, emotionally — not to talk about it, as if not saying the words would make the reality less frightening. Jake picked up his rifle from next to Lou and moved to the port, leaning his back against the rough wood next to it. "Anybody see where the shot came from?" he called out.

"I think it might have been the roof next to the saloon," a shaky voice answered. "Yeah," another agreed. "Either there or the second floor of the hotel."

Jake fed a round into the breech of his Sharps. *I should have told them,* he chided himself. *I could have warned the men . . . but about what? How? Tell them not to fire from the ports?* He eased the rifle barrel out the port, put the butt to his shoulder, and shifted into firing position, eyes slowly sweeping the saloon and the hotel next to it. *Should I have told them that there are probably a couple or more men in Mott's band who had seen a great deal of combat during the war — maybe even had been sharpshooters? That those men are deserters with their battle skills still intact, just as my own are? What good would that have —*

A scream of pain from the front end of the freighter stopped Jake's thoughts. The young man at the port held both hands to the side of his face, blood streaming from between his fingers. "Hell's fahr," he shouted. "Ain't nothin' but a scratch. Scared me, is all."

Sinclair caught a quick glimpse of sunlight on metal at a second-story window of the hotel. The glass was crusted with dust and dried dirt — impossible to see through. He placed his round in the center of the pane and when the glass exploded inward he saw a figure slammed toward the back of the room. As Sinclair reloaded, two shots tore into another outlaw as he passed by the now empty window frame. "Good shooting," Jake called out.

Each man had left the Galvin Ranch with a full canteen and a pocketful of deer or beef jerky. By midday much of the water had been drunk and a good part of the jerky eaten. The boxes of ammunition piled in the center of the wagon floor were holding up well, although the men had been firing essentially nonstop. A runner who'd weaved his way to the center wagon from the one closest to Fairplay's second saloon reported two Night Riders dead, three wounded. A runner from the other wagon reported one dead, two wounded. The best guess was that nine or maybe ten outlaws had been killed.

Sinclair worked his big rifle methodically through the afternoon, seeking out targets, taking good aim, and killing outlaws. His face smarted from gunpowder blowback, his eyes reddened and teared almost constantly, and his right shoulder ached dully from the pounding recoil it had been taking all day. There was no way to cushion or reduce the recoil: Each .54-caliber bullet fired transmitted the power of a strong punch through the cherry wood stock. Jake was pleased to trade the power, range, and accuracy of the Sharps for a sore shoulder and a face that felt a tad scalded. The freighter smelled of gunpowder, sweat, and blood, and the air was somehow thick, turgid, unmoving. Jake moved up and down the length of the wagon offering what encouragement he could. These men weren't used to combat at all, much less sustained battles. They were tired, spent, those who had killed turning over what they'd done — ended another human being's life — in their minds. Sinclair stopped behind Mason Trott, a clerk from Moe's general store, and watched as the young man pretended to aim but, a moment before pulling the trigger, angled his barrel sharply upward. He jacked another round into the chamber and flinched as Jake put his hand on the younger man's shoulder. "What's the problem, Mason?" he asked quietly, crouching next to the rifleman. "Why're you wasting ammunition? That last shot of yours must have been thirty feet over the hotel roof."

"Jake," the young man began, his eyes locking with Sinclair's. "Jake — I — I can't do it. I'm a Christian man, I'm a deacon in my church, I teach kids there. I teach them that killing is bad, wrong, a foul sin, an affront to Jesus Christ. I believe that with all my heart. I know these outlaws are evil, but it's the Lord's own will that'll dictate when their lives end." He swallowed hard. "You're right. I'm wasting ammunition and endangering my friends. I've thought it over. I'm going to make a run for it, get back to Lou's place, pray there with the women and kids. It's where I belong — it's where I should be and want to be."

Sinclair's grip on Trott's shoulder tightened. "You can't, Mason. You wouldn't get ten feet. Look: I'm almost out of ammunition for my Sharps. You set your rifle down here and go on back and look after Lou, OK? I'll take over this port. Lou's been coming in and out of consciousness. Talk to him, pray with him if you want. I've been loosening the tourniquet every so often. You can take over doing that. After dark you can make it to the other wagons, look to their wounded. But trying to hightail it out of here now is suicide. There's no sense in you getting killed when you're needed here, right?"

Sinclair watched as Mason Trott hustled back to where Lou was stretched out at the rear of the wagon. *How many others of these guys aren't shooting to kill, can't bring themselves to sight in on another man? I've seen it in every battle, boys who can't — won't — take a life, shooting way high so their pals won't know.* A quick flash of anger and frustration surged through him and he fought to back it down. *These boys are civilians,* he chided himself, *and they're doing a hell of a job. Outlaws are going down, regardless of those who can't kill.*

There was another problem chewing at

Sinclair: Mott hadn't been seen in a few hours. The windows of the buildings facing the street had long since been shattered by gunfire, and the faces of the gunmen could be occasionally seen behind the frames. No one had seen Mott. *Best bet is that the son of a bitch is lying low in the hotel. There's no way he'd run — his men would scatter without a leader. Scum like them would flee like scalded cats if they didn't have someone to tell them what to do and how to do it. There are lots of windows in that hotel — maybe he's moving around from room to room and keeping his head down when he isn't shooting. But no matter what, he's not going to walk away from this town if I have anything to do with it.*

Sinclair glanced at the half-empty case of dynamite surrounded by boxes and cases of ammunition in the center of the wagon. The explosive sticks were a quick answer — but a stupid and counterproductive one. The fire started early in the day when Jake had dynamited the sheriff's office went out when it reached an alley and couldn't jump the gap to the next structure, but use of dynamite now in the saloons, hotel, or other buildings could level Fairplay — leaving dead farmers and clerks who'd died for a town that had burned to the ground.

Through the afternoon the exchanges of gunfire had slowed, steadied, become an almost monotonous background of sounds. Jake had fired the last of his .54-caliber cartridges and his Sharps was now as useless as teats on a hay rake. The outlaw he'd targeted with his final round through the big gun hung out of a second-story window of the hotel, arms limp and motionless, blood draining down the gray clapboard in a crimson stream from the shattered clump of hair and bone that had once been his head.

Sinclair looked off to the west. Twilight clouds had gathered and a vagrant breeze had progressively become a stiff wind, creating whirling dust devils in the loose grit of Main Street. Daylight was dying rapidly and that fact worried Jake. In full dark the battle would have an entirely different structure. Mott's men would no longer be pinned inside buildings — they'd be free to move about the unlighted streets. The thick wooden protection of the wagons rose only four feet or so from the freighter floors. In the dark, the outlaws could fire downward from the rooftops, and the results of that would be devastating. Muzzle flashes made good targets, but they were useless if the outlaw fired and ducked behind a parapet or threw himself to the side.

Jake's eyes again followed the railroad tracks to the point where the distance merged the parallel rails of steel together into a single line. He breathed a long sigh of relief at what he saw there. Even against the darkening sky, the white smoke of the locomotive, worried and chased about by the wind, was visible.

A barrage from the saloon and hotel brought Sinclair's attention back to the battle. The bursts of white light from the muzzles of the outlaws' guns were distinct now, sharp-edged against the rapidly falling night. Jake pumped a few shots out of the port with Trott's rifle, not really sure of his targets or the results of his bullets, aiming only at the flashes.

The burgeoning darkness seemed to energize the outlaws. Firing that had become sporadic was now steady and insistent. Slugs poured into all three wagons, and some rounds found the ports. A gray-bearded older man toward the front of the wagon slumped to the floor, his right eye socket pumping gushets of blood. "Looks like a damn pasture fulla fireflies out there," the rifleman next to Sinclair observed. "They got us by the eggs for true if we don't take the battle to them sons-a-bitches, Jake. We gotta get outta these crates an' attack."

"Not yet," Sinclair said, loud enough for everyone to hear. "We'll attack — but not yet."

The eerie, lonely sound of the train whistle rolled through the town as if fleeing from the single sun-bright headlamp of the locomotive as it chugged toward Fairplay. "Here we go," Jake said quietly, almost to himself. Then he shouted, "Mason — run to the other wagons and tell them to be ready to attack when they hear a stick of dynamite go off. I want half the men from each freighter on each side of the street. Hurry now — you'll be safe in this light. But haul ass!" Trott scrambled over the rear gate and was gone. Sinclair crab-walked to the dynamite case and grabbed a single stick. He cut the fuse with his sheath knife, leaving it barely an inch long.

The train whistle sounded its mournful note again as it approached the town, slowing, brakes screaming in a metal-against-metal screech. "Looks like the boys intercepted the train just like we planned," the man next to Jake shouted, voice jubilant. "Hot damn!"

Sinclair watched the locomotive and the three cattle cars it hauled disappear behind the buildings across from him. He checked the load in his Colt and jacked a round into Mason Trott's rifle. He took several lucifers from his pocket, clenched them in his teeth, heads facing out, clutched the stick of dynamite, and hefted himself over the rear gate and out of the wagon. His boys laid down a volley as Jake moved to the center of the street, snapped a Lucifer to flame with his thumbnail, and touched the fire to the fuse. He pitched the dynamite within a heartbeat of lighting the fuse, its trail of sparks going straight up rather than arcing toward the buildings. The explosion ripped a hole in the darkness, a jagged, searing, white-hot gap above the street. The report was more of a tearing scream than the thunderous boom of dynamite in an enclosed space. Before the blast had the time to echo, the heavy thudding of shotguns from behind the buildings began, the firing of the twelve-gauges the Night Riders from the train carried melding with the rifle and now pistol fire of their partners from the wagons. Inside the saloon, the hotel, and several other buildings, there was sudden chaos. Outlaws screamed, cursed, firing wildly at the new invaders as the men from the wagons swarmed in through blasted-to-hell doors, front and display window frames, the glass shattered long ago in the early part of the Night Riders' attack that morning.

A hard grin set on Sinclair's face as he charged toward the hotel. There was, he knew, a turning point in every battle — a good or bad order, a quick but telling charge, or a devastating swing in strategy. This rough but effective pincers movement was that tide-turning moment. The double-ought buck from the shotguns tore into the outlaws, spinning, hurling, flinging their bleeding bodies about in macabre, jerky dances of death as lead poured into them from both front and back.

Jake stopped outside the front door of the hotel, peering across the street to the fight there. Night Riders were moving in on the clusters of outlaws firing hard, heedless of return fire. An attack yell that sounded very much like the Confederate war cry that Union soldiers had learned to fear went up from the Night Riders as they began to taste success, as Mott's men began to falter, to turn tail and run.

Sinclair, firing his rifle from his waist, levering in round after round, shoved his way into the hotel, stumbling for a moment over a collapsed beam, pushing past overturned chairs and tables of the lobby to the stairway to the second floor. The hammer of the rifle snapped sharply against the receiver, out of ammunition. Jake tossed it aside and continued up the stairs yelling, "Mott! Where are you? I'm coming after you, Mott!"

Pistol in hand, Sinclair threw himself out and down as he reached the landing, skidding over the polished wood floor, putting two slugs into the chest of the outlaw he knew would be waiting from him. Jake gained his feet, snatched up the dying outlaw's rifle as he passed him, and followed the corridor from the landing. There was a window at the end and a figure was most of the way through it, ready to jump to the low roof over the depot entrance behind the building. Jake fired the rifle and the outlaw jerked as the bullet struck his chest and then toppled over the window frame and slammed into the roof below. He dropped a second panicked outlaw as the man fumbled with a Colt, trying to jam cartridges in it, spilling more of them on the floor from his trembling fingers than he slid into the cylinder.

There were two doors — two rooms — on either side of the corridor that led to the window. Mott was in one of them — he had to be. He hadn't been on the first floor and he'd been seen shooting from the second-story windows.

"Mott — come out and face me like a man!"

Jake stood against the wall to the side of the first door he came to, preparing to slam his rifle butt against the door handle. The light was dying very rapidly now; in a few moments it'd be too damned dark to see a thing. Mott's voice from the end room startled Jake.

"You're doing this all wrong, gunman! I'll give you half the town. We can run it together. I've got the men, the guns — I've got the whole damned town scared shitless! The two of us can . . ."

"You got nothing, Mott. Nothing. Your boys — the ones that're still standing — are running like the scared rats they are. It's all over, Mott."

"Don't be a goddamn fool! There's everything we need here. We can —"

"I'd rather kill you myself, Mott, but my men would like to see you hang just like you strung up Billy Galvin. Take your choice, outlaw."

There was what seemed like a long silence from the end room. The fight downstairs continued, the booming of the shotguns and the crack of pistol and rifle fire slightly muffled by the flooring.

"I'm faster than you are, gunman — and

329

better than you'll ever be. I'm offering you a chance to live. You'd best take it." The voice was hard, without a taint of fear.

"Come on out and we'll see about that."

"I'll kill you dead, gunman."

"You going to hide in that room or you going to step out here and take care of things, Mott?"

"No matter what, you ain't gonna hang me. You gotta know that. I'll draw against you, gunman. And while you're bleeding out I'll go through that window and move on. There's lots of other towns for me."

"Let's do it, Mott. No more talking." Sinclair's voice was tight, controlled.

The corridor had fallen into almost complete darkness, although the ambient light outside would silhouette Mott's form if he left the room. Jake tossed the rifle aside and rested his right hand a pair of inches above the grips of his Colt.

"I'm comin' out slow to face you. Then I'll kill you."

Sinclair didn't respond. The room door creaked loudly and he could hear Mott's boots scrape the floor. The door stopped for a moment and then the hinges squeaked again. Jake moved his right foot back a few inches, settling himself, breathing deeply. The door stopped again. He could hear

Mott's slightly raspy breath, fast and shallow. It would be now, Sinclair knew.

He was right. The door crashed open and Mott dove out low, pistol already firing, slugs hissing past Jake's body as he drew and in the same motion threw himself to his left. The smallest bit of time before his shoulder slammed into the wall he fired at the mass of Mott's body, absorbed the impact with the wall with his shoulder, and fired twice again. The sound of gut punches told Sinclar all three of his bullets had found their mark. He moved forward, pistol extended in front of him, not completely certain how badly Mott was hit.

The outlaw's pistol was on the floor a few inches from his hand. Mott was stretched his full length. The blood gushing from the middle of his chest looked black in the dim light. Lower on his body a dark stain was spreading quickly at about belt level. Mott's voice was a gurgling whisper. "You son of a bitch," he rasped.

Sinclair looked down at the outlaw for a moment. "You still going to kill me?" he asked quietly.

He thumbed back the hammer and put a bullet into Mott's right eye.

The scene in the street was a grim one as

Sinclair walked toward the store with the Sharps he'd retrieved from the wagon. Men loaded their dead neighbors into one of the freighters, their movements ghostlike and quiet in the light of the many lamps and lanterns that'd been lit. Jake moved through the front door of Moe Terpin's mercantile — the door hanging from a hinge, penetrated in a dozen places by ragged bullet holes — and found his way to the rear of the store by the flickering illumination of the lanterns outside. His boots scuffed over broken glass, penny candy — licorice strips, cinnamon bears, peppermint sticks that all sent their individual scents up to him — to the back office. He placed the Sharps on Moe's desk, nudging aside a ledger, an ink pot, and a handful of invoices, flyers, and bills with the rifle's barrel. After a moment he turned away and left the mercantile.

Two Night Riders were helping Lou Galvin into a buggy with a pair of outlaw horses standing in the traces. Jake strode to the older man.

"You're looking fair to middling, Lou," he said.

Galvin managed a smile. "You did good for us, Jake," he said. "When we get back to my place the boys will want to drink with you, thank you."

Sinclair nodded.

Lou grunted in pain and held Sinclair's eyes. He sighed. "You won't be there, will you." It was a declaration, not a question.

"No."

"I didn't think so. We won't forget you, son."

Jake nodded again. "Nor I you."

There were lots of outlaw horses behind the still-smoldering sheriff's office and jail. Jake selected a tall buckskin gelding.

When he got to Galvin's ranch it didn't take him more than a few minutes to shag the buckskin on his way and to saddle Mare. She was ready to run.

So was Jake Sinclair.

ABOUT THE AUTHOR

Paul Bagdon is the author of more than thirty published novels, under his own name and pen names. He is a contributing editor with *Writers Digest* magazine, and an instructor for Writers Digest Online Workshops. He lives in Rochester, New York, where he teaches creative writing to adults in a local school system. He is currently at work on his next Western novel.